DANGEROUS SLEUTHING

Terror stricken, Amy ran blindly and blundered into the marsh. Ankle deep water and gooey mud slowed her down. The barking of the dogs changed and became higher pitched, more excited. They splashed into the water after her.

Amy glanced over her shoulder and saw their bodies arc into the air, each giant leap bringing them a yard closer. They'd be on her any minute.

She shimmied up an aspen sapling. The big lead Doberman charged and vaulted upward in one fluid motion. His teeth scraped her ankle and caught in the cloth of her running shoe.

He ripped it off as he fell to the ground and backed off for another lunge . . .

GRAVE SECRETS
A Dr. Amy Prescott Mystery

LOUISE HENDRICKSEN

ZEBRA BOOKS
KENSINGTON PUBLISHING CORP.

To my children, Sharon Newton and Tom Leiker—two of the finest individuals I know—and my mother, Viola Bjornson, a great lady. She kept the faith.

Prologue

A metallic click jolted Simon Kittredge awake. Dazed, he groped for the pistol at his side, until a rifle barrel jammed into his gut.

"Make a move flatlander and I'll blast your innards."

A chill seized Simon. *I can't die yet, I have to prove . . .* His fingers closed around the butt of his .38.

"Watch him, Bear. He's got a gun."

"Don't worry." Moving shadows became men beneath a pale night sky. "Sonuvabitch'll never use it." A big man loomed over Simon and rammed down his boot heel.

Simon heard a bone in his right arm snap. Then he heard a scream. His scream.

A kick jolted his spine. "On your feet, wise guy. Let's see who the hell you are." Large hands dragged Simon from his sleeping bag.

"What do you want?" Simon tottered and fell against the man's bulky body. "Why—" An open-handed cuff silenced him.

"Them's his pants beside ya, Bear. Git his wallet."

A flashlight gleam pierced the darkness. Simon registered masked faces.

"Says here, he's Simon Kittredge."

"He with the other one?"

Simon swayed. *The other one! What other one?*

"Christ almighty, he's a goddamned reporter. Works for *Global News Magazine* out in Seattle."

"Holy shit! That's all we need."

Supporting his throbbing arm, Simon faced the one with the Tennessee mountain drawl. "You guys have the wrong man. I'm just a fisherman who happens to be a writer."

"Cut the jawin', Kittredge." The Tennessee man took cord from his pocket and jerked Simon's hands down in front of him.

Simon choked on his scream and dropped to his knees. "No!"

"Shesh your trap." He clamped Simon's wrists together and bound them.

The one called Bear hung the strap of Simon's camera around his thick neck, tossed Simon's gear into the middle of the sleeping bag, and flung the improvised sack over his shoulder.

The tall, skinny one gouged Simon in the ribs. "Move it, we gotta fur piece to go."

With only brief stabs of torch light to guide him, Simon stumbled into the darkness. Thorns and jagged rocks ripping the soles of his bare feet, he scrambled up hills, slithered into brush-filled ravines and slogged waist deep in a foul slimy swamp.

Blood pounded in his head. Cold air stung his lungs. His captors heckled him, urged him to a swifter pace. A swinging branch smashed into his arm. He reeled, staggered, and fell. The rifle barrel caught him, jabbing into the pain. He gagged on his vomit. "Stop!"

The man prodded him again. "Hike your ass. We ain't got all night."

With tears running down his face, Simon staggered on. *How long? How long?*

Simon squinted and saw a faint glow ahead before a sack was drawn over his head. He'd gone only a few steps when a low growl sounded.

"Christ almighty, some pea-brain let the dogs out," Bear said. The growling rose to a snarl. "Get back, damn you." Something hard thudded against flesh and a dog's high-pitched yelp followed. "That'll teach him."

A short way farther on Bear let out a curse. "Stupid camera got hung up in the brush."

"Shuck the no-good thing."

"Can't. He coulda taken pictures."

Simon shuffled forward. He couldn't see through the gunny sack, but with each step he could tell the light got brighter. From all sides came the steady chunka-chunka-chunk of countless large engines. The men stopped. Chains rattled, metal clinked against metal, gate hinges creaked. Off to the right, he imagined he heard the murmur of voices.

Simon felt the wires of a Cyclone fence press against his shoulder and the side of his head. Now he knew where they'd brought him. He'd found the place that morning. Watched it from the woods most of the day.

One of the men poked him. He trudged a few feet and heard the gate clang shut behind him. The light became much brighter. They thrust him through a door and prodded him down what seemed like a hall.

"What'll we do with him?" Bear asked.

"What about the timekeeper's office? Nobody's used it since they closed the place down."

Rusty hinges creaked and Bear said, "Yeah, this'll do.

Those white-shirted bastards ain't paying us to think. Just deliver."

They wrenched Simon sideways, backed him onto a chair, and began to bind him. He drew a ragged breath. "Take it easy, damnit. I'm not going anywhere."

Bear gave a wheezing laugh. "Ya got that right." He cinched the rope a notch tighter around his legs. "That's it, pard. We're out of here."

The door slammed. Simon listened to an instant of silence. Biting the pain, he worked the sack off his head with his teeth, nose, and chin. On his right, the drawers of a file cabinet hung open, their contents spilling onto a floor littered with papers, file folders, and grimy supply books. To his left sat a dented metal desk. Dust-covered scratch pads, a jumble of pencils with broken leads, and a two-year-old calendar.

His shoulders sagged. *Thought you were going to show your old man how great you were, didn't you, Kittredge? Going to nab the con men who skunked him, get his money back, be your daddy's fair-haired son for the first time in your whole damn thirty-four years.*

He scanned the plywood-lined room. Near the baseboard of a wall, half hidden by the desk, he spied the edge of a small ivory-colored box.

Adrenaline speeded his pulse. *Keep calm. Think it through.* He clamped his lip between his teeth and tipped the chair back and forth. Gradually he managed to work himself closer to the desk. *Good.* He twisted the chair back from side to side. The rope bindings set up a see-sawing motion against his bare chest. His teeth sank into his lip until he tasted blood.

Bracing, he lunged right, then left, and heard a creak. More precious minutes dragged by before the round, wooden, spindles pulled out of their sockets and his ropes slackened enough for him to get his arms loose.

Without pausing to free his hands and feet, he fell forward, taking the chair with him, and landed on his injured arm. Flashes of color pierced his brain. He fought to keep from blacking out. "Jesus, not now ... not now."

He blinked to clear his vision and peered into the narrow crack between the desk and wall. A break at last. The box he'd spotted was a phone jack.

His heart pounded in his ears as he traced the cord until it disappeared into the shadowy recesses under the desk. He plotted his next move, clenched his jaw tight, and put his hands under the desk. Working blind, he felt along the floor. Nothing. He inched closer, reached out and strained until a moan wrenched from his throat.

He rested his cheek on the splintery floor boards, turned until he lay parallel with the desk and tried again. He had it! Relief made his fingers weaker. He had difficulty closing them on the flat plastic line.

Slowly, ever so slowly, he tugged the line toward him until coils of it began to gather near his midriff. Sweat stung his eyes. He gritted his teeth so hard his head hurt. A frantic pull, a noisy clatter, and a phone detached itself from under a pile of trash behind the desk.

He drew it to him, sent up a quick prayer and maneuvered the receiver to his ear. A dial tone! Tears sprang into his eyes and he didn't give a damn.

No sense in calling Rock Springs' police chief or his deputy. He'd asked them for help when he first arrived and had gotten nowhere.

He felt the room slowly turning gray at the edges and lay back to gather his strength. He'd call Amy, she'd know what to do. He closed his eyes and his mind began to float. *Forgive me, Amy. I truly thought I loved you . . . until I met Erika. Meant to tell you, when you met my plane in Seattle.* His bitter laugh made a harsh sound in the silent room. *Meant to . . . until I looked into your trusting brown eyes . . . then I didn't have the guts.* He snorted in disgust. *That makes me as big a bastard as your ex-husband, doesn't it?*

He groaned and pressed his head on the desk's cold steel until his mind responded. By contorting his body, he got the receiver into place and held it steady with his knees.

Perspiration slicking his hands, he punched in the 800 number of the Prescott's forensic investigator's office.

Just as Amy's taped message began, his thoughts blurred and he failed to make out her words. *Stay alert. This is for keeps.* He began a halting report and was interrupted by a beep. He hadn't waited long enough. A terrible tiredness came over him.

He took a shaky breath, then another. "Screwed-up again, Doc. Need . . . help." Darkness closed over him. "Sun . . . rise," he mumbled. "Ruby-eyed . . . ra—a—ven . . ."

Chapter 1

Amy rushed to Carson Flight Service's counter and pulled her ticket from her purse. "I'm Dr. Amy Prescott and I'm late," she said. "Fog socked in Seattle–Tacoma Airport. We couldn't get off the ground."

The clerk snatched up a phone, punched some buttons, and snapped, "Dr. Prescott's here."

Beside Amy, a young man fastened tags to her suitcase and forensic satchel. "Let's go lady, the pilot's about to take off." He triggered the automatic glass doors and vaulted through the opening. Out on the apron, a tall, broad-shouldered man ambled unsteadily toward a two-engine commuter plane. The baggage clerk dashed off in the same direction.

Amy hitched up her skirt and sprinted after him, her high heels clicking a rapid tattoo on the pavement. She'd only known Simon a year, but she'd learned early on that he couldn't resist a meaty story regardless of the danger involved. The sound of his garbled words on her answering machine this morning had started her imagining terrible things.

Soon now, she'd be in Rock Springs. Once on the scene, she'd find him and send him off to Erika, his new love. As she ran, she gloried in the exertion, the rush of wind against her cheeks. Each stride she took brought her closer to Simon. The thought eased the harried sensation she'd carried in her stomach since her journey had begun.

In her haste, she failed to notice the crack in the pavement. She tripped, pitched forward, and landed on all fours. Cinders, gravel and bits of concrete ground into her palms, cut her knees, shredded her stockings.

"Damn," she muttered. "Damn, damn, damn." She clamped her teeth on her lip and pried herself off the pavement. Her battered and bleeding knees made it difficult to stand, a minor detail compared to her acute embarrassment.

She averted her eyes from passengers who might be watching, picked up her purse, and hobbled up the steps at the rear of the plane. Inside, single seats extended down each side. Men filled seven of them. She walked up the aisle and apologized to the pilot for detaining him.

He shrugged. "Won't be the first time or the last."

Quailing inside, she faced her fellow travelers, took a breath, and smiled. All returned it, except one man. He sat with his head braced against the wall, his eyes half closed. From force of habit, her mind registered his description: male, Native American, at least six feet in height, 170 pounds, medium build, jet black hair and eyes—the type of man her women friends called, "a hunk."

As if in answer to her appraisal, he let his gaze travel up her slender 5'7" frame to her short brown hair. When his eyes shifted to meet hers, he lifted one shoulder in a gesture of casual indifference. Thus, having put her in her place, he slumped down in his seat and tilted a battered, low-crowned, Stetson over his face.

Heat flooded her cheeks. *Same to you, mister.* Good-looking men's smugness irked her. Throughout their four-year marriage her ex-husband, Mitch Jamison, had used his handsome face and body to attract a steady stream of sex partners. If she ever married again, the man would be homely as a basset hound.

She raised her chin and marched down the aisle. With the kind of luck she'd had today, it came as no surprise the only vacant seat lay across the aisle and one row back from the dark-eyed man.

As she passed him, she got a strong whiff of bourbon and pressed her lips together. Alcohol and drugs had been another of Mitch's weaknesses. She slid into her seat and fastened the belt across her lap.

After the plane took off and settled into its flight pattern, the gray-haired man in front of her turned around. "I'm Dr. Miles Leibow." Wet, pouty lips separated his mustache from a skimpy beard that failed to conceal his double chin. "This your first visit to Silver Valley?" His bellow overrode the rumble of the plane's engine.

She stopped pawing through her cavernous purse in search of the extra nylons she always carried and forced a smile. "Yes, it is."

"Ah!" He straightened his tie with fleshy fingers. "In that case, I must ask you not to judge our area by the landscape around the airport when we land." His small, watchful eyes peered from behind thick rimless glasses. "Noxious emissions." He nodded knowingly. "The smelter disrupted the intrinsically balanced ecosystems."

Intrinsically balanced ecosystem? The pompous buzz words grated on her already frayed nerves. "Really?"

She extracted a pen and a small black notebook from her bag, hoping the doctor would take the hint and discontinue his shouted conversation.

"Oh absolutely. Since it's September, you can't tell as easily, but believe me the topography has improved remarkably."

"Hm-m-m that's nice."

"Isn't it though." He cleared his throat noisily. "Takes know-how." He tapped his forehead with a manicured fingertip. "Pressure in the right places pays off. Regrettable, but necessary, if you expect progress."

"So politics fuels fires even in Idaho. Amazing!" Amy opened her notebook.

"Oh, they acted as if the whole project was their idea." He thumped his chest with his fist. "But my committee and I know who really lit the fire."

"I see." She dated a blank page in her notebook.

"How far are you going?"

She hesitated, unsure whether she wanted her fellow passengers to know her plans. Finally, she decided anyone who really wanted to find out would do so anyway. "Rock Springs."

The dark-eyed man jerked and his knees dislodged from the seat in front of him. The heels of his scuffed western boots came down hard on the floor.

Dr. Leibow swiveled his head in the man's direction and without lowering his voice an iota said, "Looks like the redskin's got a snootful. You'd think they'd at least have brains enough to know they can't handle the stuff."

She scowled at the doctor and waited for the Indian to tell him what he could do with his opinion. Instead, he acted as if he hadn't heard. She stared at his back. *Do something!* When he didn't she cringed with shame, not for him but for mankind. His placid acceptance had to have come from a lifetime of slurs.

She leaned toward the doctor. "Why should they? We Anglos haven't learned, and we've been at it a hell of a lot longer." She held his squint-eyed glare until he flushed and dropped his gaze.

"Watch your mouth, girl. Talk like that'll get you in trouble around here." Holding himself ramrod straight, he turned his back to her.

Narrow-minded bigot! She tried to put the incident out of her mind, but each time her glance wandered to the Indian, she got a knot in her stomach.

America, land of freedom and equality. What a laugh.

A man up front turned his head. He had a long, sharp-planed face that looked as if it would break into ice shards if he smiled. His half-hooded eyes flicked over her and she felt her flesh creep.

She ignored him, forced herself to relax and began to mull over the profound changes that had taken place in her life. In a short span of time, she'd acquired a divorce, a degree in medicine, and a degree in forensic pathology. A week after getting her pathology degree, she'd started work at the Washington State Crime Laboratory in Seattle. For the next two years, she'd labored to pay off her ex-husband's old debts.

Four months ago, she and her father, a former medical examiner, had gone looking for an office. They found what they wanted in Ursa Bay, a town thirty miles north of Seattle.

She smiled as she remembered the two of them admiring the gold-edged sign in their front window. Dr. B.J. Prescott and Dr. Amy Prescott, Forensic Investigators—that moment had been the fulfillment of their dreams.

The plane bucked, bringing her back to the present. She sighed, gazed down at her notebook, and wrote Simon's name beside the date. Below, she started her usual who, what, where, when, how, and why questions.

Who had a motive to harm Simon? Three weeks ago, Simon's father had summoned him home from Central America where he had been on assignment. Simon had detoured through Seattle to apply for his vacation from *Global News*. He'd asked her to dinner and they'd talked non-stop for three hours.

Last October, before he left the States, she and Simon had started a relationship. Both of them had hoped their feelings were based on love and not just their intense physical and emotional needs. In the past ten months, his trips to Seattle had been at wider and wider intervals. Recently, his letters had dwindled to a trickle, and in them he made frequent references to another journalist named Erika Washburn.

Amy had felt him slipping away and wondered what qualities she lacked. She must have a major flaw of some kind. Why else would she be incapable of holding a man's interest and affection?

Amy frowned at the few words she'd written and retraced Simon's name. Although a talented writer, he considered himself a literary failure, a feeling fostered by a domineering father who'd totally ignored his youngest son's achievements. It had been a bittersweet experience to witness Simon's exhilaration over his father's call for help.

During dinner and while they talked later in the lounge, she had noticed a short, nondescript man watching them. When she'd brought him to Simon's attention, he'd sluffed it off.

"I think he's a government agent," he said. "They often put a tail on you when you enter a sensitive country. He's been following Erika and me for weeks."

"How can you be so casual about it," she asked. "What if he's following you for some other reason?"

"Erika reported it to the American Embassy, but nothing changed. After awhile, we ignored him and concentrated on getting the story we'd come after."

"I don't like it. I don't like it one bit. For all you know, a drug baron in one of those Central American countries could think you're getting too nosy. Maybe the guy following you is just waiting for the right time and place. Did you ever think of that?"

"Well, yes, I did."

"So?"

He grinned at her. "I talked to some friends. They're going to check with a couple of sources and let me know if they learn anything."

After leaving Seattle, Simon had contacted her twice. His first call had come from his boyhood home in Coeur d'Alene, Idaho. He'd been shocked to learn swindlers had conned his father into buying phony stock in a silver mine.

Simon's next call had come from Rock Springs, a small town in northern Idaho, where the trail of one of the swindlers had led him. Simon had told her he was staying at the Riverside Motel. He hadn't mentioned the man tailing him either time he phoned and she'd forgotten to ask him.

Under the "Who?" heading, Amy wrote, "Man Shadowing Simon" and "Swindlers." She turned to a new page and labeled it "What?" What had happened? Had

Simon come too close to the swindlers? She shivered. Or had the man stalking him found Rock Springs an ideal place to carry out his orders?

Chapter 2

The plane settled to a smooth landing at Filmore Airport. Amy stayed in her seat until the other passengers filed out. As she ventured onto the top metal step, she paused to regard a spare, multipurpose building at the edge of the apron and swore under her breath. If they had a car rental desk, she'd be surprised.

Moving with a halting, stiff-legged gait, she joined the others who'd gathered beside the plane's luggage compartment. As she stooped to grab the handle of her forensic satchel, one of the men took it from her.

"You're a lifesaver," she said with a smile. "I wasn't looking forward to carrying it with these. She turned her hands palm side up, revealing abraded skin peppered with large blood blisters.

The man gave a low whistle. "They'll be sore tomorrow." Concern etched his thin, haggard face as he touched the deepest abrasions. "Easy to get infection with ground-in dirt. When we get to Rock Springs, come into the pharmacy and I'll dress them."

She observed him more closely, noting his waxy, ivory-tinged skin and the yellowish cast to the whites of his eyes and made a curbside diagnosis of cancer. Guilt engulfed her for having let him take the heaviest of her two bags, but she knew it would do him more harm if she attempted to retrieve it. "I have a first-aid kit, Mr. . . ."

"Pennington, Will Pennington." He set down her bag and lifted his blue golfing hat, revealing his hairless head. "I own Valley Pharmacy in Rock Springs."

"Thanks for offering, Mr. Pennington. Is there a town near the airport where I can rent a car?"

"Afraid not," he said. "Most of us ride the bus to Rock Springs."

"Then I guess I'll ride the bus, too."

A horn honked and a gray Mercedes swept by them with Dr. Leibow at the wheel. In the medical world, some doctors take and some doctors give. Dr. Leibow struck her as a taker.

"Will you be staying in Rock Springs long?" Mr. Pennington asked.

She searched her mind for a logical cover story. "Depends," she said quickly and flushed. She wasn't a good liar. "I'm a . . . a vacationing photographer."

His lips curved into a pleasant smile. "Then you'll be around for a good long time. The scenery in these mountains is spectacular." He opened the door to a waiting room that looked no bigger than a large office and reached out for the bag she held. "I'll give your luggage to the bus driver."

"I'll need this one." She gestured to her torn stockings.

He nodded. "See you on the bus." With a tip of his hat, he went to join the waiting passengers.

Amy hurried into the women's rest room and locked the door. After hanging her navy-blue blazer on the doorknob, she washed up and changed her nylons.

Then, she took a shoulder holster and a .38 Smith & Wesson Special from her suitcase. Events during the past year had convinced her someone in her profession needed to be armed whether they liked it or not.

She dressed quickly and rushed outside to find the bus parked in front of the building. The men had already boarded. Gripping the suitcase handle in her aching hand, she mounted the steps and paid her fare.

Passengers filled all the seats except two. The one behind the driver tempted her, but her defiant nature made her ignore it. She worked her way to the rear of the bus where the tall, black-haired man sat. He had assumed his spine-crippling slouch and tipped his hat over his eyes.

She cleared her throat. "Excuse me, sir . . ."

He tilted his hat back, glanced up at her, and she felt a tingling rush that took her breath away. "Is that seat taken?" she asked softly.

The irises of his dark eyes contracted slightly, otherwise his face remained impassive. He pulled in his long legs and made a sweeping gesture with his hand.

"Thank you." She raised her bag to set it on the rack above his head. Midway the handle twisted, tearing open one of the large blood blisters in her palm. She gave a quick little gasp. Before she could lower the case to the floor, several drops of blood spattered his worn jeans.

He glanced down at his pant leg, then up at her with another of his enigmatic looks. To her utter horror, her lip chose that moment to tremble. Her face burned with embarrassment and she murmured, "I'm sorry." His gaze intensified but he gave no reply.

"Don't waste your breath on him, lady." The man across the aisle got to his feet. "Let me take that." Muttering under his breath, he placed her suitcase in the overhead rack and sat down again.

Amy balled a tissue against her oozing blister, sidled into the seat by the window, and sank down. Her throat hurt and her chest felt as if it had an inflated balloon inside. When would she learn to stop making noble gestures? This character wouldn't know one if it fell on him.

She let out a long sigh. Since she'd divorced Mitch, she'd become touchy, bullheaded, and overly independent—traits that had precipitated every one of the arguments she and Simon had had. He'd accused her of carrying a chip on her shoulder and daring everyone to knock it off. She gave another sigh. He was probably right, as usual.

Her seat companion's gentle snore caused her to glance sideways. Instantly, her investigative instinct took over. Hair a bit long but clean and shiny. Lean face, high cheekbones, slightly arched nose, full lower lip, strong chin—an eye-pleasing combination, she admitted reluctantly.

She frowned slightly as she studied him. His appearance raised a number of questions. Although his face and the tops of his forearms were brown as saddle leather, the rolled sleeves of his blue chambray shirt revealed portions of pale beige skin on the undersides of his forearms. Conclusion: he wasn't a full-blooded Indian, and his work kept him out in the sun.

On one of his long slim fingers he wore a ring, a red gemstone nested in interlaced strands of fine silver, a superb piece with exquisite workmanship. Intriguing.

Her glance traveled down his faded blue jeans to boots made of brown belly-cut alligator. She pursed her lips in a silent whistle. In a Tony Lama Boot Shop, she'd seen a pair that cost over six hundred dollars.

You certainly aren't poor, mister. She noted the bunched muscles in his thigh, the tense lines of his body. *And you aren't asleep either. So just what kind of a game are you playing?*

She took out her notebook, turned to the page marked "Who?" and wrote, "Who is this man and why is he pretending to be something he isn't?" She could think of nothing more to add, so she returned the notebook to her purse and directed her attention to the passing scenery.

Steep rocky hills with whorls of fall foliage latticing their thick evergreen mantle hemmed the narrow valley. At intervals, corrugated tin buildings clung precariously to ocherous scabs of earth jutting from precipitous slopes.

After letting off passengers in the mining towns of Kellogg and Wallace, the bus turned up Nine Mile Canyon and wound its way over Dobson and King's Pass. Along the way, she spotted numerous mines, each sporting a hoist shack and a towering headframe. Tunnel scars and tailings dotted the slopes as if giant gophers had been at work.

By the time they reached the small, secluded valley on the other side, the September sun had begun to slip behind the Coeur d'Alene Mountains. The last slanting rays threw the devastation left by dredge and hydraulic mining into stark relief—ragged hillsides, mounds of denuded rock, downed trees with dead, bone-white roots.

Weather-beaten cabins straggled up every valley wall and perched on barren, pockmarked ledges above the valley floor. Some lacked a roof or a door, others had props driven into the ground to hold them up.

As the valley broadened, old Victorian houses appeared. Each of the places teemed with activity. Men wielded paintbrushes, straightened picket fences, and repaired broken steps. Women in faded dresses washed windows, pruned overgrown shrubbery, and filled wheelbarrows with clippings and weeds. Ragged children raced from one bonfire to the next.

The bus pulled to a stop in front of a long, brown building. A sign suspended from glistening yellow trim indicated they had arrived at Rock Springs' bus depot.

The man beside Amy stood up, lifted a striped camouflage backpack from the overhead rack, and followed the other men out. When they'd gone, Amy wrapped a handkerchief around her hand and retrieved her suitcase.

The depot rested on a four-foot-high cement foundation. She climbed wide wooden steps to a platform constructed of newly sawn planks the color of beaten egg yolk. A pungent, resinous odor rose from the sun-warmed wood to blend with the depot's smell of new paint. *Rock Springs must be prospering,* she thought.

Stepping carefully to avoid cracks between the new planks, she moved across the platform to a phone booth and called her father.

"Whew," he said. "I'm glad you're there. I've been on edge ever since you left."

"I'll try to keep you posted," she said. "But I may not phone every day. I don't know who I can trust, so I won't be calling from the motel."

"I sure wish I could have come with you."

"Now, Dad, we agreed not to fret about each other. Remember?"

"I know, but Simon manages to get involved with some pretty bizarre people."

"And so do we."

"Maybe, but ours are usually dead." He gave a feeble laugh. "You be careful now, won't you?"

She reassured him, left the booth, and pulled open the depot's heavy oak door. A man wearing a black suit coat, its sleeves slicked with age, sat on a high stool behind a brass wire screen. He finger-combed tufts of white hair over his pink scalp. "May I help you, young lady?"

From her conversation with Simon earlier in the week, she already knew the motel situation. Now she needed to find out more. "Does anyone in town rent rooms?"

"Not that I'm aware of." He gave his white shirt cuffs a little jerk. "And I know most everything that goes on in this man's town."

"Can you recommend a motel?"

He smiled. "The Riverside's all we've got. It's not too bad, considering."

She cocked her head. "Considering?"

"Well . . . it used to be first rate before Ted Zeigler took over." He chuckled. "Course he's only had it a couple months."

She grimaced. "Gee, thanks."

His inquisitive eyes traveled over her. "Stick around a few months. We'll have a deeeluxe ski resort to offer you."

She forced a smile. It'd been a long, long day, and it was far from over. "Sounds great. Did the bus driver bring in a satchel with the name 'Prescott'?"

The clerk slid off his stool and ducked below the counter. In a minute, he bobbed up again. "Yep."

"Can I leave my bags here for a while?"

"Sure thing, little lady. I'll be here until nine."

She slid her suitcase through a square hole in the

counter, thanked him, and wandered outside. She gazed down the deserted street, wondering where to start. This morning, after getting Simon's message, she'd called his parents' home in Coeur d'Alene. His mother had answered. Not wanting to alarm her, she'd kept the conversation casual.

By the time she'd hung up, she'd gathered two pertinent facts. They hadn't heard from Simon in three days, and he'd rented a red Volkswagen minivan so he'd have a place to sleep if he didn't find lodging during his journey.

Smiling faintly, she strode down the platform. A red minivan should be easy to spot in a town this size. Her smile broadened. Simon would say, "A piece of cake, Doc."

She neared the steps and caught sight of a movement in the shadow of some trees. The tall, dark-haired man ambled toward her and started up the steps. Suddenly, her high heel sank into a crevice between the planks. "Shoot! Of all the—" She lurched forward and began to fall.

He caught her under the arms, but she had to grab him around the waist to keep from sinking to her knees. *Klutz!* Her cheeks flamed, perspiration beaded her forehead and upper lip.

He righted her and they stared at each other. Now he knew she was packing a gun.

So was he.

Chapter 3

She teetered on one foot. The average guy didn't have a pistol tucked into the band of his pants. Why did this man? Her former seat companion's beetle-browed frown indicated she'd aroused his curiosity, too.

Their eyes met and she felt him probing the deepest recesses of her mind. She tried to look away but couldn't. Finally, with concentrated effort, she stretched her lips into a smile. "This doesn't seem to be my day." The words came out in a soft, breathy timbre, and suddenly she longed to crawl under the platform. Her delivery endowed the trite remark with the sensual essence of a Marilyn Monroe. *Damn it!* Why couldn't she be more at ease with men?

"Lean on me and I will rescue your shoe." He spoke slowly, his voice quiet and deep, spacing his words as if each held equal importance.

His closeness magnified her shyness, but she made herself rest her hand on his broad back. He worked the wayward heel to and fro, causing his muscles to ripple under her palm. The sensation triggered a reaction she refused to identify.

After several minutes, he pulled the shoe free. "You

are in luck," He held the shoe steady while she slipped it on. She tested her weight and winced.

"You should have a doctor look at that ankle."

"I am a—" she began and thought better of it. "Yes, thank you, I will." Without thinking, she proffered her hand. Immediately she became aware of the crude handkerchief bandage covering her palm and tried to hide it in a fold of her skirt.

"May I see?" He stretched out his arm.

"It's nothing."

He wiggled his fingers slightly and waited until she complied. He examined her injuries and shook his head. "I'll send someone to carry your luggage." He gestured to a bench in front of the depot and helped her over to it. "Wait here."

"Thanks, Mr. . . ."

He started to descend the steps. Halfway down, he turned. "Nathan Blackthorn. Most everyone calls me Nate."

Twenty minutes later, a teenaged boy rushed onto the platform. He gulped in a big breath. "I'm Yancy Wahsise." His outgrown Rock Springs Raiders T-shirt hit him above the navel, leaving a two-inch gap between it and his patched jeans. He lifted a skinny arm and pushed back loose strands of black, shoulder-length hair. "Nate Blackthorn sent me."

She smiled to put him at ease. "Did he tell you I'm so clumsy I'm dangerous to be around?"

"No ma'am. He said to look for a pretty lady with brown eyes and short brown hair."

"Oh." A warm glow gathered in her chest. Disturbed by her reaction, she snatched her purse from the bench. This was neither the time nor the place for such nonsense. She straightened her skirt and moved toward the depot door. "My luggage is inside."

Yancy collected her bags and, with her hobbling along beside him, they set off down the darkening street. Five days ago, when she'd talked to Simon on the phone, he'd told her his room number at the Riverside. This morning her father had phoned the motel pretending to be Simon's editor at *Global News*. He'd been informed they didn't have a guest by the name of Simon Kittredge, nor had he been at the motel earlier in the week. Why had the man lied?

Apprehension choked her for an instant and she tried to reason it away. Simon hadn't said he was in danger. Yet she couldn't forget the tone of his voice on her answering machine, or his garbled words. What had they meant? She wrestled with the possibilities. Then she resolutely pushed them from her mind. She must keep a clear head.

A neon sign with two unlighted letters marked The Riverside's paved entrance. Built of peeled, varnished logs, the one-story structure had been laid out in a U-shape. One side edged the river, the middle section had its back to a field, and a warehouse shared an alley with the portion on her left. Like the depot and all the other houses on the street, these buildings had been built on abnormally high foundations.

Yancy stopped beside the unit marked "Office." "I should be able to manage from here on," she said.

He scratched a swollen mosquito bite on his arm as he pondered her suggestion. Finally, his gaze lifted to meet hers. "Nate said to see you to your room."

"Well, okay. This shouldn't take long." A bell over the door jangled as she entered. Two chairs with worn brown upholstery flanked a table overflowing with dog-eared, coverless magazines. A row of dead flies lay on the windowsill. She sighed and moved to a wooden counter, where a brass sign announced in large block letters that Ted Zeigler was the owner.

Nearby an old-fashioned hotel register lay open. She darted a glance down the dark hall—all clear. With pounding heart, she leafed through the pages, searching for Simon's name. Nothing. She scanned them again looking for erasures—still nothing. She ran a fingertip down the center of the book and felt a stubby edge. A page had been cut out. At the sound of a door slamming, she turned the register around and pushed the buzzer attached to the desk top.

A hulk of a man filled the distant doorway and lumbered toward her, swinging thickly muscled arms. "Yeah?"

"Are you Mr. Zeigler?" she asked, hoping to establish whether or not he had been the man who'd spoken to her father.

He rested his hands on the counter and leaned toward her. "Can't you read?"

She met his scowl with one of her own. "The sign says Ted Zeigler is the owner. You could be an employee."

"Humph! Only ones who work here are me, my old lady, and a maid. And she don't show up half the time." He hunched his shoulders and leaned forward. "You trying to sell something or what?"

"I'd like a room on the river. One with a kitchen if you have it."

"Why didn't you say so instead of beatin' around the bush?" He folded his arms. "Forty dollars a night. No checks. No credit cards." He pocketed the money she gave him before he handed her a pen and spun the register to face her. Suddenly, his eyes sharpened. Drawing his bushy eyebrows together, he peered past her and pointed a tobacco-stained forefinger. "What's that Injun kid doin' here?"

"He carried my bags from the bus depot."

"Don't want his kind hanging around here. Bad for business."

Amy's grip tightened on the pen, but she kept silent and went on writing. She listed the address of her father's summer home on Lomitas Island. Whoever was responsible for Simon's disappearance might get suspicious of someone who came from the same area as Simon.

Zeigler studied what she'd written and tossed a key on the desk. "Follow the sidewalk," he said with a careless wave of his hand. "It's halfway down."

She rejoined Yancy outside. "That man could use some lessons in how to handle people."

Yancy muffled a snicker with his hand. "You can say that again."

She unlocked the door to number five and asked Yancy to put the suitcase on the webbed rack. The square room had an early American motif. A compact kitchen with maple cabinets took up one corner. A round wooden table with two captain's chairs stood near a sliding glass door that led out onto a patio. With a groan, she kicked off her high heels and limped across the brown tweed carpet to a bed that looked as if it'd been made by an inept child. "Is there a restaurant close by where I can get a sandwich?"

"The Golden Goose Cafe is a block down the street." Yancy watched as she explored the bones of her foot and ankle. "Maybe I'd better get it for you."

She sagged with relief. "Oh, that would be . . ." she

began and changed her mind. "No, I've taken up too much of your time already." She took five dollars from her purse and held it out to him. "Your parents will be wondering where you are."

He glanced at the money, shook his head, and backed away. "I don't have any parents. I live with my grandmother."

"It's dark out and you don't want to worry her."

The boy's face twisted and for a moment she thought he might cry. "She's sick, awful sick. We tried Winterhaven Hospital, but old Doc Leibow wouldn't let her in. Said she didn't have insurance or money to pay." He scuffed the toe of his sneaker on the rug. "Some friends took her to the hospital in Silverton. They're keepin' her for ob—ver—sa . . . to look her over."

A lump filled Amy's throat. She knew how he felt. She had gone through a shattering separation when she was a child.

She coughed to cover her emotion. "So Mr. Blackthorn came to stay with you while your grandmother's away."

"Well . . . no, not exactly. He's going to stay, but he didn't know she was in the hospital."

She remembered how the man had reeked of alcohol and frowned. "I'm sure your grandmother wouldn't approve of you letting a stranger stay in your house."

Yancy grinned. "I haven't seen much of him since he got out of college, but Nate's not a stranger. He was a friend of my father's."

A college man! A fine lot of good an education had done him. Suddenly, an unreasoning rage took hold of her. He'd sat right there and let Leibow treat him like a second-class citizen. Gutless. That's what he was. Probably the kind who let people walk on him, then complained about it later. Without thinking, she blurted, "The man's been drinking, you shouldn't be around him."

Yancy lifted his head. "I thought you . . ." He thrust out his chin. "Nate doesn't drink. Never has. Never will. That's what killed my dad and Nate hates the stuff. He says if he ever catches me drinking, he'll nail my hide to the barn." He drew himself up and met her glance with a challenging one of his own. "Nate could do it too. He's some kinda guy."

The boy's words fanned her anger. Yeah, some guy— the do-as-I-say-not-as-I-do kind. She curbed the churning inside her chest and spoke quietly, "If you'll get me a sandwich and cola, I'll buy one for you, too."

The boy regarded her with a patient expression. "I don't need a sandwich. Nate said . . ."

She knotted her fists. "I don't care what he said. This is between you and me. Okay?"

"If you say so . . . but I don't think he's going to like it."

She gave him the money. "Take your time, I'm in no rush."

As soon as he had gone, she opened her suitcase and tossed clothes she'd be needing on the bed. The first-aid kit and cosmetic bag she took into the bathroom. After removing her contacts and donning the tortoise-framed glasses Simon hated, she ran warm water into the sink, scrubbed embedded dirt from her abrasions, and spread on antibiotic ointment. Today, she must have set a record for awkwardness.

With a plastic bag in hand, she went to the refrigerator and dropped several ice cubes inside. She arranged pillows on the bed, lay down with the cold pack on her propped ankle, and leafed through her notebook. Under

"Why?" she printed Ted Zeigler's name. Beneath it, she wrote, "Why would he cut a page from the register? What reason did he have to conceal Simon's stay at the motel? Could there be a connection between Zeigler and Simon's call for help—if so what?"

She'd just printed "Minivan" across the top of a page when a knock sounded and she found Yancy had returned. "Good heavens, Yancy, you can't have eaten in that short period of time." She waved him into the room.

He set a sack on the table and counted out her change. "I decided not to. Nate doesn't say much, but when he does, he means it."

"But I only wanted to repay you for helping me."

He regarded her as an adult would a not-too-bright child. "I carried your bags because Nate asked me to. I got your sandwich because I wanted to." He squared his shoulders. "I didn't expect to be paid."

His sense of dignity shamed her. "I'm sorry. I should have known." She sat down, unwrapped the roast beef sandwich, and gestured to the chair opposite her. "Have you seen a red minivan around Rock Springs lately?"

He stood beside the table idly rubbing his left shin with the toe of his right sneaker. "Uh huh, a Volkswagen. Looked new, so I noticed it right off."

The bite she'd taken stuck in her throat and she took a gulp of cola to wash it down. "When?"

"Let's see . . . I was at the park watching the workmen build a foot bridge across the river." He chewed his lip. "About four or five days ago, I think. It stopped in front of the police station and this Anglo got out and went inside."

Amy set down her sandwich. "Could you describe him?"

"I didn't see his face."

"Oh . . ." Her shoulders slumped in disappointment.

"He was tall . . ." Yancy began hesitantly, "but not as tall as Nate and . . ." a wide smile lit his face, "and his hair was kind of reddish and he wore a cap . . . a . . . a green cap. The funny, floppy kind those guys from England or . . . or Ireland wear in the movies."

Simon. He loved driving and golfing caps. She leaped up, grabbed Yancy's hand, and pumped it up and down. "Thank you." She sobered. "Did you ever see that minivan here at the motel?"

Yancy shook his head. "Us kids used to play baseball and soccer in the field behind the motel before Mr. Zeigler bought it. Now, he won't let us anywhere near the place. He even tried to keep us from playing in the dry riverbed after they changed the channel."

She stared at him. "You mean, I asked for a room on the river and there isn't even a river out there?"

He nodded. "Every spring and fall it flooded the town."

"So that's why the buildings have high foundations."

"Right. Last spring, they changed the channel so they could make the old one deeper." He gave a bored shrug. "Sunday, after Mayor Vanzandt and Judge McAllister blow the dam, the river will be back in the old channel again." He moved toward the door. "I'd better go. Nate'll be expecting me."

She walked along beside him. "Thanks again, Yancy. If you should ever need a favor and I'm still here . . ."

"Yeah, sure," he mumbled and slipped out.

She closed the door and leaned against it. Had Simon gone to the police for assistance in finding the swindlers, or did he have another reason? She returned to the table and picked up her sandwich but realized she was too keyed-up to eat. To fill time, she changed to dark pants and a turtleneck, then cleaned and reloaded her .38.

Minutes dragged by and her nerves stretched tighter. While she fiddled away her time, Simon could be in desperate need of help.

Calm down, she told herself. *Panic causes sloppiness, and you can't afford that.*

She unlocked her forensic satchel, assembled the necessary items, and placed the compact tote bag on the bathroom counter. Nearby, she arranged her contact case and a roll of elastic wrap.

Her preparations complete, she set her alarm for 1 A.M., turned out the light, and lay down to wait.

Chapter 4

She must have dozed. When the alarm sounded, she jerked upright and stared into the darkness, wondering where she was. An instant later, the day's events flooded her mind and she came wide awake.

Groping her way to the windowless bathroom, she closed the door, turned on the light, and put in her contacts. After wrapping her ankle with an elastic bandage, she put on shoes and stood in front of the mirror. Dark makeup and a broad streak of black grease paint along each cheekbone hid her fair complexion so she could blend into the shadows.

She regretted the measures she sometimes had to take, but in the past year, she'd learned the frustration of trying to fit her needs into those of some officious law officer. Unfortunately, the importance of her mission didn't make her actions any less illegal. So be it. She worked her fingers into ultra-thin black leather gloves and switched off the overhead fixture. Simon needed her.

She went out the sliding glass door, eased over the patio rail, and lowered herself to the dewy lawn below. An asphalt path separated a line of quaking aspens from the riverbank. Eerie light from a pallid half-moon cast the landscape into shadows of graveyard gray.

She checked her holstered gun for the fourth time in ten minutes. The retired burglar who'd coached her had said she'd get to the point where she'd get a thrill out of adventures like this. No way. Not ever. She crouched and scuttled upslope through ankle-deep grass. As she ran, she counted patios—six, seven, eight. They ended at ten, where a metal garbage dumpster occupied a paved area. It separated the right leg of the U-shaped complex from the short row of units at the foot.

She rounded the corner of number eleven, and a faint sound brought her up short. She held her breath. Silent as death, a shadow from above glided over the grass and swooped into the field in front of her. A high-pitched squeal pierced the stillness. Then, its great wings lifting in stolid, funereal beats, the owl rose into the air with his struggling prey.

Amy let out a quivering breath and hurried on to unit twelve, the room number Simon had given her. She studied the curtained glass doors for several minutes. *Please, don't let it be occupied.*

A shiver traveled along her spine. The big guy in the sky hadn't looked after the small creature in the field. She sighed. Dad would say, "God helps those who help themselves."

She hitched up pants that slid low on her slim hips, pushed her tote bag between the balusters of the patio's guard rail, and climbed over.

In her mind, she had rehearsed how she'd jimmy the glass door. To her surprise, she found it ajar. A maid's oversight, Zeigler's sloppiness, or something more threatening? She listened for several minutes. When she didn't hear voices or movement, she drew her gun and slipped through the drawn curtains.

No illumination came through the insulated drapes, but enough filtered from spaces at the top and sides to assure her no one lay in the bed. One worry banished. Relieved, she moved forward a few steps. With the .38 locked in a straight arm stance, she swung in a slow half-circle.

Uneasiness stirred at the base of her spine, worked its way upward, and settled between her shoulder blades. She inhaled and let the air out slowly. Someone was in the room.

She released the pistol's safety catch and took a step backward. She searched the darkness for a black mass. Where was he? She felt a movement of air against her nape and started to swivel around.

A man grabbed her from behind and pressed a knife to her throat. "Easy. Not a sound."

She went rigid, her heart hammering her ribs.

"Give me the gun."

Blackthorn! Why here? Why now? How? . . . Her mind went numb from overload.

He tightened his choke hold. "I do not want to hurt you, Dr. Prescott, but I will."

Blackthorn's flat, unemotional tone snuffed out any hope of a counterattack. She let him take her gun.

He turned on the lamp beside the bed and her scalp prickled. The clothes he wore resembled her own except for one chilling detail. He wore a tight-fitting hood and only the whites of his eyes and the gleam of his teeth showed through the narrow slits in the elastic cloth. He held her gun on her while he slipped his knife into an ankle sheath.

She wet her dry mouth and steadied quivering muscles. *When cornered, attack.* "What are you doing here?"

He made a broad gesture with his gloved hand. "Kittredge, same as you."

"Who are you? How do you know why I came here?" She narrowed her eyes. "And what do you want with Simon?"

He sat on the arm of a chair. "If you intend to check his room, you had better get a move on." His voice, although soft, carried a note of command.

She clenched her fists. No man told her what to do, not anymore. "Where's Simon? What have you done with him?" She folded her arms and glowered at him.

He lifted one shoulder. "I was not aware he was missing until a few hours ago." He stood up, seeming to tower above her in his black garb. "You are wasting time, doctor."

She weighed her options. Left to his own devices, he might destroy important evidence. Yet the possibility of providing him with clues to Simon's whereabouts filled her with apprehension.

A quick appraisal convinced her she couldn't escape unless he chose to let her go. "My equipment is on the patio." Without a word, he fetched the cloth bag and laid it on a chair.

The room held a small dresser, a night table, two vinyl chairs, and a bed. She examined the furniture with a magnifying glass and found they'd been wiped clean. The drawers and the stripped mattress yielded nothing of any consequence.

Underneath the bed, she discovered two small lumps of tightly compressed mud. When she groped behind her for the sack of supplies, Blackthorn shoved tweezers and one of her polyethylene evidence bags into her hand. To her surprise, he'd filled in most of the pre-printed label with inventory number, date, victim's name, time, and location.

She surveyed him with a raised eyebrow. Where had he learned to label evidence? Under "Description" she wrote, "Dried mud, 1 cm × 1 cm × 1.5 cm found under right side of bed." She signed her name, placed one of the squares inside, and held out her hand for another envelope in which to package the second lump of mud.

"Did Kittredge phone you?"

"His name is Simon. He's a person, not some medical-case history."

He leaned closer, his eyes glittering. "Did you hear from him?" He came down hard on each word.

Her smoldering temper rose a notch. She swiped bangs out of her eyes with the back of her hand and scowled. "Why should I tell you anything? I don't even know who you are." His exasperated grunt gave her a perverse sense of satisfaction.

"You will just have to trust me."

"Why? Give me one reason."

"I want to help you find him."

"And if we do, then what?"

"That depends on his answers to my questions."

"I see." *Simon held some sort of key.* She finished examining the carpet around the bed and moved to the closet. "Do you know who swindled Simon's father?"

He shook his head.

"Hm-m-m." *Maybe he's telling the truth and maybe he isn't.* She plucked strands of hair from a splinter protruding from the doorjamb and waited while he labeled an envelope. "What about the man that followed Simon and Erika from Central America?"

He turned his hands palm up. "I know you're very

good at what you do, but you don't know what . . ." he smoothed his black leather gloves over his knuckles. "You may need me."

She regarded him for a long moment. "I've managed to look after myself for a good portion of the last thirty-one years."

"We must find him as soon as possible or . . ."

She pressed her hand to her stomach. "Don't say it." Simon was all right. She swallowed a rush of panic. He had to be. She would not consider any other possibility.

Gathering her gear together, she pushed open the bathroom door. A familiar aroma brought a rush of memories—the two weeks she and Simon had spent together last fall, the life-threatening experience they'd lived through, and, most poignant of all, the tender moments they'd shared.

A squeezing sensation invaded her chest and tears stung her lids. She sank down on the edge of the tub and gazed up at Blackthorn who stood in the doorway. "Zeigler claims Simon didn't stay at this motel." Although she stretched her eyes wide, a tear escaped. "I know he did. A friend of Simon's in Paris created that cologne you smell especially for him." Her nose began to run and she sniffed.

Blackthorn tore off a handful of toilet tissue and passed it to her. "Did you register under your real name?"

She nodded and blew her nose.

"That wasn't wise. Zeigler talks. Someone in town may connect you with the article Kittredge . . . uh, Simon wrote about you and your father for *Global News.*"

"You have a file on me?" she snapped. "Why? Simon hasn't done anything. What are you after?"

"If someone connects what you do with why you're

here," he said, ignoring her question, "you could be in danger."

"That's my problem." She blew her nose again and at the same time noticed a glimmer at the bottom of the wicker wastebasket. She upended the basket, tapped the sides gently, and packaged shiny glass splinters that fell onto the tile floor.

A fifteen-minute inspection turned up nothing more. After stowing the collected objects in her bag, she set it on the bed and faced him. She drew herself up to her full height and met his gaze squarely. "I'll take my gun now."

He tilted his head and his mouth widened in a grin. She scowled at him. *Arrogant clown, how dare he make fun of me.*

He removed her pistol from inside his belt, handed it to her, and pointed to the bag she carried. "If you learn anything helpful, would you let me know?"

She lifted her chin. "Sharing is a two-way street."

He gave a solemn nod. "True, but sometimes circumstances do not allow—" he stiffened. "Someone's coming." He turned off the lamp. "Get in the closet, and *stay* there."

She did as he directed and peered through a crack. A second ticked by. Her pulse quickened until its beat thundered in her head. Suddenly, the outside door burst open, the light flashed on, and Zeigler stalked inside.

Before the motel owner could cry out, Blackthorn lunged at him. The fingers of Blackthorn's left hand sank into Zeigler's fleshy neck while his right rammed the big man's chest with pile-driver force. Zeigler crumpled like a poleaxed bull. Blackthorn caught the man's limp body and lowered him silently to the floor.

Her breath whistled from her lungs. *Good God!* This afternoon Blackthorn had sat meekly and taken Dr. Leibow's abuse. What kind of a man was he anyway?

Chapter 5

Next morning, Amy swung her feet to the floor, stood up, and let out a groan. Even though her ankle felt better, her bruised knees protested with every step. She put on her glasses and hobbled out onto the patio. The early morning sun slanted through quaking aspen leaves arrayed in golden autumnal splendor and bathed her in gilded light.

She filled her lungs with crisp clean air and gazed around her. A clanking noise far off to the west attracted her attention. Grasping the rail, she leaned farther out, trying to locate the source of the racket. She winced and drew back. For a moment, she'd forgotten her swollen hands.

Her gaze wandered to the grassy slope she'd traversed the night before. Blackthorn wanted to question Simon. Did that mean Simon was involved in something illegal? She raked fallen leaves into a pile with her bare toes. Not Simon, he was too intelligent, too honest, too . . .

A sigh escaped her. Did she ever really know him? When he'd declared his love for her, hadn't she harbored doubts? And hadn't those doubts proven well justified?

She shut her eyes. After what Mitch had done, she'd lost her trust in men. She hadn't wanted to love again. In truth, she'd been relieved when Simon had found another lover. Being a friend was much easier, and safer.

She sighed again and switched her thoughts to Blackthorn. Not much hope of getting any answers from him. What an enigma he'd turned out to be. He frightened her, yet he also intrigued her.

She frowned. *Silly woman. Must you always clutter up your life with some man?* She made a sound of disgust, went inside, and took off her pajamas.

With a critical expression, she peered at her naked image in the dressing-table mirror. Simon claimed she had a terrific body. But, then, he'd thought the same about his deceased wife Julie and Mona Sanders, the woman he'd fallen for after Julie died. He probably thought the same of Erika. Simon wasn't a great judge of women.

Amy expelled a long sigh. When she and Simon met, she'd been trying to recover from her divorce and was up to her eyeballs with feelings of rejection. She shrugged. No doubt Erika had an equally fascinating problem for Simon to solve.

She showered, attended to her abrasions, and wrapped her sprained ankle. Rest and ice packs had reduced the swelling. She peered into her suitcase at the clothes she'd packed. What role should she play today? Feminine? Yes, very definitely, but not excessively so. Practical? Yes, that too. She snapped her fingers. She'd be a housewife out doing her shopping. No one would pay her the slightest attention.

She put her shoulder holster next to the skin and donned a roomy gingham-check blouse. A denim skirt, low-heeled walking shoes, tortoise-shell glasses, and a faint trace of lipstick completed her guise.

Before leaving, she put the specimens from Simon's room in her forensic satchel and shoved it through a trap-door she'd found in the closet ceiling. Probably Zeigler didn't feel too frisky this morning. Nevertheless, she didn't intend to take a chance on him going through her things.

Once she'd hidden anything that might give away her mission, she slipped on a jacket, draped a camera strap around her neck, and set off.

When she reached the bridge spanning the river, she saw evidence of the task Rock Springs had undertaken. The river looked at least two hundred feet wide, and cemented rock covered the walls and the bottom of the fifty-foot deep channel. Deepening a river that size must have been an expensive undertaking for a small town. Two dump trucks loaded with boulders thundered by, interrupting her observations.

Midway across the arched bridge, she stopped and stared with delight. Double, three-foot-high walls made of cobblestones edged the river on both sides. Soil filled the spaces between the walls and chrysanthemums in shades of apricot, yellow, and rust spilled over the sides. Beside the wall ran a wide asphalt path that led through a green belt adjacent to the river.

She snapped a picture and started along a sidewalk. A spacious town square paved with pillow-shaped, terra cotta-colored cement bricks lay on her left and a tree-dotted park on the right. Concrete benches sat under the trees. Huge bowl-shaped planters made of cemented pebbles and planted with showy, red-leafed shrubs rested at intervals around the town square.

Everywhere she looked, she saw something built of

stone or some product of stone: pools, miniature waterfalls, light standards, playground equipment. Even the walk on which she stood displayed different patterns of hand-laid stone in every other square. The sights so engrossed her, she scarcely noticed the shabbily dressed gardener leisurely raking leaves into a pile with long strokes.

"Morning, miss," he said, touching the wide, floppy brim of his straw hat.

At the sound of his voice, she shielded her eyes from the sun, and the words of greeting she'd been about to speak died in her throat. Gray speckled his hair and full mustache, but the voice was Blackthorn's. He turned and trundled his wheelbarrow toward a small building hidden in the trees. It took all the control she could muster not to stare after him.

Why had he drawn attention to himself? Had he done it to remind her that he would keep watch until she led him to Simon?

She jumped as a red truck, jacked up high and glistening with chrome, rumbled by. Seconds later, the driver reversed and sped backward until he was opposite her.

The blond young man inside smiled broadly. "Hiya, sweet thing. What candy box did you drop from?" When she neither spoke nor looked at him, he laughed and accelerated just enough to stay even with her. "Sorry, doll, I forgot to introduce myself. I'm Holt McAllister's oldest and best looking son, Troy. I'm on my way to The Green Lantern Saloon for a Bloody Mary. Why don't you hop in and we'll have one together."

"No thanks."

He made a U-turn in the middle of the street, came

up onto the sidewalk and inched in behind her until his front bumper nearly touched her legs. "In this town, baby, you don't turn down a McAllister's invitation."

She clenched her teeth and walked on without increasing her pace. Behind her, McAllister's wide tires crushed shrubbery, tipped over planters, scraped corners off light standards. There weren't many people around, but those who were hurried about their business without stopping to gawk.

She breathed a deep sigh when she saw two police cars parked in front of a white stone building. Surely they would see the destruction the young idiot was causing and stop him. When no one came out, she strode across the street. McAllister rumbled over the curb and followed her halfway up the low steps.

She gained the top and hurried inside. The heavy glass door closed behind her with a resounding ker-thunk. No one came to the front desk. After waiting ten minutes, she opened the metal gate, marched to an office marked "George Pike, Police Chief," and flung open the door.

A portly white-haired man sat reading a magazine, his booted feet resting on a drawer pulled out of his desk. He lowered the magazine and peered through black-framed glasses. "Sumpthin' eating you, little sister?" he said in a thick Southern drawl.

"A man named Troy McAllister is harassing me."

"Whoa now, sister. Don't get yourself all riled. That boy is just funning you."

"Oh, he is, is he?" She gripped the edge of his desk and leaned toward him. "Then you don't mind if he mashed your back fender."

The chief's spider-veined face turned purple and the

heels of his western boot thudded to the floor. "Norm!" he bellowed. "Norm Hollenbeck, get the hell out here."

A rangy, sandy-haired man with a modified Poncho Via mustache came through the door. He yawned, stretched, and scratched his ribs. "Yeah, what's up, George."

"I thought Holt told you to ride herd on those damned boys of his."

Norm blew out a gusty breath. "You expect me to follow those two half-assed bubbleheads to every bar and cathouse in the county?"

Anger flared in Chief Pike's pale blue eyes. "Whatever it takes. And if you don't do it right, I'm not the only one who's going to chew your ass, boy." His sagging cheeks quivered. "Now you get out there and see what that ornery no-account Troy has done this time."

Scowling at her, Norm left, slamming the chief's office door behind him. Chief Pike shifted his fiery gaze to her. "As for you, sister. We don't need no fillies swishing their tails on our streets and rousin' the sap in our boys. You best take care of your business right fast and move on."

Amy stared at him, her disbelief turning to disgust.

"What you staring at girl?"

"You." Her gaze traveled from his rumpled blue pants to the peak of the white Stetson hat resting on the back of his head and her lip curled. "Police usually look after the public's safety." Her gaze captured his. "Evidently Rock Springs has a different set of values."

He bounded to his feet and leaned across his desk. "Now you looka here, Ms. Prescott . . ."

He knew her name! There went her plan to blend in with the citizenry. Frustration churned inside her as she stalked out of the building.

Norm Hollenbeck stood on the broad stone steps shouting and waving his arms at Troy McAllister. Troy backed his trunk into the street, crunching another of the police car's fenders in the process. He laughed, revved the truck's motor to a high-pitched scream, gave Norm the finger, and took off.

Norm turned, saw her watching, and came toward her. "If I were you, I wouldn't spend a lot of time in Rock Springs. Troy gets real mean when he doesn't get what he wants."

Chapter 6

Amy lingered beside the police station door until Norm gained the top step. "Thanks for the advice, officer." She smiled, hoping to make a friend in enemy territory. "I'll give it some thought."

His gaze traveled over her, then he nailed a tuberose bush with a stream of tobacco juice. "Maybe there's some hope for Troy after all. His taste is sure as hell improving." He winked at her and went back inside.

Amy blew out her breath. Nothing like causing a public incident to create good community relations. At this rate, she'd have to turn in her private investigator's permit.

As she went down the steps, she glanced over at the park. This whole ludicrous charade must have given Nate Blackthorn a good laugh. Her spirits lightened when she saw no sign of his shabby, bent figure.

She sauntered through the town square, stopping to peer into windows. Chief Pike probably had obtained her name from the clerk at the bus depot. Maybe he did it routinely to keep track of newcomers. She hoped so. He didn't appear to be the type who'd take kindly to someone peeking under the rug in "his" town.

The two-story building ahead of her had "1890" incised on the keystone. Its red brick walls had been sandblasted until they resembled the muted pink of new skin. Workmen ambled in and out of the lower story's double oak doors, carrying grayed barn boards.

"What're you doing?" she asked a hard-hatted workman.

The man passed his palm over his lined face. "The judge wants the rooms divided." He put one hand behind his head, the other on his hip and took a couple of mincing steps. "They're going to be bo—teaks you know."

She laughed and pointed to the building next door. "That his, too?"

"Yeah, Judge McAllister owns them and three of the local mines." He pointed to a canyon. "Owns the smelter up Detter's Gulch too. Had to close it down when the silver started petering out though." A lopsided grin made white furrows in his florid skin. "Damned cryin' shame." He chuckled. "And one he rightly deserved."

Amy regarded him speculatively. He seemed to relish McAllister's misfortune. "Are some of the mines still working?"

He hooked his thumbs into the front pockets of his worn jeans that clung precariously to nonexistent hips. One of his hands had two fingers missing. "Yeah, a few of the small outfits. The judge's Lucky Boy is closed, but a crew's still mucking at his Queen Bee. And I hear tell they're doing some exploratory cores at his China Lady." He frowned and pulled at his lip. "Holt's been mighty close-mouthed about what they're finding though."

"Is Holt McAllister a real judge, or is that just a nickname."

"A *real* judge?" The man's harsh laugh sounded as if it had been torn from deep within his wiry frame. "Depends on whether you're for the people or the county." He gestured toward a big, white-pillared house on the hill. "That's where his honor lives. Us folks down here muck his mines while he sits up there buying cars, Arabian horses, and condos."

"Were you a miner before you became a carpenter?"

His face took on a grim expression. "I was a shifter at the China Lady until two years ago."

"A what?"

"A shift boss. They closed it down after . . ." his eyes became watery and his Adam's apple bobbed several times, "after the explosion that . . . that took my two boys."

His grief touched her, and she found it hard to keep her eyes from tearing. "I'm sorry, Mr. . . . ?

"Dworski. Jared Dworski."

She stuck out her hand. "I'm Amy Prescott." She pressed his large, callused palm between both of hers. "Losing one child would be awful, but two . . . I don't know how you stood it."

"Raised them all by myself from the time they were eight and nine," he rasped. "The inspectors called it an unavoidable accident. It wasn't and Holt damn well knows it." His mouth twisted into a sneer. "That's why he's got me overseeing all these pissy-assed projects of his."

Amy glanced at the men moving in and out of the gutted building. "Do all these men work for McAllister?"

He leaned forward, enveloping her in yeasty-beer

breath. "The whole damned town works for him. In one way or another." He squinched up his eyes. "Thought you'd know that after talking to Pike."

"You don't seem afraid of him."

He shrugged. "He could fire me. But he won't."

"I see." She tilted her head and studied him for a moment. "Did you happen to notice what his son did awhile ago?"

"Couldn't hardly miss it."

"Does he get away with stuff like that?"

"Regular as All Bran." A smile crinkled around his eyes. "Most of the women around here kowtow to him."

She squared her shoulders. "Not this woman."

His grin broadened. "Did my heart good to see a lady with some spunk."

She smiled and started moving away from him. "Nice talking to you, Mr. Dworski. I'm on my way to have breakfast."

"Try Verna's Special. It's a doozie."

"Perhaps I will. The fresh air has given me an appetite. Thanks for the suggestion."

Farther along the block, a picture of a coyly strutting yellow goose in a chef's hat dominated the top portion of a white, freshly painted, clapboard building. Below, large black letters informed her she had arrived at The Golden Goose Cafe.

Inside, high-backed booths deeply upholstered in marshmallow vinyl-flanked walls covered with blue and white checked paper. She'd no sooner sat down than a slender woman arrived with a glass of ice water, a coffee carafe, and a menu.

"Morning." She filled Amy's cup, set down the carafe, and gave her oversized glasses an impatient shove. "My name's Edna Wakefield." She tucked a wayward tendril of dark hair behind her ear. "Too bad you had to meet up with one of the McAllister boys your first day in town."

"Yes." Amy pasted on a smile. Doing an investigation in a town where everyone knew everyone else's business could have its drawbacks. "Chief Pike seems to think it was my fault."

"Humph, you might know it. Old George ain't about to butt heads with the judge." She wrote down Amy's order and went off toward the kitchen.

Amy took her notebook from her purse and made entries while she sipped her coffee. One thing she knew for sure, she'd get no help from the law in this town. Yancy had seen Simon go into the police station, so Simon must have discovered the same thing. She put down Jared Dworski's name and also the waitress's for future reference.

When Edna returned with her breakfast, Amy showed her a picture of Simon. "Has this man been in here?"

Edna pushed her glasses into place and studied the snapshot. "Uh-huh, he's been around about a week." She puckered her forehead. "Last time I saw him was Wednesday . . . I think." She snapped her fingers. "No it was Thursday. I remember 'cause he had me make two peanut butter and jam sandwiches to go." She snickered. "I told him that was our schoolboy lunch."

Simon loved peanut butter. Amy gripped the handle of her cup and tried to lift it to her mouth. Her hand shook and coffee sloshed onto the table. "Was . . . was he with anyone?"

Edna scratched her head with her pencil. "Saw him talking to half the people in town. That man was plumb full of questions. Never saw him with the same person twice." Her eyes sharpened. "He a friend of yours?"

Amy nodded. "Simon and I—his name's Simon Kittredge—we planned to meet here and spend part of our vacation together." She sighed. "Now I can't find him and . . . and I'm worried."

Edna sank down in the seat opposite her. "Gee, that's too bad." She reached across and patted Amy's hand. "He probably went fishing and lost track of the days."

Amy pretended to be cheered. "Maybe you're right. He loves to fish. Got any ideas where the fishing is especially good?"

"From what I hear there's lots of places. I'll ask our customers if any of them has seen him."

"Uh . . . I'm Amy Prescott, but I'd rather you didn't mention my name. You know how guys are about possessive wives and girlfriends." She held out the snapshot. "Keep this, I have another." She took a swallow of orange juice. "How come there's so much construction going on all over town?"

"It all started when we got the grant."

"Oh? What kind of a grant?"

Edna shrugged. "Don't ask me." She beckoned to a white-haired woman who'd just entered.

The woman hung up her jacket, smoothed her blue uniform over well-padded hips, and came over to where they sat. "Got a problem?"

Edna shook her head. "This is Amy Prescott. She's new in town. She was asking about all the improvements." Edna waved toward the front window. "Since you're on the Rock Springs Rejuvenation Committee, I thought you'd like to tell her."

She slid out of the booth and the other woman took her place. "Amy meet Verna Jensen," she said. "She owns The Golden Goose." The bell over the door jingled as a tall man dressed in a blue suit and carrying a briefcase came in. "Keep in touch," Edna said and headed up front.

Verna smiled broadly, showing dimples in both plump cheeks. "You may be sorry you got me started. George," she dimpled again and her skin turned a pretty pink, "Mr. Pike, the police chief, says I'm as persistent as a bible salesman." She giggled and put her hand over her mouth. "That man has such a way with words."

"Yeah," Amy said. "I noticed." She took a bite of toast and waited for Verna to cream and sugar the cup of coffee she'd poured herself. Vaguely she was aware of the waitress asking the gentleman in the adjoining booth for his order. When he spoke, Amy nearly choked on her toast. She hadn't seen Nate Blackthorn come in, but the voice certainly sounded like his. She became so engrossed, she didn't catch Verna's first words.

"—applied for the grant." A tiny furrow appeared between Verna's china-blue eyes. "At least that's what Mayor Vanzandt told those of us on the committee."

Amy took a wild guess. "You say the mayor applied for the grant?"

"Either him or someone on the town council, I think. But I'm getting ahead of myself. First, Mayor Vanzandt offered five hundred dollars to the person who could come up with a plan to rejuvenate this old burg. Wanda Reece's husband, Frank, had mashed his leg at the mine. He needed something to keep himself busy, so she talked him into working on the project with her." Verna got to her feet. "Come see what they did."

Verna beckoned her to a far corner where a four-by-eight sheet of plywood sat on two sawhorses. "You may have noticed we have an overabundance of rock. Frank suggested we buy a rock crusher and give the whole area a face-lift." She ran a stubby fingertip along a miniature copy of the street outside. "Frank proposed stone, cobblestone, or some by-product of crushed rock be used wherever possible."

"Fantastic. From what I saw on the way here, you've certainly done wonders."

Verna glowed. "By the time we're through Rock Springs will be a place to be proud of." She glanced toward the kitchen. "I've got pies to bake." She smiled. "They're huckleberry. Stop in this evening and have a piece.

Amy lingered by the display a moment longer, then swung around and scrutinized the man in the booth adjoining hers. He wore a blue suit, and brown wavy hair and a small mustache. He raised his head and his blue eyes met hers. He couldn't be Blackthorn.

The man's right eyebrow rose a trifle and he shrugged one shoulder. Amy dropped her gaze and moved on by him. Yesterday, on the plane, Blackthorn had made a similar gesture. She slumped down in the booth and pressed her fingers against her temples. Perhaps, she was getting paranoid.

A gray-haired man pushed open the front door and hobbled down the row of booths. He greeted everyone by their first name and stopped occasionally to inquire about someone's health. He jerked his body forward with each step, his face darkening as his weight shifted. When he reached Amy, he said, "I'm Dr. Paul Chambers." He peered at her and grinned. "You're pretty like your mother, but by damn I'd still know you were old B.J.'s daughter."

Amy's cheeks grew hot. "Dad didn't . . ." She waggled her head. "What am I going to do with that man? I swear he's got a friend or an old school chum everywhere I go." She looked up at him and smiled. "Which one are you?"

He groaned as he lowered himself onto the seat opposite her. "B.J. and I roomed together in college. Haven't seen him since I ran into him years ago at a medical convention. Is he still full of Old Nick?"

"Oh, yes. He's fifty-six and has the energy of a twenty-five-year-old." She sobered. "Knowing Dad, he probably suggested you keep an eye on me. Right?"

Amusement lit his eyes. "Nope. He just asked if I'd give you some tips on where to get some good wildlife pictures."

She relaxed her tensed muscles. "That would be helpful."

"I've got an even better proposition." He laughed at her startled expression. "Since you're going to be here awhile, why don't you stay in my cabin? It's nothing fancy, but it's better than putting up with Zeigler's guff."

"No, no, I couldn't do that." She drew her brows together in exasperation. When she got back home, she and her father would have to have a serious talk. "I wouldn't want to inconvenience you."

"Not at all. Not at all. The cabin is fifty yards behind my house. I'll never know you're there." He hit his elbow on the table, flinched, and massaged it. "Maybe, if you're not too busy, we could have an occasional chat." He leaned forward and lowered his voice. "In Rock Springs, stimulating conversation is hard to come by."

She chewed her lip. Maintaining secrecy when Zeigler had a key to her room was definitely a problem. "Well, I guess it'll be all right."

* * *

In less than thirty minutes, she'd checked out of the Riverside Motel, stowed her luggage in Dr. Chambers's station wagon, and taken the seat beside him.

"My place is within walking distance of town," he said as he put the car in gear. "Granddad bought the ten acres of virgin timber before they discovered silver. He built the cabin, then later on the main house."

"Carpenters made them to last in those days," she said. "The Prescott family home is on Lomitas Island. Originally it belonged to Captain Thaddeus Prescott, a grandfather with numerous 'greats' in front of his name." She laughed. "He had some rather nutty notions. You wouldn't believe some of the odd—" His strange expression stopped her.

He ran a finger inside his collar. "My granddaddy had . . ." he licked his lips and swallowed, "some . . . uh . . . peculiarities, too." His eyes lost focus and a tic twitched a muscle in his cheek, pulling the corner of his mouth into a leer.

The hair on the back of her neck rose, and she gripped her fingers together. What kind of a situation had her father gotten her into?

Chapter 7

Dr. Chambers shook himself, and his expression became genial. "It'll be nice to have a woman around the place again. My wife's been gone ten years." He peered at her. "Matter of fact, you remind me of Mora."

He turned down a lane and parked in front of a somber, two-story house. The slate-gray paint, shuttered windows, and high, untrimmed shrubbery gave it a guarded appearance.

"Excuse my housekeeping," he said as he let her inside and showed her around.

Oak wainscoting and wallpaper in shades of blue predominated in all shadowy rooms except for the one he'd outfitted as an examination room. With a slight groan, he sank down on a stool. "I have chondrocalcinosis." He glanced up at her as though to see if she understood the word's meaning. She did, but she didn't comment. "It's a disabling joint disease," he said. "If I don't feel up to going to the office, patients who must be seen come here."

She nodded. "Dad has had to cut back, too," she said and hoped her father hadn't told him he'd switched from family practice to forensic medicine.

She found the rest of the house unremarkable except for one detail: the side where the doctor had his study abutted a sheer rock wall at the base of Whitecrest Mountain. She shivered, unsure whether the damp chill of the room or the oppressive gray stone was the cause. Apparently, the threat of avalanche hadn't frightened old granddad.

The cabin lay some distance from the house. Built of lodge pole pine, the weathered building blended so well with the wooded surroundings, it could scarcely be seen.

After Paul, as he'd urged her to call him, pointed the way, he pressed the key to his camouflage Army-surplus jeep into her hand and took off for Winterhaven Hospital to see a patient.

Amy explored the cabin. The rustic decor reminded her of her father's beach house on Lomitas Island—pine paneling, stone fireplace, braided rugs. Here, one large room served as kitchen, dining, and living quarters. Through a door in the side wall, she found a generous-sized bedroom with an adjoining lavatory-shower.

She stowed her suitcase under the bed, hung up her jacket, and converted a small corner table into her laboratory. When assembling her forensic satchel, she'd selected the lightest and most versatile microscope she could find. It sufficed for most field procedures.

She arranged a glass fragment taken from Simon's bathroom under the microscope's objective and peered through the eyepiece. Amber residue coated the chip. This she would have her father send to Simon's friend in Paris for analysis of the cologne's ingredients and comparison with Simon's special scent.

She studied another of the glittering shards to determine its ream markings, hardness, density, and optical properties, information she would need if she should find a person with glass embedded in their clothing or shoe soles.

A tremor went through her. She wouldn't have to go that far unless Simon was dead, and she refused to dwell on that prospect.

She cross-sectioned two of the reddish-brown hairs she'd found in Simon's room. All elements indicated the hair had come from a Caucasian with type B, Rh-positive blood. *The same as Simon's.* To narrow the possibilities even further, she added quinacrine. When the Y chromosomes began to fluoresce from high concentrations of the dye, she sighed with satisfaction. The hair belonged to a man. Her gut feeling told her that that man was Simon. If worst came to worst, someone else would have to disprove her findings.

She glanced at her watch, took off her glasses, rubbed her eyes, and got out the two soil samples. When the outcome involved a friend, the time-absorbing tests frayed her nerves.

She adjusted her camera and took close-up and magnified views of the two pieces of soil. Mud had been deposited in layers as the person walked about. If the soil came from Simon's shoes, and it could have—he liked trail boots with deep-lug soles—she might learn where his investigation had led him.

She positioned one of the segments under the microscope and began to tease black leaf-mold thicknesses apart with a dissecting needle.

With infinite care, she examined and listed each minute particle—feces from a small animal, yellow and orange lichens, a quarter inch of conifer needle, the tip of a porcupine quill, a bit of snail shell. Her hand shook as several shiny fish scales came to light. Under closer scrutiny, she found the scales to be the same cycloid shape as salmon and trout.

She could scarcely believe her good fortune. While doing her specialty forensics, she'd been amazed to learn fish scales had growth rings similar to those of trees. With these scales as reference, a specialist—if one existed in the area—could calculate the fish's age, size, and even where he came from.

Ushering up a prayer, she prepared a slide to take with her.

At the Fish and Game Department in the nearby town of Creston, Amy stated her problem and the receptionist ushered her into an office.

As she entered, a short, middle-aged man rose from behind a green metal desk. He came toward her with his hand outstretched. "I'm Ivar Stenrud," he said with a faint Scandinavian accent.

"Amy Prescott," she said giving his hand a firm shake.

He motioned her to a chair. "What can I do for you. Miss Prescott?"

She ran her tongue over her dry lips. Telling lies made her nervous. "I'm . . . doing research for a class I'm taking at the University of Washington." She reeled off a few of the facts she knew about fish scales and set the slide she'd mounted in front of him. "Can you tell me what kind of fish these belonged to and where it came from."

He smiled. "Sure can." He led the way into a small, adequately equipped laboratory. "Hope the smell of dead fish doesn't bother you."

Amy remembered some of her postmortems and smiled. "I've smelled a lot worse."

He set up the slide and gave her a sideways glance. "I'm the closest thing to an expert you'll find in these parts."

"An expert." She beamed at him. "That's wonderful."

He smoothed his hand over thinning blond hair. "I find fish extremely interesting." He bent his head over the microscope. "They have the same number of scales when they're born as when they die."

"You mean the scales just grow bigger as they do."

"That's right." He moved to the side. "Notice that most of this fish's growth rings are approximately the same width."

She peered through the eyepieces. "Is that significant?"

"Very. It reflects the condition of its habitat." He did some figuring on a calculator. "This fish had reached a length of approximately fifteen inches. He's over three years old and from a fast-growing species."

Her nerves began to twitch. "Any clues to where he might have been caught?"

"Several. He's experienced little stress, which means he had a plentiful food source in water of unvarying temperature. I think he's a *Salmo trutta*. They thrive in warm, sluggish streams and ponds where few other trout can live."

She jiggled one foot impatiently. "What's that tell you?"

He readjusted the microscope and stood back. "Look at the tightly woven rings in the center." While she did as he instructed, he turned to a shelf and took down a three-ring notebook. Plastic fish-scale replicas filled the pages he leafed through.

"Ah," he said at last. "Now compare what you see with this." He indicated a replica labeled "Brown Trout *Salmo trutta*, Source: Colby Creek."

Suddenly, all of the strength drained out of her. Her knees went weak and wobbly. At last, a place to start looking for Simon.

"What do brown trout eat?"

"Hm-m-m," he said and stroked his chin. "Well, a large one will feed on amphipods, isopods, and insect larvae such as mayflies and caddisflies."

She'd found no insects in the soil sample. "Is that all they eat?"

He turned off the microscope light and leaned his back against the counter. "Their diet also includes lampreys, minnows, frogs, and snails."

The piece of snail shell. A glow of accomplishment spread through her. "Thank you. Thank you very much." She could scarcely wait to get on her way. "I certainly appreciate the help you've given me."

Mr. Stenrud put away the three-ring binder. "You planning on going to Colby Creek."

"I thought I might."

"The road's washed out." He cocked his head to one side. "You may have to hike eight or nine miles."

"No problem," she said with an exuberant wave of her hand. "I'm used to it."

After bidding him good-bye, she made two stops, the first at the Ranger Station to pick up maps of the area and the second to buy groceries. While there, she phoned her father.

"I'm making a little progress," she said and gave him

a quick run-down on what she'd been doing since she arrived. She didn't mention Nate Blackthorn.

"Sounds promising," B.J. said, "What do you think of Paul?"

She hesitated, searching for the right note so he wouldn't detect her qualms. "He seems like a nice person."

"Seems? What do you mean 'seems'?" He blew out his breath. "Amy, are you holding out on me?"

She pressed her forehead to one of the Plexiglas panels that surrounded her on three sides. "Now, Dad, you're overworking your imagination again. I can take care of myself."

He grumbled something she couldn't catch, then said, "You stay in touch, hear?"

She drew boxes inside boxes around the edge of a notebook page. Somehow, some way, she had to convince him not to be so protective. "Tomorrow, I'm going to Colby Creek, so I may not check in for several days."

"All right, but watch it, okay?"

She promised and replaced the receiver. The current of her father's compelling desire to see her happily married and the mother of children ran just beneath the surface of all their conversations. His yearning expression when he saw a small child tore at her heart. Meanwhile he had too much love and only her to lavish it on.

The sun had disappeared behind the distant peaks of the Bitterroot Mountains by the time she pulled the jeep into its place beside the garage. Paul was standing beside his station wagon. "Get some good pictures?" he asked.

She surreptitiously patted her purse, hoping to find her camera, yet in her mind's eye she could see the Minolta Maxxum sitting on her bed. In the future, she'd have to be more careful.

"I've just been scouting the area," she said quickly. "Have the deer and elk come down from the mountains yet?"

Paul hobbled over to the jeep and rested his arm on the fender. "I heard an elk bugle yesterday morning."

"Got any suggestions where I might see some?"

"Try Davis Creek Road. It heads into the foothills near Horseshoe Peak. I used to bag an elk in there every season."

"You wouldn't happen to have a backpack you could lend me would you?"

"Lordy Moses, do I." He triggered the automatic garage door. "Come along and I'll show you." He pointed to one wall of the two-car structure. "I've got the whole shooting match—tent, backpacks, sleeping bags, and guns of all kinds. My God, you wouldn't believe the number of guns I've got. Use whatever you want. My hunting and fishing days are over."

Amy picked up a camouflage knapsack and said, "This will do nicely." She took her wallet from her purse. "I'd like to pay for the use of the cabin and the jeep."

"Wouldn't think of charging you." He glanced toward the house. "My pot roast should be about done. How about having dinner with me?"

It was the last thing Amy wanted to do, but she stretched her lips into a smile. "Sounds marvelous." Mentally, she set her evening plans aside for a couple of hours. "I'll put my groceries in the cabin and be right over."

When she walked in Paul's back door, he stood at the kitchen counter pouring whiskey into a water glass. "Want a sundowner?" He continued to pour until the tumbler was two-thirds full before adding water and ice.

"No thanks. I've never been a successful drinker."

After gulping down a third of his drink, Paul sank onto a lumpy, threadbare recliner in a corner of the roomy kitchen. "There's a salad in the fridge and baked potatoes in the microwave." He groaned, leaned back, and rubbed the glass against his forehead. "Hope you don't mind if we eat in here. Using the dining room takes too many steps."

"Good heavens no. Half the time, I have my meals standing up. That is, if I remember to eat at all." She smiled. "If you'll point me in the right direction, I'll set the table."

Later, as they sat at the round oak table, she noticed that any movement caused him to grimace with pain. "Is there anything that can be done for your joint problem?"

"I've had the whole course. Now, it's a toss-up who wins, me or the pain." He stared into space. After a long moment, he sighed and his head drooped. "Some nights I sit with a gun in my hands for hours trying to get the nerve to end it."

While she struggled to find something to say, he rose and left the room. When he returned a few minutes later, he'd removed his suit coat and appeared to be in a much lighter mood. "Paul, I don't know what . . ." she began.

"Hey, what's with the long face. This is a party." He poured himself another stiff drink. "I hear you had a run-in with Troy McAllister." He arched an eyebrow. "*And* with Police Chief Pike."

She frowned in annoyance. "Aren't there any secrets in this blamed town."

He took a hefty swallow of whiskey and peered over the rim of the tumbler. "The people here, they aren't like . . ." he licked his lips. "Rock Springs is kind of isolated . . . and some people make their own laws." He avoided her gaze. "Be careful. You're a long way from Seattle."

"But I haven't done anything, Paul."

He sipped his drink in silence. After several minutes, he regarded her with a bleary stare. "Tha'sa good story," he said. "You stick to it."

Oh, swell, now I've got a drunk on my hands, just what I need. "As soon as I get the pictures I need, I'll be on my way."

An odd little smile lifted the corners of Paul's mouth. "Know what I think, Ms. Prescott?" He pointed an unsteady finger at her. "You're trying to flimflam me. I read about you and old B.J. in the *Global News.*"

"Oh?" She pushed a lump of baked potato around her plate. "I suppose I should have told you, but you know how it is when you go on vacation. The minute people find out what you do, you get involved and . . . and there goes your holiday."

She took in a deep breath. *Not bad, old girl. Pretty soon you'll be lying as convincingly as a used-care salesman.*

"So-o true, so-o true." He drained his glass, wiped his mouth on the back of his hand, and grinned. "Guess what?" he said, slurring his words. "I ran into that young feller."

She grasped the edge of her chair. "What young feller?"

"You know." He flung out his hand and knocked his glass onto the floor. "Oops." He glanced down at the broken pieces as though surprised, then continued. "Simon . . . Simon . . . what's his name?"

Amy leaned forward. "You met him? Where? What day?"

He gave her a sly look. "Ah, *now* I've got you interested in old Paul." He put his moist hand over hers. "Haven't I, honey?"

She stifled the urge to jerk away. Instead, she clutched his fingers. "Help me, Paul. Simon and I planned to spend our vacation together, but I can't find him."

Paul patted her hand. "Poor little girl's lost her lover." He beamed at her. "Too bad. Guess you'll just have to snuggle up to old Paul." He reached out to put his arm around her and fell off his chair.

She swore under her breath, knelt, and got him to his feet. "What did you and Simon talk about?"

"Help me to my bedroom and I'll tell you."

She gritted her teeth. "Tell me, then I'll put you to bed." She'd flunked her self-defense course in her confrontation with Blackthorn, but handling this souse would be a snap.

He aimed puckered lips at her cheek. She turned and his kiss landed on her ear. "Be nice to me, sweety."

"Sure. Sure. Just tell me what he said." She draped his arm over her shoulder. "Which way?" He pointed to the hall and she steered him toward it. During her four-year marriage, she'd put Mitch to bed more times than she cared to remember.

Paul chuckled. "Been a coon's age since a good-looking woman's had her arms around me."

She halted. "If you don't tell me about Simon, I'll drop you right here."

"Okay. Okay. He asked if anyone in Rock Springs had been flashing a lot of money."

She eased him through the door he indicated. "What did you tell him?"

"Us mountain people don't say much to strangers." He rubbed his cheek against hers. "But we're not going to be strangers for long, are we, sweety?" His fingers caressed her breast.

She yanked away nearly upsetting his nightstand. "You know who Simon's looking for, don't you?"

He teetered back and forth. "Maybe I do. Maybe I don't." He patted the comforter. "Let's discuss it in a . . ." he smirked, "in a hor-i-zon-tal position." He stuck out his arms.

She stepped aside, bumping the off-kilter nightstand so that the drawer slid out. She caught it before it fell. Inside, on a small tray lay a piece of surgical tubing, a syringe, a vial of morphine, and a blood-splotched cotton ball.

"Good God, Paul. What have you been doing?" She pushed up his shirtsleeve. A Band-Aid covered the most recent injection site and needle tracks dotted the vein.

"It's a crap shoot, sweety. It's either that or," he put his finger to his head and pulled an imaginary trigger. He sat down on the comforter. "Ted Zeigler says someone broke into one of his motel rooms last night." He peered at her. "I'm betting it was you." He winked. "You keep my little secret, sweety, and I'll keep yours." He chuckled and flopped back on the bed. "For now."

Chapter 8

Amy paced her bedroom, her boot heels thudding on the worn rag rug. One of the men responsible for swindling Simon's father lived in Rock Springs. Paul's sly remarks had convinced her of that fact. To find Simon, it looked as if she might have to track down the con man first.

She wiped damp palms on her jeans, wished she could be as cool as investigators on TV, and glanced at her watch—9:30. By ten, Rock Springs's most popular gathering place ought to be full enough for her to get lost in the crowd.

She took a last-minute inventory: twenty-dollar bill in her pants pocket, pistol strapped to her ankle, what else? Her purse with all her I.D. lay on the bed. She hid it with her forensic satchel.

This morning before leaving the cabin, she'd discovered a trap door beneath a bureau in a corner of the room. As she lifted the lid to the root cellar, she noted the oil she'd squirted on the rusted hinges had cured the squeak. She tossed her purse inside. The square cement-sided hole made an ideal cache.

She slipped on her denim jacket and glanced around

the room once more. If she didn't go now, she'd lose her nerve. She hurried out the door and scurried along the murky, overgrown path.

As she drew even with the garage, she gave the jeep a longing glance. She'd better not risk using it. The noisy motor might rouse Paul out of his drunken slumber.

When she reached the main thoroughfare, she learned that Rock Springs's modernization program had not extended past the town square. Here on the outskirts only an occasional porch lamp glimmered. The thick darkness stifled her, made her breath rasp in her throat.

She tried to hurry, but the rubble-strewn roadside and Saturday-night traffic made it impossible. For safety's sake, each time a vehicle approached, she crouched in tall weeds.

Twenty minutes passed before she glimpsed The Green Lantern Saloon and heard a plaintive country song. Inside a split-rail fence, dust-coated cars and trucks filled a parking lot. She winced as pea-gravel rolled beneath her feet and threaded her way through the maze of vehicles until she reached the barn-like building. Unpainted, vertical slab-wood covered its weathered, windowless walls. Two rusty kerosene lanterns wired with electricity and fitted with green globes provided the only light.

Suddenly, the plank door in front of her burst open and a couple of men staggered out. Mud smudged their clothing and a week's growth of whiskers bristled on their chins.

When one saw her, he swept off his battered western hat and made a deep bow. "Good evening, beautiful creature. Me and Omar are goin' out to the truck to get us a snort of juniper juice." He smacked his lips. "Want to come along?"

She took a step backward. "Sorry, I'm meeting someone."

He grinned. "That's all right, darlin'."

His friend caught hold of his arm. "Let's go, Dewey, I gotta pee so bad my ears are about to pop."

After they'd crunched off into the darkness, Amy pulled open the tavern's door and slipped inside. A pungent odor of beer and cigarette smoke filled her nostrils.

She sidled by a long bar where men and women stood two and three deep all talking at once. She found a vacant table, sank onto a chair, and glanced around. A few feet in front of her, couples stomped and whooped to the three-piece band's spirited rendition of "Cotton-eyed Joe."

In a remarkably short time, considering the crowd, a waitress clad in a fringed, red leather miniskirt and an equally brief, fringed bra came to ask what she wanted to drink. Amy ordered a beer and took Simon's picture from her jacket pocket. "Have you ever seen this man in here?"

The woman leaned forward, spilling a golden fan of hair over well-rounded breasts. "Yeah, he was here Monday. Came back the next afternoon and asked me to go out with him Friday night." She flipped back her hair. "Bought myself a new dress and the sucker never showed up."

Never showed up. The words echoed inside Amy's skull. "That's not like Simon."

"Humph, him and his smooth talk. Should have known a man like that couldn't be trusted."

Amy regarded the young woman closely. "Are you acquainted with the person he's trying to find?"

The waitress held up her hand. "Forget it, lady. I don't know nothing about nobody." She took off for the bar. When she returned with Amy's beer, she gave Amy change and left without a word.

Amy sighed and peered around at the revelers. Her glance encountered that of a heavily bearded man with bushy hair. He sat with his chair tipped back against the wall. She lowered her gaze. If she played it cool, no one would bother her.

Someone joggled her table, tipping over her beer. She stood up to avoid getting a lap full and the bottle rolled off onto the floor. She looked up at a young man who looked vaguely familiar. "Thanks a lot."

"Sorry," he said. "How about a dance?"

"Not tonight," she said. "I'm waiting for my date."

"So let him wait for you instead."

She shook her head. "He wouldn't like that."

"Ah, come on."

"No, thanks." She fixed a smile. "Maybe some other time."

Someone grasped her shoulder and she turned to find Troy McAllister scowling down at her. "You don't learn very fast do you" She tried to move away, but the pressure of his hand kept her in place. "You'll do whatever me or my brother Dean wants. Got that?"

She glanced from one to the other—the same features—except that Dean had a receding chin. Apprehension tensed her spine, but she shrugged it off. Surely the manager wouldn't allow any rough stuff.

She met Troy's stare. "Take your hand off my shoulder." She lowered her voice and spaced her words. "I don't like threats, and I don't like you."

"Well, now ain't that a shame." His lip curled and he

flung a glance at his brother. "Think she'll get the message if we have a little two-on-one out in the woods?"

Dean learned down and whispered, "Ever played sandwich, doll face?" He licked his lips and his eyes darted right and left. "Whoo-ee, Troy, hope she's as good as that last one. She was something else."

They're serious! Amy stabbed her boot heel into Troy's instep, spun, and aimed a kick at his shin. He sidestepped, seized her right arm and twisted her wrist into a hammer lock. In a well-timed move, Dean wrenched her left arm into the same hold. "Let go of me," she yelled and kicked at them.

Troy grinned at the people who glanced up from their beer. "She's just riled 'cause I didn't give her enough lovin' last night."

"He's lying," Amy shouted and struggled to get free. "I don't even know him."

"Show her who's boss," one man said, the rest laughed. The women looked the other way. The band increased its tempo.

Troy and Dean tightened their grip and she let out a scream. They smiled at everyone, lifted her feet off the floor and started through the crowd. "Help me," she screamed as they rushed her past the bar.

"What's the matter, Troy?" some man yelled. "Can't you control your woman?"

Troy laughed. "That'll be the day." No one made a move to help her and in seconds the front door slammed shut behind them.

She screamed and Troy slapped her. "Open your yap again and I'll ram your teeth down your throat."

The slap fueled her anger. "Damn you." She ignored the pain in her wrists and threw her weight against first one then the other. "You won't get away with this."

"No?" Troy's humorless laugh sent prickles along her skin. "That's what you think." They hauled her across the lot to his truck. "Hold her, Dean." He released his grip on her arm and fumbled for his keys.

Amy tore her hand free and gouged Dean's eyes. He yelped and let go of her. She swung around, rammed her knee into his groin, and he collapsed onto the gravel.

Before she could stoop and pull her pistol from its ankle holster, Troy backhanded her. She reeled and caught her balance on a car door.

"Stupid bimbo." Troy strode toward her, both arms outstretched.

She butted him in the stomach. Her head struck his belt buckle. Pain ricocheted through her brain. For an instant, red dots whirled in the blackness behind her lids. She staggered, caught herself and dived beneath the truck. Her heart hammering her ribs, she wriggled to the other side, leaped up, and ran. In her haste, the loose gravel rolled and she landed hard on all fours. She scrambled to her feet.

Troy came after her, brandishing a baseball bat. "You've had it, bimbo."

Her mouth went dry. She dodged between some cars. He followed, smashing windows and headlights in his rage. Her eyes blurred, and as she ran she swiped at them, her fingers coming away wet and sticky with blood. Even if she got a chance to draw her gun, she couldn't hang on to it or see well enough to shoot. Troy swung at her, she ducked, scuttled around a van and tried to get back to the tavern door. Troy barred the way.

She wheeled and plunged past a row of cars. Her head throbbed. Every breath seared like flames. She stumbled, collided with a bumper, veered, and darted between two large U-Haul trucks. The side of the building blocked her exit. She skidded to a stop, breathing hard. No way out. She whirled to face Troy.

He backed her to the wall and jammed the bat beneath her chin. "Gotcha, bitch. You gonna give me what I want or do I have to work you over first?"

"Don't even think it, buck-o." The thickly accented voice issued from the darkness behind Troy.

"Who the hell?" Troy wheeled around.

Amy grasped hold of the truck fenders on either side of her, levered herself up, and kicked him in the back. He pitched forward onto his knees but only for a second. The next minute, he sprang to his feet and began to swing the bat at her and a man who kept just out of his reach.

"What's the matter, boy. Didn't your daddy teach you to fight like a man?" The man taunted and danced away when Troy flailed at him.

Amy wiped away blood that streamed down her forehead, clouding her vision. When she could see clearly, she recognized the bushy-haired man with the full beard who'd stared at her inside. He wore suspenders and cut-off pants like a logger. She drew her pistol and waited. Her legs trembled so badly she could hardly stand. If she killed a couple of Rock Springs's solid citizens, that pea-brained sheriff would slap her in jail before the gun quit smoking.

"Come on, hot shot," the man urged. "Show me how tough you are."

Troy lunged, his feet slipped, and he missed. Before he could regain his balance the other man darted in, jerked the bat from his hands, and flung it into the darkness. "Now, let's see what you can do."

Troy bowed his neck and knotted his fists. "I'll kill you, you dirty sonuvabitch."

The man swerved and Troy's headlong rush went by him. Troy crouched. "She's mine, damn you."

"Not this time, McAllister." The bearded man whacked him alongside the neck with the side of his hand. As Troy's knees buckled, his attacker grabbed him by the shoulders and rammed his knee into his groin so hard it lifted Troy off the ground. Troy sprawled in a silent heap on the gravel.

The bearded man stepped over him and strode toward her.

Amy gripped her .38 and braced her shaky arms. "Take one more step and I'll shoot."

Chapter 9

The bearded man stopped. "Relax, Dr. Prescott," he said in a quiet voice. "I'm Nate Blackthorn."

She sagged against the tavern wall. "What do you do, change disguises three times a day, whether you need to or not?"

He drew closer and stooped to eye level. "Are you all right?"

"I am now."

"Good." He moved to the rear of the truck and peered out. "They've found Dean. Let's get out of here—and fast."

They crawled to the other side of the U-Haul truck, sprang up, and raced into the darkness. With him leading the way, they sprinted down a winding lane, through a thicket of brambles, and into a woods. To her amazement, when the trees thinned, she found they'd arrived at the rear of the cabin.

Once inside, Blackthorn insisted on pulling all the shades before she switched on the lights. "No one must know we are connected in any way or who I am. Some people in Rock Springs would welcome an excuse to torch the homes of my friends."

She slumped onto a chair and sat with her arms hanging limp, her legs splayed out. "What's the matter with these people? They watched those two scuzzballs drag me out of that place and never raised a hand."

He shrugged. "They, like city folks, avoid getting involved." He leaned down and peered at her scalp. "You have quite a gash there."

"I rammed my head against Troy's belt buckle."

"You should ask Dr. Chambers to take a few stitches."

"No way. I've done enough wrestling with him for one night."

"Old Doc Chambers made a pass at you?"

"He gets amorous when he's drunk. Tomorrow, I'll have to move back to the motel."

"Can you keep him in line for a few more days? You'll be much safer here."

"I'm not so sure about that. Paul knows who I am and why I'm here."

"How come?"

"He's read that magazine article Simon wrote about me and Dad. Paul talked to Simon earlier this week and I suspect he knows the man Simon's looking for. Anyway, when Zeigler told him someone had broken into one of his rooms, Paul figured I was the culprit." She found a tissue and scrubbed a rivulet of blood on her face. "He's using the information as bait."

"Bait?"

"Yeah, bait. To get me into bed. Beats me what he thinks he's going to do when he gets me there. He's a doper and a drunk. It's got to be wishful thinking." She heard a strangled sound, glanced up, and caught his expression of amusement. "It's not funny, Blackthorn."

He sobered. "If you have a mosquito-nosed forceps, I

can knot some strands of your hair. That will hold the laceration closed."

She peered at him again. The man was full of surprises. "Fine with me." She shuffled into the bedroom. As she passed a mirror, she caught sight of her blood-smeared face and tousled hair and grimaced.

She bent down on bruised knees and managed to lift the root-cellar lid. When she leaned into the hole, her head felt as if it would explode and her swollen hands refused to obey her commands. After two attempts to get the heavy satchel out, she gave up.

She went to the doorway. "I'm afraid I'll have to have your help."

"Oh?" He eyed her suspiciously and plodded across the room.

She shifted from one foot to the other. What was his problem? Surely, he didn't think she was a sex-starved female.

He halted ten feet from her. "What do you need?"

"My satchel. It's in the root cellar. I can't get it out."

"Is that all?" He circled around her, took out the satchel, and set it on a chair.

She noticed Paul's knapsack leaning against the night table and kicked it under the bed. "Thanks." She unlocked the bag and took out the things she thought he'd need. As she handed them to him, she remembered the apprehension she'd felt in his presence the night before. For some reason, between then and now her fear of him had been replaced by a fascination she preferred not to analyze.

She snapped the bag shut. "I'll have to rinse my hair in the kitchen sink. I'm a little too shaky for the shower."

He stood so close she could feel his warmth and a

kind of electric-force field that made her pulse beat faster. She swayed toward him but caught herself before she touched him.

He swallowed, a dry clicking sound in the quiet room, and started to inch past her. "You have . . ." His body brushed her and he drew in a quick breath. "You have been through a bad time." He made it to the doorway and strode into the other room.

What a strange man. He seemed more scared of her than she was of him, she thought as she collected shampoo and towels in the bathroom. When she joined him, she found he'd arranged scissors, foil packets of Betadine scrub, gauze sponges, and forceps on the kitchen table.

She inspected his display with a puzzled expression. "Have you done surgery?"

"Enough to get by."

Enough to get by? She set the towels and shampoo on the counter, took off her jacket, and turned on the warm-water faucet. "Did Dean see you?"

"He tried to get up as I came by. I changed his mind."

"Changed his mind?" She braced herself for the sting of the laceration, wet her hair, poured shampoo into her hand and began to work up a suds.

"Neither of the McAllisters will want to think about women for at least a week."

"I see." She rinsed and groped for a towel. He shoved it into her hand. She wrapped the towel into a turban. "Will their friends come looking for me?"

"They might. Men can get some crazy ideas when they've been drinking." He pointed to a chair he had set beside the table. "If it's all right with you, I'll stick around for a while." He ran water and scrubbed his hands.

"I'd like that." She settled herself on the chair with a wan smile. "I've done a lousy job of looking after myself lately."

He removed her towel and began to part her hair with his fingers. "I doubt Dean would agree, Dr. Prescott."

"Call me Amy."

He tore open a package of gauze and cleaned her pulsating wound with Betadine. When satisfied, he pushed several packets of gauze sponges toward her. "Will you sponge for me, please."

They worked in silence for a few minutes, finally she could contain her curiosity no longer. "It was too dark to see last night. How did you know it was me in Simon's room?"

"You sat beside me on the bus, so I knew you used camomile shampoo."

"You could smell the odor of my hair?"

"Yes."

"What about the gun?"

"You had just cleaned it."

She'd have to remember that in the future. "Where were you standing?"

"Across the room."

"You couldn't have been. How did you get behind me without me hearing a sound?"

"Years of practice." He picked up the scissors and snipped some hair. "My parents were both school teachers, so I spent a great deal of my childhood with my grandparents. My grandfather started initiating me into the old ways as soon as I could walk."

"Amazing."

"Not really. Our creator gave all of us exceptional abilities. Most people don't realize they have them." He stood back a moment and looked at her in an odd sort of way. "Yesterday, on the bus, you gave me a good going over. What conclusions did you reach?"

She pursed her lips. "You weren't asleep for one." She glanced up at him, wondering how much to say.

"And?"

"You're part Caucasian."

"Mother was French Canadian. My father is Nez Perce. Go on."

"Your work keeps you out in the sun."

"You might say that."

"You wear expensive alligator boots and also a costly handcrafted ring, so you aren't poor."

"Foot comfort is a high priority in my . . . with me." He tied another stitch. "I made the garnet ring."

"Beautiful work. Are you a silversmith?"

He shook his head. "I like working with gold and silver."

"Does your family live near Rock Springs?"

"My mother died when I was sixteen. My father and grandparents are in Orofino."

"Orofino? I don't think I've heard of it."

"It is a small lumber town at the foot of the Bitterroot Mountains, about a hundred miles south of here." He laid down the mosquito forceps. "Your hair is holding the wound's edges together nicely."

She began to clean off the table. "Thanks, Nate." She stopped, the name didn't feel right on her tongue. "Do you mind if I call you Nathan?"

"My mother and grandparents always have."

"Your maternal grandparents?"

"No, I haven't met them. They disowned my mother when she married my father."

She stared at the floor for a moment before lifting her head to look at him. "I see."

He went to the door. "I'm going to check around outside." He slipped out.

She had finished blow-drying her hair when he returned.

"All clear for now. Did you learn anything helpful from the specimens you took last night?"

"Some. The hairs came from a man with the same blood type as Simon's. In one of the mud squares, I found feces, lichens, a conifer needle, the tip of a porcupine quill, and a bit of snail shell."

"Mind if I take a look?"

"We-ell, I don't usually . . ."

"Just the lichens, the feces, and the conifer needle. I might be of help. I studied forest and land management in college."

"Well, all right. I'll get them."

"I can do it."

"No, no," she said hastily. "I'd rather no one handled them but me." More importantly, she didn't want him to see the fish scales. With his resources, heaven knew what he might figure out.

She put the microscope on the kitchen table and the mounted specimens beside it. He folded his long frame onto a chair and fitted a slide under the objective.

She washed and dried the instruments he'd used, glanced at his absorbed countenance and scrubbed the sink. When he still hadn't uttered a sound, she said, "Would you like some coffee?"

"M-m-m-m," he said without looking up.

She filled the percolator, darted a glance over her

shoulder, measured in coffee, glanced his way again, and set the pot on the burner. "What do you think?"

"Pika scat."

She took two mugs from the cupboard and walked over to him. "I beg your pardon."

"Some people call them coneys or whistling hares. You see them on the talus slopes high in the mountains. Their feces look like black tapioca." He positioned another slide under the low-power objective, took a long look, and switched to high power. "Now, we are getting somewhere."

She dug her hands in her pockets, took them out, paced to the stove and back. "What is it?"

"This is not a true conifer needle." He stood up. "See that little gland on the upper side of the scale-like leaf?"

"Uh huh."

"Both the Rocky Mountain and the Western juniper have that particular feature. But if it were Western juniper, it would have a droplet of resin."

"Okay, so the leaf's from Rocky Mountain juniper. How does that help?"

"It ties in with the Pika scat. That species of juniper grows on dry, rocky promontories in the mountains where few other trees will even take root."

Amy squeezed her palms together and laced her fingers tightly. "The lichens cinch it, don't they?"

"Seems likely. Now, all we need to find out is where Simon started from." He rested one thigh on the edge of the table, let his leg swing and regarded her with a stern expression. "I know you went to the Fish and Game Department."

She frowned. "I thought I saw Yancy while I was using the phone booth at the bus depot. Have you got him spying on me?"

"Yancy works there. Sweeps the floor. Dumps the trash." He narrowed his eyes. "What did you learn?"

She squirmed with discomfort and rubbed the back of her neck. "The mud sample contained several fish scales. I hoped someone at the department could tell me what kind of fish they came from."

"Yes?" When she made no reply, he scowled fiercely. His bushy wig and false beard made him look twice as threatening. "And?"

"I'm not going to lead you to Simon."

He sighed and sat down across the table from her. "Two men are missing, Amy."

"Who besides Simon?"

"A man named Henry Cummings."

She folded her arms and thrust out her chin. "That's not my concern."

"Maybe and maybe not." His gaze met hers and she read something in the depths of his dark eyes that set off an alarm bell in her head.

"Have you discovered something?"

He didn't answer immediately, and her fear grew. "Tell me."

"I found Simon's car at the bottom of Silver Lake."

Chapter 10

Amy stood motionless, scared to move for fear she'd crumble into pieces. From the moment she'd heard Simon's message, she'd worried this might happen. She'd thought she'd prepared herself, but she hadn't

She gulped in air. "Was Simon . . ." Her voice trembled. She steadied herself and tried again. "Was he inside?"

He shook his head. "No suitcase. No papers. No personal items of any kind." He hesitated for a moment, then went on. "I searched the entire lake shore, but—"

She wet her dry throat. "Yes, I know. It takes longer for a body to surface when the water's cold." She sank onto a chair. "What happened to Simon's luggage, his camera, and his laptop computer?" Her voice rose. "He never went anywhere without his computer." She eyed him narrowly. "How did you know where to look?"

"Pure luck. One of our people happened to be hiking in the hills above Silver Lake about four o'clock this morning. He saw the Volkswagen racing down the road. That section's very narrow and winding and full of potholes, so he figured the driver might be headed for trouble. Trees screened the car from sight for five or ten minutes, then he saw it go off a cliff and land in the lake."

"Did he see anyone in the water or on the cliff?"

"No, but I found a couple of footprints close to where the car went over."

Amy massaged her forehead, her throbbing temples. She would not believe Simon was dead, not until she saw his body. "You think it was accidental or . . . or deliberate?"

Nathan looked puzzled. "Could have been either one. Why?"

She chewed her lip, tried to think of a plausible answer. "Maybe . . . he wasn't in the Volkswagen." She laced her fingers together, tightening them until they ached, "What if someone kidnaped Simon then . . . then dumped his car."

He gazed at her with a gentle, concerned expression. "I suppose it could have happened that way."

She rose, poured coffee into their cups and set the pot on an iron trivet in the center of the table. "The waitress at The Golden Goose says he bought a take-out lunch Thursday."

She cradled her cup to warm her cold hands. "Dad and I have apartments in the same building as our office so we don't turn on our answering machines until we go to bed about eleven. Sometime between eleven Thursday night and six o'clock Friday morning, Simon left a message."

She took a gulp of coffee. "He said, 'Screwed up again, Doc. Need help.' The next words were faint and kind of garbled."

"Could you make them out?"

"They didn't make sense."

Nathan sat forward. "Tell me anyway."

"It sounded like, 'Sunrise, ruby-eyed raven'."

"Sunrise," he murmured. "Ruby-eyed raven. Hm-m-m, you're sure it was him?"

"Positive, the name 'Doc' is a private joke between us."

"Did his voice appear to be normal?"

"I played the tape over and over." She shivered and chafed her arms. "Each word seemed to be wrenched from him."

"Then the message could hold some clue to his whereabouts."

She shivered and sipped her coffee. "The bar girl at The Green Lantern says she saw Simon Tuesday. He asked her to go out with him Friday night. He didn't show up."

She closed her eyes for a moment, then raised her gaze to meet his. "I'm scared."

He moved his hand as if to touch her fingers but withdrew it. "We'll find him." He stared at the wall as if he expected the answers to be written there. Several minutes passed before he brought his attention back to her. "What kind of fish did the scales come from?"

Amy sighed and surrendered. She had to trust someone. "A brown trout. The man at the Fish and Game Department says it probably came from Colby Creek."

"You're planning on going there tomorrow."

It was a statement, not a question. She should have known he was much too observant not to have noticed her day pack in the bedroom and her sack lunch on the counter. "Yes."

"Do you have a map of the area?"

"I got some at the ranger station."

"Good." His gaze grew more intent. "It would be best if we went together. Agreed?"

"I suppose." She shoved back her chair and went to get the maps.

At four-thirty the next morning, she huddled in the semidarkness waiting for Nathan. Silver Lake lay only a few miles from where the road forked and traveled up Hot Springs Gulch to Colby Creek. Consequently, she and Nathan had agreed to meet at the lake so she could make a dental stone cast of the footprint he'd found.

She blew out a breath. It turned white in the icy air. She scrunched down in the jeep's seat and put her hands in her arm-pits to keep them warm. Nathan had said it would be safer for both of them if he walked. She hadn't liked the idea. The lake was at least ten miles from town.

Birds stirred in the pines and began to chirp. Down on the mist-shrouded lake, a loon called and fell silent. Out of the silvery-gray stillness came the clear metallic bugling of an elk. The sound filled her chest, made it hurt. She shifted her position and was surprised to see Nathan standing a few feet away.

The elk's bugle came again and Nathan listened with a rapt expression until the last notes faded. "I've missed that sound," he said softly. "When I'm away, the longing grinds inside me like an achy tooth."

"Yes, I know," she said, and he looked at her with surprise. "I often hike the Cascades and the Olympics."

"Really? You look so feminine, so . . . so fragile."

"Fragile! That'd gave my cousin Oren a laugh. He and I spent out entire childhood exploring every inch of Lomitas Island. We even climbed the cliffs and dove off them into the sea." She smiled. "Something that'd scare me to death if I knew a child of mine was doing it."

He smiled back. "After seeing you sprint for the plane the other day, I should have known you were athletic."

Warmth suffused her skin. "I'm not usually so clumsy."

He opened his mouth as if to speak, closed it, and motioned to a plastic sack on the seat. "Is that your casting equipment?" At her nod, he lifted it out. "Follow me."

Today he looked almost his normal self, except that he had heavier eyebrows, a full mustache, and a faded green baseball cap. Much to her dismay, she again felt a quickening of her pulse. She picked up her camera and tagged along behind him.

Distracting, she muttered to herself. And unprofessional. The middle of an investigation was not the time to get romantic notions. Such foolishness could get them both killed.

Nathan reached a clearing and pointed to a circle of stones roofed with twigs and pieces of bark. "I thought that would help preserve the best print." He set the sack nearby.

She walked to the cliff's edge and looked over. Below, the water looked black and formidable. He came to her side. "The car came to rest about twenty feet down and the water is murky."

She let out her breath. "No one would have found it."

He scanned the eastern horizon. "You'd better hurry. Dawn is not far away."

She knelt in the dew-dampened dirt and removed the covering he'd made. Inside, she found a well-defined print of the right foot. She made a sketch of the area in her notebook, recorded date, time, location, weather conditions, and type of soil.

After snapping several photographs, she measured the print. "Size 13, triple E width. That's a break. He doesn't buy his shoes from the same source as other men in the country." She glanced at Nathan. "I estimate he weighs about two-eighty."

"At least." Nathan picked up a dry twig and leaned forward. "See this right here. The leather of the shoe splays out over the sole. What do you make of the print's odd shape?"

Amy studied it from several angles. "I'd lay odds his large toe is missing."

Nathan struck himself in the forehead with the heel of his hand. "Of course." His brows drew into a scowl. "I should have seen it myself."

"Why? You'd probably see one print like it in a lifetime." He still seemed troubled, so she tried again. "Besides, I had a slight advantage. When I was an intern, I had a diabetic patient who'd had a toe removed. I remembered the twisted appearance of his shoe." She spread her hands. "And I'm only guessing, he could have some other foot deformity."

Nathan gnawed his lip and continued to scowl. "I seldom make a mistake."

She met his gaze square on. "I do. Lot's of them. It keeps me humble."

An unexpected grin brightened his face. "Yes, teacher. I get the message."

The morning breeze shifted fine grains of sand into the indentations. She knew she'd have to hurry. After removing a couple of large pieces of debris, she set out the materials she would need.

Nathan squatted opposite her, cupping his hands around a five-cell torch so the light could be seen by no one but themselves. "How long have you been at this?"

"That's rather a long story." She fitted a metal frame around the print. "My mother left my father and me when I was eleven. Not long afterward, my father gave up his family practice and became Lomitas Island's medical examiner. When he didn't have anyone to look after me, I went on cases with him."

She measured dental stone powder and water into a Ziploc bag and began to mix it by squeezing the bag. "His work fascinated me, so in college I studied pathology, medicine, and forensic science."

She poured a thin layer of the soupy mixture into the depression and sat back on her heels. "I worked at the Washington State Crime Laboratory in Seattle for two years while I took extra classes in the forensic specialties." She tested the surface of the thickening dental stone with a fingertip and poured in the remainder of the concoction. She cleaned the Ziploc bag and returned it to her pack. "Now, my father and I have our own forensic investigation business."

"Does that keep both of you busy?"

"Starting to. Often the Crime Lab gets so inundated with work the attorneys hire us to process evidence." After inscribing the date, item number, and her initials in the dental stone, she lifted the hardened cast from the surrounding soil and wrapped it in paper. "We can go now."

He tipped the torch and its beam flashed upward for an instant. "Your face is bruised." He touched a sore spot on her cheek. "Who hit you? Did somebody come by after I left."

"Troy smacked me a couple of times outside the Green Lantern."

He made a sound deep in his throat. "I should have cut off his cojones."

She grinned at him. "Last night, I'd have helped you."

The lines in his face softened. "Yes, I believe you would have." He picked up her sack of supplies and led the way back to the jeep.

Deep ruts in the Colby Creek road made travel slow and spine-wrenching. Shafts of sunlight were filtering into the canyon by the time they reached a washout so deep and treacherous they could go no farther in the jeep.

Nathan studied several sets of tire tracks leading off into the trees. She crouched at his side. "The same car that went into the lake," he said, outlining the tread. "Looks as if Simon came here twice."

She examined the dried mud in one set of tracks and the still moist soil in the other and nodded, "Evidently, a couple of days apart. Question is, did he meet his abductors here or somewhere else?"

Nathan went over the ground where the driver had parked. Russet cottonwood leaves littered the ground to a depth of several inches, making his search for footprints twice as difficult.

Finally, he gave up and focused on the washout. Sand and small rock defeated his efforts. "We might as well hike up the canyon. Maybe I'll run into his tracks." He unloaded their packs and drove the jeep into some underbrush, where the vehicle's camouflage colors blended with bark and leaves.

She shouldered her knapsack and hooked her camera strap around her neck. "Hope we don't meet any nosy people."

"We might not," Nathan said. "Rock Springs is having a big celebration today."

"That's right. I'd forgotten this was Sunday." She

worked her way to the bottom of the wash. "Yancy said something about the mayor blowing a hole in the dam so the river can return to its original channel."

Leaping from boulder to boulder, she reached the other side of the turbulent stream that cut through the roadbed. "I have to admire the public-spirited people of Rock Springs." She clambered up the bank. "They've certainly done a lot to improve the looks of their town."

"Yes," he said. "So it would seem."

She waited for him to elaborate. Instead, he set off at a rapid pace. He walked bent over and zigzagged from one side of the narrow lane to the other, otherwise she would have had trouble keeping up with him. His gaze swept the gravel roadbed, the black humus shoulder, the bordering shrubbery, and the trees towering overhead, missing nothing.

Half an hour passed in the peaceful, quiet woods. The only sounds—bird calls, a gurgling brook, and chattering squirrels.

Nathan paused and pointed to a lightning-scarred pine. *"Weptesh,"* he whispered. He spread his arms and in slow rhythmic beats mimicked the movement of great wings.

She searched the tree limbs and failed to see anything until a bald eagle stirred and took flight. Two hundred yards farther on, he paused to show her a set of tracks on the stream bank.

"Yak'-i-ma," he said. "Black bear." He held his fists at each side of his head as a bear would his paws.

"How long ago?" she asked in a hushed tone.

He got down on all fours and signed for her to do the same. As she took her position across from him, their eyes met and for an instant something pulsed between them. Nathan shifted his gaze and directed her attention to some mashed grass in the bear's paw print. With long, graceful fingers, he demonstrated the manner in which the blades of grass slowly lifted. When she indicated she understood, he put his closed hands side by side and shook them once.

Ten minutes, she mouthed. He nodded and her eyes went wide. She scrambled to her feet and peered into the shadowy woods. A smile tugged at the corners of his lips and a flush rose to her cheeks. How ridiculous she must seem to him.

He sniffed and signed for her to do the same. She inhaled and detected a faint but definitely rank odor. She nodded and tried to ignore the prickling hairs at the nape of her neck. Nathan's black eyes sparkled at her response and she felt a glow at having pleased him.

"In Washington," she said. "Yakima refers to either the town of Yakima or the Indian tribe. Is it a Nez Perce word?"

"It is Shahapti. The Nez Perce, Umatilla, Palus, Tenino, Klikitat, Yakima, Wanapum, and Kittitas are all part of the same linguistic group." He pulled a piece of foxtail from its coarse base and chewed on the succulent end. "Besides those, I speak the tongues of six other tribes. Languages have always been easy for me."

He sat down on a sun-warmed log. She chose a flat-topped boulder several feet away. "Tell me about the Nez Perce."

He gave her a guarded look. "Our Indian name is *Nimipu*. It means 'We the People.' Nez Perce is a French word for," he smiled with his eyes and put his right forefinger under the tip of his nose, "pierced noses."

She cocked her head and tried to picture a thin sliver of seashell protruding from each side of his nasal septum. "I'm glad it's no longer the custom. I like your nose just as it is."

He flushed and changed the subject. "Sometimes, speaking so many languages has its advantages. If a Nez Perce expression does not translate into English, I cheat and use one from another tribe." He shrugged. "If that does not suit me, I may use German, Russian, Japanese, Vietnamese or Spanish."

She regarded him quizzically. A person wouldn't learn that combination of languages by happenstance. Had the slip been accidental, or had he decided to trust her?

"Must be useful." She flung him a mischievous glance and pursed her lips. "Especially if you work for a government agency." His pupils flickered slightly and she knew her probe had hit close to home.

"I would not know about that." He settled his knapsack more comfortably and moved on.

She followed close behind. Off to her right, on one of Star Mountain's jutting ridges, the bleached and rotting timbers of a hoist shack and mine headframe littered the escarpment. Piles of rock dotted the mountain's sides where tunnels had been dug. Water gushed from one of them and tumbled over boulders to join Colby Creek.

From time to time, Nathan stopped to test the temperature of the stream. She remembered what the Fish and Game man had said about brown trout thriving in warm water. She hadn't told Nathan; however, it didn't surprise her that he knew.

Five miles up the steep incline, the lane narrowed to a brushy path. Two hours went by before Nathan found a quiet stretch of creek that pleased him. He set his pack under a tree and she followed suit. He removed his jacket and shirt, put a finger to his lips and beckoned for her to follow. He chose a spot deeply shaded by willows and elderberry. Bare to the waist, he wriggled on his belly until he reached the bank, draped his arm over and dangled his hand in the tea-colored water.

She stretched out in a little hollow downslope where she had a good view and rested her cheek on folded arms. From time to time, she glanced at his hand undulating in the current like a piece of pond weed. Mostly she watched his face, the line of his sensual mouth, the way the skin pulled tight over his cheekbones, carving each feature into sharp relief.

Fifteen minutes passed. He didn't move. A mosquito whined in her ear and buried its stinger in her neck. She longed to scratch the itch, only she didn't dare. Hidden rocks pressed into her flesh until they felt like boulders. She closed her eyes and tried to let her mind float. Her plan didn't work. Nathan invaded her thoughts.

"Got him!" Nathan shouted. "Look at him, Amy." He held aloft a wriggling fish.

"Is it a brown?"

"Sure is and a whopper at that." Suddenly the fish spurted from his fingers. He grabbed for its tail as it made a slithering path through the grass. He lost his balance rolled down the slope until his body bumped into hers. "Whoops. Sorry," he said.

She heard a rustling sound and saw the fish flopping in the tall grass nearby. "I'll get him." She squirmed out from under Nathan and caught hold of the fish's tail.

Nathan chuckled. "No way. That's my fish."

She laughed and got a better grip. "He's mine now."

"Don't be so sure." Nathan lunged for her. They wrestled in the grass until he flipped her onto her back. "Now, I gotcha." A grinning Nathan sat astride her middle, his hands holding her arms outstretched. "That will teach you to—"

The smile faded from his face, but his gaze continued to hold hers. "Mihewi," he said softly. Slowly, as if he wanted to control the gesture but couldn't, he brushed his fingertips from her temple to her chin. "Sun Woman." Flames smoldered in the depths of his eyes. His breath quickened and his nostrils flared.

Warmth spread through her body, melted her bones, throbbed in her veins. *This can't be happening. I can't want a man I scarcely know.* She moistened her lips. His gaze shifted to her mouth, his flush darkened, and he bent his head. His lips hovered inches from hers. Her pulse drummed in her ears, the air thinned.

Suddenly, he thrust himself away from her, hurried to where he'd left his pack and strode up the trail.

He *had* wanted to kiss her. Surely, he must have seen she felt the same. What had made him change his mind? She pushed herself erect, put the fish in her pack, and set off after Nathan.

She'd been hiking along a steep grade for thirty minutes or more when he materialized on the path in front of her.

"I've found the place." He gestured to a dark, shaded pool behind him. "This is where Simon caught the fish."

Chapter 11

Amy didn't bother to warn Nathan not to compromise the area, she knew he wouldn't. He plowed through a thicket of mountain laurel and entered the grove of ponderosa pine by an indirect route. She plodded along behind him, her limbs weighted with guilt. She'd let this man drive all thought of Simon from her mind. She must make certain it didn't happen again.

Padding over thick layers of dropped pine needles, Nathan paused beside a sapling. "Porcupine," he said, touching a gnawed section about four feet from the ground. "They like the juicy inner bark."

"Are you sure? Couldn't it be a beaver?"

He shook his head. "Too high. Porcupines climb, beavers don't. Simon fished from that bank over there," he said with a brief gesture.

She approached carefully, watching where she placed her feet so as not to destroy something of importance. Numerous prints overlay each other in the soft, damp soil at the pond's edge. Her lungs clamped shut for an instant before she allowed herself a long sigh. All the prints had been made by deep-lugged trail shoes.

She looked up at Nathan. "Have you gone over the area?"

"I thought I should wait."

"Thanks, I appreciate that. If you'll start on the right side of the clearing, I'll take the left. We'll meet in the middle."

A concentrated silence fell over the sun-speckled enclosure. A covey of quail skittered out of the bushes, their head plumes bobbing. They surveyed Amy with bright eyes, gave a loud screech and scampered away.

Light glinted on something at the base of a hollow tree. Crouched, her eyes never leaving the ground, Amy worked her way forward. When the object came into full view, she gave a small cry.

Nathan swung around. "Find something?"

"Simon's jackknife and plastic bait box are still here."

"Easy now." Nathan straightened his back and massaged his neck muscles. "They could belong to anyone."

"No way." She held up a green plaid cap. "See this. It's Simon's favorite. He's had it for years." She gulped. "He'd never have forgotten his lucky cap."

Nathan's calm, controlled gaze met hers. "His luck is still holding. He's given us a starting point." He bent and continued his catlike stalk.

Amy stowed Simon's belongings in her knapsack and started a meticulous search, for what she didn't know. Their combined skills had given them a couple of breaks, but she couldn't be sure they'd get another.

A grunt of satisfaction from Nathan brought her head up. "What now?"

"Come see what you think."

She joined him at the far side of his section. "Something important?"

He broke off a branch and pointed to a spot some distance in front of him. "That look familiar?"

"Nathan, it's . . ." She clutched his arm. "It's the same print as the one I cast at the lake."

"Now take a look at his." In a sector of the forest floor where water oozed through moss and maiden hair ferns, a patch of leaf mold revealed more prints. "The man with the twisted shoe is carrying something."

"He's left-handed. See how much deeper the left foot is embedded." She leaned closer. "No, I'm wrong. His deformity prevents him from using his right foot for carrying any weight, so he has to use his left instead." She shifted her gaze and made out another set of prints. "Someone's with him. A much thinner man."

"And long-legged," Nathan added. "Notice the length of his stride."

She eyed the odd, rolled effect at the outer edge of the sole. "Rubber boots. How old would you say the tracks are?"

"Two days at the most."

Two days ago, a couple of men had come to this clearing. Had they met Simon? She hugged her elbows and peered into deep shade. "Oh, Lord." She pointed a shaky finger. "Those must be Simon's tracks." She took a deep breath. "He's barefooted."

"Yes," Nathan said in a quiet, noncommittal tone and she realized he'd let her make the discovery on her own to lessen the blow. He crouched down beside her. "The way I read the sign, Simon was in his sleeping bag when the two men attacked him. So they must have come looking for him."

"Which means their paths crossed somewhere else."

"Well . . . could be, or these men may be just hired

hands. One thing is certain. They were never in the military or law enforcement."

She drew her brows together in a puzzled frown. "How can you know that?"

"Simon's hands are tied in front of him. Of course, that may be because . . ." He glanced quickly at Amy and slipped off his backpack. "You'll need your casting material. While you're doing that, I'll scout around a bit."

Amy studied him for a moment. "You're holding something back."

"It will keep."

She set her lips in a thin, hard line and stood up. "Don't treat me like a child."

"Amy," he ran a hand over his face. "You're already worried. Knowing more won't help."

"I'll decide."

Nathan opened his mouth, then closed it. "Notice how he's putting more pressure on the balls of his feet and curling his toes under. Now watch." He hunched his shoulders, held his hands together low on his abdomen, and took four or five steps.

A cold leaden weight landed in her stomach. "He's injured."

He observed her with a concerned expression. "Probably not seriously. I didn't find any signs of blood."

Her mind snatched at the thin hope he'd offered. "Simon's been in tight spots before. He'd surely know better than to antagonize his captors." She raised pleading eyes to his. "Wouldn't he?"

"If they gave him a choice." Nathan shouldered his pack. "I will be back in an hour."

When he returned, she had finished and was wrapping the casts. He took them from her and put them in his knapsack. "I followed the tracks until they entered a swamp, but couldn't find where they came out." He checked his watch. "It's one o'clock. With these high canyon walls, it can get dark by four-thirty. All right with you if we continue the hunt for a couple more hours?"

"I'm ready when you are."

Conifers gave way to quaking aspen, then to Scouler willows as they descended to the canyon floor. Nathan cut one of the willows and whittled off branches as he strode along. Magpies scolded from the tops of trees as the two intruders passed by.

Rushes, cattails, and stunted willows spread across the valley and up an adjoining gulch. Amy forged through knee-high marsh grass until she slipped off a tussock and her feet sank into the mud. "Phew." She wrinkled her nose. "Foulest smelling swamp I was ever in."

"Mineral hot springs," he said. "There are lots of them in these mountains. We cross here." He handed her the sturdy staff he'd made. "You may need this. Watch where you step. There may be quicksand.

Leaping from one island of matted willow roots to the next, they made it to the other side. For well over two hours they swatted deer flies and slogged through muck where they sometimes sank up to their knees. Still they found no trace of the three men's footprints.

Finally, Nathan called a halt. "I'll come back tomorrow and stay until I find them."

"Just another hour, Nathan. We might find their tracks any minute now." She straightened shoulders that sagged with weariness. "Then, we'll know which direction they headed."

He shook his head. "This bog is too treacherous to

navigate in the dark. Any other time I would chance it, but not tonight. I couldn't find anyone to stay with Yancy."

She raised an eyebrow. "Isn't he a bit old for a sitter?"

"I meant someone to stand guard."

"You're kidding. What in the world for?" She slapped a stinging gnat on her cheek and another on her neck.

"Tell you later." He jerked his head toward the low end of the marsh. "We'd better get out of here before you're covered with bites."

They reached solid ground before the sun sank below the ridge. After they'd rinsed a pound of stinking mud from their shoes in a stream, Amy inquired about Yancy.

"The night my cousin, Sarah Wahsise, went to the hospital," Nathan said as he led the way up the hill to the trail, "the boy stayed with friends. While he was gone, someone ransacked the house."

"Must've been someone who knew them."

"I thought that, too, at first. Friday, her purse was taken from her room. The nurses found the contents scattered around the parking lot. Her wallet still contained the two twenty-dollar bills she had when she came in."

"Weird."

"And another detail bothers me. When Yancy went to The Golden Goose for your sandwich Friday night, he thanked Verna Jensen for the elderberry wine she'd left on their back porch the week before. Verna said she hadn't made any wine this year."

"Maybe another friend left the wine for her."

"Sarah is a proud woman and all of our people know it. She wouldn't accept a handout unless she could give something in return. Right now she's hit rock bottom. No friend of hers would risk making her feel worse."

"So why are you worried?"

"The person who broke into her house didn't touch Sarah's silver jewelry, but he did take the wine bottle."

"Do you think the wine has some connection with Sarah's illness?"

He shrugged. "She's in a coma."

"Is she going to die?"

"The doctor says there isn't much hope." Nathan lifted the baseball cap he wore and ran his fingers through his hair. "The whole thing is crazy. Sarah is a tiwata-a-tom, what you people call a shaman. One of the best. She would have taken care of her health."

"Maybe Paul would know if she had a medical problem. I'll ask him." She thought over all that he'd said. "Why would anyone want to harm an innocent old lady?"

"Remember that mock-up of Rock Springs Verna showed you?"

"Yes, lots of detail. Easy to see why it won the contest."

"After you and Dr. Chambers left the restaurant yesterday, I took a look at it."

Nathan held back a low branch so she could pass. "This gets a little complicated. Sarah's husband died about six years ago. He left a piece of land to Yancy. When Luke, Yancy's father, got cirrhosis of the liver and knew he wouldn't live long, he made me and Sarah the boy's legal guardians. Sarah wrote me a month ago. She'd been getting letters saying the land was going to be sold for back taxes."

Nathan turned to Amy with a scowl. "That can't be true. I've paid those taxes with a cashier's check every year." His mouth twisted. "Guess what I saw on that mock-up? Yancy's land sits right in the middle of the new resort's ski runs."

"Oh, my God!" Her temper rose to match his. "Those damned corporation people thought they'd pull a fast one and she'd never know the difference. Anyone ever try to buy the land?"

"Some real estate salesman came to see her last spring. Said he had a buyer who wanted the land for an investment. The man offered her about a third of what the land is worth. She said she wouldn't sell at any price."

She put her hand on his arm. "I'm afraid you'll need a good deal more than what you've got before anybody will listen."

"I know," he said and fell silent.

Thunder grumbled somewhere in the gathering darkness and distant lightning glowed in the sky. Amy began to limp. Although she hadn't been hiking in a month, she had kept jogging to stay in shape. Evidently, her body hadn't gotten the message. With each step, she felt as if needles were being jammed into the muscles at the back of her legs. Her toes dragged, and she stumbled and would have fallen if Nathan hadn't caught her arm.

"Did you eat lunch?"

"I forgot."

"For a doctor, you don't take very good care of yourself."

"So everyone tells me." She slipped off her pack. "Would you like a smooshed peanut butter and jelly sandwich?"

He chuckled. "Sure. It's been a long time since I've had a smooshed peanut butter and jelly sandwich." He took a bite. "M-m-m dee-licious. You miss the little things most when you're away." He stopped chewing and stood still, his head cocked to one side.

"Something wrong?"

"Dogs. They're running something to ground." He shuddered. "I'd rather take on a grizzly than a pack of dogs with a thirst for blood. I've seen them rip an animal to shreds just for pleasure."

Amy forgot her tiredness and lengthened her stride. "Let's hurry."

When they reached the jeep, she gave him the key. "Maybe you can miss some of the chuck holes I hit this morning."

At the edge of town, Nathan pulled over to the side of the road and got out. "I'll hike up to Colby Creek tomorrow and stay until I find something definite."

"I'm going with you."

A double beat of silence passed between them. "Would it do me any good to argue?"

"No."

He let out his breath. "You are a difficult woman, Amy."

"I had four years of being told what I could and couldn't do. And of being smacked if I didn't." She lifted her chin. "I've earned my independence."

A muscle knotted along his jaw. "He hit you? What kind of a husband was he?"

"Not much of one, I'm afraid."

He looked at her with a grave expression. "You should have a gentle man. One who can appreciate . . ." he moved the hand he had resting on the car door closer to hers, "what a fine . . ." His fingers touched hers and he jumped as if he'd been burned. "I have to go. Meet you here at four o'clock tomorrow morning," he said and vanished into the night.

Two hours later, she was ready for bed when a knock sounded. She glanced at her blue satin, man-tailored pajamas. They covered her adequately. "Who is it?"

"Nathan."

A chill caused goose bumps to pop out on her arms. Something must have changed his plans. She switched off the light and held open the door. After he'd slipped inside, she turned on a table lamp and regarded him with an anxious expression. "Is Yancy all right?"

"Yes." His eyes held hers. "The mayor blew the dam today. The river is back in its old channel." His gaze intensified and he took hold of her shoulders. "Amy, you have to be strong."

A terrible fear gathered in the pit of her stomach. "Why? What's happened?"

"This evening, Yancy and his friends discovered a man's body in a shallow pool among the river rocks."

Chapter 12

Amy pressed her arms to her sides in an attempt to steady herself. "Where is the body?"

"Across the river from the park. About a hundred yards farther downstream."

"Are they sure it's . . . Simon?"

"No, they stayed on the riverbank. In this town, the Indian boys steer clear of anything that might bring the sheriff down on them."

"Did you see the body?"

"Too dark. And too risky."

She began to shake and her knees turned weak. "Maybe it's not . . ." A sob escaped her, and then another. She clung to him and cried like a child, her tears wetting his neck.

He held her, stroked her hair and her back. "Cry," he murmured. "It'll do you good." Minutes passed and his embrace gradually tightened, bringing her close to his body. The soothing strokes grew softer, his fingers brushed her cheek and her neck.

She quieted and her body melted against his. In the languorous silence, she became aware of his pounding heart, his ragged breathing.

"Amy . . ." He pressed her to him. "I . . ." He shook his head, put her from him, and stepped back several feet. "You must go there," he said in a husky voice. "Too many people could get hurt if I'm seen near the man."

She straightened her shoulders. "This is my responsibility and no one else's. I'll get ready."

"Not now. Someone might see your flashlight. Wait until dawn. Few people are up at that hour." He peered down at her. "Think you can manage?"

She shoved back her hair and firmed her chin. "Of course, I always manage."

"I'll notify the sheriff around six. So do whatever you have to do and get out fast. If you're caught—"

"Sheriff Pike would have a field day." She tried to make eye contact, but Nathan's glance kept sliding away. "It was thoughtful of you to come, Nathan."

He brought his gaze up from the floor. "I wanted to . . ." As if drawn by a magnet, his glance lowered to her mouth, then swept down her pajama top where light glistened on the blue satin. He swallowed. "To be the one who . . ." he backed toward the door, "who told you." He switched off the light. "Go with care, Amy."

"You too."

"Be sure to bolt the door."

The click of the latch sliced through the warmth that had surrounded her moments before. Distraught, she wandered through the cabin. Pictures of Simon laying in the river flashed strobe-like inside her head. *Simon, I'm sorry. I should have gotten here sooner, hunted harder.*

Tomorrow morning, her mind stopped there and she had to force herself to finish the thought. She'd examined a great number of dead bodies—she shivered—but none of them were friends.

She wrapped her arms around herself and rocked back and forth. *I will get through this. It's just a matter of remembering a professional is a professional regardless of the circumstances.* She began to assemble the things she would need in the morning and to stow them in her knapsack.

When she finished, she checked the lock and propped a chair under the knob for extra insurance. Any night now, Troy and Dean McAllister might decide to get even.

She set her alarm, put her pistol under the pillow, and burrowed beneath the covers. To keep her mind off what lay ahead, she let her thoughts drift to Nathan. A strange emotion had swept over her while he'd held her. She attempted to relive the moment so she could put a name to the feeling but failed. Finally, sleep took over.

A few hours later, the alarm jarred Amy awake. Groping in the dark, she gathered up her clothes and dashed into the bathroom. As she washed her face, thoughts of the task ahead filled her with apprehension. *What if?* A dozen possibilities rushed at her, but she shut them out. Once launched on a course of action, she made it a policy never to back down. If you let it, fear could become a paralyzing disease.

She donned shirt, jeans, shoes, and an old jacket of Paul's that hung in the closet. In one of the pockets, she found a blue stocking hat. She pulled it on and tucked her hair up inside. At last the moment could be put off no longer. She snatched up the knapsack of supplies, slipped her camera strap over her shoulder, and stepped outside.

Black clouds hung over the canyon and thunder rumbled in the distance. Around her, fog crawled along the ground, sending gray, skeletal fingers around the buildings and into the trees. She set off through the woods, following the trail Nathan had kept to Saturday night. When she exited near town, she stayed on the back streets. Pale lights glowed in a few of the houses and the sound of a car starting disturbed the padded silence. She lengthened her stride.

Near the river, updrafts swirled the fog into billowing veils. Midspan of the bridge, an empty gravel truck rumbled out of the mist. She turned her back and stared down at branches, and other debris bobbing in the muddy water below.

When the truck disappeared around a bend, she hurried to the other side of the bridge. A sign that read *AUTHORIZED CARS ONLY, NO MOTOR BIKES ALLOWED* was bolted to a locked cantilevered gate that extended across an asphalt roadway edging the riverbank. She pushed through the turnstile. A waist-high stone wall stood between the broad track and the river's edge. She jogged along beside it so she could see over.

She felt her pulse beating as she passed the boundary of the park across the river. Here, crushed rock replaced the asphalt. In this area, no improvements had been made except for a crude path hacked through thickets of sprawling aspen, chokecherry, and wild rose briers.

Ahead, a rock slide narrowed the channel. Waves capped with foam the color of tobacco spittle plunged, whirled, and hurtled into the air as the river squeezed through the gap. She slowed her pace to peer down at massive boulders. During the night, a storm in the mountains had raised the level of the river, perhaps . . . She turned cold as she glimpsed the body floating facedown in an eddy between two rocks.

Her heart thundering, she scrambled down the bank. At the bottom, she hunkered down and wrapped her arms around her chest. *Calm down. That may not be Simon lying there. But if it is you have to do this right.* Her pulse slowed enough for her to think clearly.

She turned him onto his back and bent over him, her breath rasping from her lungs. *Oh, God. Oh, God.* It wasn't Simon after all. She steadied herself and sketched the scene in her notebook, uncapped her camera and snapped pictures from several angles. When satisfied, she squatted at the river's edge, tiny wavelets wetting her sneakers.

The dead man wore white coveralls. On the arm and legs, the tough, tightly woven material of the cotton coveralls had been ripped in a dozen places.

Because they were closest to her, she began her inspection with his bare feet. Cuts, bruises, and abrasions covered the man's toes and the soles of his feet.

The man's coarse black hair hung well below his ears. From what she could tell from his bloated features, he was either Indian or Mexican. Taking fingerprints the usual way would leave tell-tale ink stains for the coroner to pick up. Instead, she carefully dried his fingers, brushed on Elmer's white glue, and let it dry while she carried out the rest of her routine.

She took an impression of his teeth, clipped a lock of hair, swabbed one nostril and one ear, leaving one of each untouched for whoever would do the autopsy.

The man wore nothing except boxer shorts under the white coveralls. She examined him hastily but thoroughly. Some animal had bitten his arms and legs repeatedly, tearing loose large chunks of flesh.

The poor man must have suffered horrible pain. She took some close-up shots, then nicked a vein in the groin and extracted a sample of blood. The remaining procedures were completed in minutes, and once again she became aware of the world around her.

The sound of thunder had grown louder and jagged flashes of lightning sliced through the churning clouds overhead. She found a branch of long-needled pine and brushed out her footprints. Secure in the knowledge she'd done all she could, she climbed to the path and set off at a trot.

Before she'd gone far, Nathan softly called her name. She slowed to a walk but couldn't spot him among the aspen.

"Pretend to tie your shoe," he said.

When she knelt as instructed, he moved and she found he'd been standing only ten feet away. Such stillness. How did he manage it? Yesterday, she'd seen him disappear right before her eyes, yet he'd taken only a few steps.

"Was it Simon?" he asked.

"No. An Indian or a Mexican. Twenty-five to thirty years old, five foot ten, about a hundred and sixty pounds."

"How long has he been dead?"

"Twelve to twenty-four hours. Hard to tell. The water's awfully cold."

"Cause of death?"

"Not sure. Deep animal bites on arms and legs. Might have bled to death. Might have drowned." She rose to her feet and focused her camera on the park across the river. When the roll was finished, she snapped out the exposed film, inserted another and held the exposed roll behind her. "Can you have this developed privately?"

His fingers touched hers briefly. "Will do." He shoved the film in his jacket pocket. "Yancy's grandmother died last night."

She recalled the frightened look on the young boy's face when he said his grandmother was sick. "I'm so sorry, Nathan. Let me know if there's anything I can do."

"I asked for an autopsy."

"How long before you get a report."

"Three or four days." He stepped back a couple of paces. "You better go. I'll call the sheriff about the body in thirty minutes." He vanished from view.

For a short way, she ran as if pursued but slowed to a jog before she reached the gate. As she started across the bridge, she heard a clatter of stones. She turned in time to see a gray Mercedes lurch out of the Riverside Motel's entrance gate. The driver braked to a squealing stop and she recognized the man behind the wheel. *Damn!* Dr. Leibow. What a lousy time for a windbag like him to show-up. He sat watching her, the Mercedes' engine rumbling softly like a panther on the prowl.

She formed her lips into a smile and waved. "Good morning." He made no reply. She gulped down her panic. Every move she made must appear to be those of an avid photographer. Her hands shook as she positioned the tiny tripod she carried on the bridge's wide cement railing.

She felt Leibow's eyes boring holes in her back, and she longed to look over her shoulder but didn't dare. She secured her camera on the tripod and took several timed exposures of the town and the approaching storm. Time ticked by and a spot at the back of her neck began to itch. Why was he watching her? Had he seen her coming along the river path?

The instant she heard the car leave, she stowed her paraphernalia and hurried on her way.

In front of the post office, she glanced around. Then she darted inside the outer door, dropped a bubble-pack envelope filled with all the small physical evidence she'd gathered thus far into a mail chute, and sauntered out. The dental stone casts would have to be sent to her father later on.

Up the street, she saw the "OPEN" sign go on in the window of The Golden Goose Cafe—an ideal place to await developments. The bell over the door tinkled as she went inside.

Edna came toward her with a big grin wreathing her face. "Amy, am I glad to see you." She picked up a coffee carafe and escorted Amy to a booth. "Is it true?" she asked, her eyes bright with curiosity.

Amy picked up the menu and opened it in case she needed something to shield her face. "Is what true?"

"Did you really bust the McAllister boys' balls?" Edna hunched over the table. "All by yourself like they say you did?"

Amy met her gaze. "Wouldn't you, if you thought the guys intended to rape you?"

Edna bobbed her head in vigorous agreement. "The no good bastards should've been castrated at birth." She took out her pad. "How about pancakes, eggs, and sausage?"

Amy pulled off the stocking hat and fluffed out her hair. "Sounds great."

Edna shoved her pencil back into her pocket. "Breakfast's on the house. Now that you've got the ball rolling," she winked to make sure Amy caught the double meaning, "maybe the people in this town will get off their butts and do something."

"Hope you're right, but don't count on it."

Edna gave a long sigh. "I know." The bell on the door tinkled as a tall man with silver gray hair came in. "Oh, oh, it's the judge," Edna whispered. "Watch yourself." She took off for the door at a fast clip.

Edna seated the man near the front windows, brought him a carafe of coffee, and hurried toward the kitchen to turn in her orders.

Amy went to the rest room and scrubbed her hands twice. As she returned, she was conscious of Holt McAllister's gaze following her. She sank onto the booth's padded seat, cradled her mug in both hands, and took a gulp. The hot brew didn't quiet the tremors inside her.

A couple of minutes passed before she heard his footsteps. She kept her eyes on the table until he stopped beside her.

"Are you Amy Prescott?"

She counted to five slowly before raising her head. "Yes." She let her gaze meet his. "What can I do for you?"

He perched on the edge of the seat opposite her. "I'm Holt McAllister." He paused, his icy-blue eyes searching for a chink in her composure. "*Judge* Holt McAllister."

"Oh?" She took a sip of her coffee and dabbed her lips with a napkin. "I've heard quite a lot about you since I arrived in Rock Springs."

A muscle worked along his jaw. "And I've heard too damned much about you." He drew heavy gray eyebrows together and thrust out his jaw. "None of it good. Who the hell gave you the right to . . . My boys are in the hospital on account of you." He knotted his fist and shook it at her. "You're going to pay for what you did to them."

She stood up, rested her hands on the edge of the table, and leaned toward him. "See the bruises on my face." He tried to turn away. "Look at me, damn you." She bent her head so he could see the gash in her scalp.

"Those predatory beasts you call 'boys' did all of that. They planned to take me into the woods and rape me."

He reared back in the seat his nostrils flaring. "That's a dirty goddamned lie."

"You think so? From what the two of them said, they've worked that same rotten routine a number of times."

"That's your story."

She narrowed her eyes. "It sure is." She let her gaze travel over him. "You may be a good judge, *Mr.* McAllister, but as a father you're a miserable failure."

"Why you," spittle flew from his mouth, "smart-ass bitch." He leaped to his feet. "You'll get yours. I'll see to that."

She let his angry retort roll off her. "I defended myself against a couple of perverts," she said in a quiet voice. "If you think you can make a case out of that, you're welcome to try."

"It's your word against theirs and everybody in town will back them up."

"Will they, judge? I don't think you're foolish enough to put that to a test."

"Go to hell." He stomped back to his booth.

Her quivering knees gave way and she lowered herself onto the seat. She might have made things worse by standing up to him, but he needn't think he could walk all over her like he did everyone else.

When Edna brought her breakfast, she gave her a thumbs-up sign. Amy glanced at her watch—6:15— things should start popping any minute now.

With one eye on the street outside, she buttered her pancake, put her egg on top, and poured syrup over all. A police van drove past, no lights, no siren. She ate slowly. Once they opened the gate, it wouldn't take them long to drive to where the body lay.

Forty minutes passed. She'd long since finished her breakfast and had drunk enough coffee to last her a week. Finally, she rose, waved to Edna, and ambled outside. No curious crowd hung around the gate across the river. No pedestrians clustered here and there on the street. She started back to the cabin. By afternoon everyone would be talking about the dead man and it'd be easy to slip in some questions.

Half-way home, drops of rain began to pepper the dusty road. She ran the rest of the way. At the cabin, she put all the casts she'd made into a box and took them into the woods. Earlier, she'd spotted an abandoned well house that was nearly overgrown with brush. Being careful not to disturb the shrubbery, she set the box inside and covered her tracks on her return trip.

She'd no sooner gotten inside than the sky opened up. Rain beat down so hard and fast she could scarcely see out the window. Lightning cracked, thunder roared, the earth shook, and she expected huge rocks to come crashing down Whitecrest Mountain any minute.

In the midst of the tumult, a knock sounded on her door. She turned the knob, the wind snatched the door from her fingers, and it smacked against the wall.

Police Chief George Pike stood on the front step, water pouring off the rim of his white, ten-gallon hat. He stalked inside and pointed to a chair. "Sit down, sister," he said, his southern drawl less pronounced than the first time they'd met. "I want to talk to you. And I'd better get some straight answers."

Chapter 13

He'd found out she'd examined the dead man. Amy closed the door, taking her time so she'd be calm when she faced him. "What's the problem, Chief Pike?"

He yanked off his hat and slapped it against his thigh, showering the rag rug with droplets of water. "Woman, you been stuck in my craw ever since you hit this town." His watery-blue eyes narrowed. "What were you doing at the river this morning?"

Amy let her breath out slow and easy. "Photographing the gathering storm. Did you see the clouds? Charcoal, midnight blue, pansy purple, plum cordial. Magnificent. Just magnificent. Such power. Such——"

"Poppycock!" He snatched her camera off the table, ripped the film from its cartridge, and dropped the exposed strip on the floor.

Amy planted herself in front of him. "You can't come in here and destroy personal property for no reason."

"Oh, no?" He jammed knotted fists on fleshy hips and glared at her. "You're up to something and I intend to find out what it is." He stomped around the room, opening cabinet doors, dumping out drawers, tossing cushions off the couch.

She watched him in silence, wondering why he didn't just ask if she'd seen the dead man. She followed him as he worked his way into the bedroom. He yanked the blankets off the bed, up-ended the mattress, growled, and began on the closet.

With all the racket, she didn't hear Paul until he appeared in the bedroom doorway. His clothes were rumpled, his hair awry, his eyes bloodshot—and he held a rifle. She sidled into a corner.

"This your cabin, George?" Paul roared.

"Butt out, Paul." Pike continued flinging clothes out of the closet without bothering to glance at Paul.

Paul strode over to the closet and kicked the door closed. It smacked Chief Pike in the rump. He let out a bellow. "You crazy old souse!" He backed out and wheeled to confront Paul. At the sight of Paul's raised rifle, his eyes bugged. "Have you gone crazy?"

"Yeah, I'm crazy. Real crazy." Paul swayed and caught hold of the bedstead. "What's your excuse?"

Chief Pike bristled. "I'm here on official business."

Paul rocked onto his toes and back on his heels. "You didn't wipe your feet, George. I don't like people coming into my house without wiping their feet."

"Don't be a damned fool. I phoned Lomitas Island where this . . ." Pike's jowls turned purple and he jabbed a finger at Amy, "this smart-mouthed female claims she's from. The sheriff says she and her old man make a habit of sticking their noses into places where they ain't wanted. I'm not standing for that, ya hear?"

Paul's mouth stretched into a cold, thin-lipped smile. "Why George," he said in a soft, slow voice. "We're just simple country folk here in Rock Springs. We don't have anything to hide." He regarded Pike with narrowed eyes. "Or do we."

Color climbed Chief Pike's thick neck and mottled his face. "She . . ." he shook his finger at Amy, "did grievous harm to those poor McAllister boys. Could have ruined their manhood. Maimed 'em for life."

Paul snorted and waggled the rifle barrel. "Git your fat ass out of Amy's bedroom. Haven't you got any decency?"

The chief scuttled by him and took a stand in the main room. "I want her out of Rock Springs before she causes any more trouble."

Paul advanced on him. "You're so full of shit your brain has ossified. Omar and Dewey were out in The Green Lantern's parking lot having a snort of white lightning. They saw those two whelps roughing her up, saw her give them exactly what they deserved."

"Dean and Troy claim she had help."

Paul jammed the rifle into his belly. "And you believed them, didn't you, you spineless bastard? You know Omar and Dewey are honest as the day is long." He thrust out his bewhiskered jaw. "Are you going to stand there and say they're lying?"

He shoved Pike into a chair. "If you're so hot about law and order, why don't you get off your behind and find out why Sarah Wahsise died? That woman never had a sick day. Only medicine she ever took was a little digitalis for her palpitations."

Pike smirked. "Whooee! Who'd a thought it. You and a shriveled-up old squaw. Sinking pretty low aren't you, Paul?"

"Low!" Paul's fingers whitened on the gun barrel. "She was the daughter of a chief. Her family settled here over a hundred years ago." His voice quieted and he accented every word. "Sarah was only fifty-nine."

"Humph! A wonder she lived that long. Dirty and

stupid, that's what they are. Ain't a one of 'em knows sic'um about taking care of themselves."

"A lot you know, you red-necked sonuvabitch." Paul's Adam's apple worked. "A cleaner person than Sarah never lived. She was a medicine woman. She probably cured more people in this valley than I ever did."

Pike eased himself out of the chair. "Okay, okay, don't go popping a blood vessel. Soon as I get time, I'll look into it." Keeping a watchful eye on Paul, he backed toward the door.

"You tell those McAllisters if they come sneaking around my property, I'll blow their brains out."

"Now, Paul, you don't mean that."

"Huh! Just let 'em try me. This town has been my life. I owe it something." An odd little smile twitched his lips. "I don't plan on being around a helluva a lot longer. Getting rid of those two mongrels before I go to glory would be a fitting gift."

Pike drew himself up and puffed out his chest. "You better watch your mouth. Holt ain't a man you want to get riled."

Paul raised the rifle. "And you're just itching to tell him about this little conversation, aren't you, George?"

Chief Pike paled and reached behind him for the doorknob. "No, no . . . not me, Paul. I won't say a word." He jerked open the door and scurried onto the porch. "Not a single word."

Paul made a sound of disgust. "Get out of my sight."

Minutes later, a car motor roared to life, tires spewed gravel, and the police chief sped away.

Paul propped his gun against a chair, sank down on the couch, and massaged his temples. "You got some aspirin, Amy? My head's about to burst."

Amy brought two tablets and a glass of water from the bathroom. "When is Sarah Wahsise's funeral?"

He tossed back the pills, drank the water, and handed her the glass. "Tomorrow at two. Why?"

"I'd like to send flowers."

He lifted his head and stared at her. "Why? You didn't know her."

"I just want to." She began to clean up the mess the police chief had made.

Paul levered himself off the couch and picked up his rifle. "That business about done me in. Guess I'll go lie down."

She put her hand on his arm. "Thanks for side-tracking the chief."

He smiled wanly. "That goggle-eyed old goat needed a good shaking up. Maybe it'll put his brains in gear." He crossed the room and gazed through the open door-way at the rain sheeting off the roof. "But knowing old George, I doubt it." He groaned, hobbled out, and closed the door behind him.

Amy fixed herself a tuna fish sandwich and paced the room as she ate it. The torrential downpour banished any hope of them finding the tracks of Simon's abductors. Now, she didn't have a thing to go on . . . except. . . . She took Paul's old jacket from the closet and dashed out into the storm. Someone in Rock Springs must know the man with the deformed foot.

Her tennis shoes squishing with every step, she hurried along Main Street. At Valley Pharmacy, she cleaned mud from her shoes on the floor mat and glanced around—shelves and display islands held a pot-pourri of goods, everything from greeting cards and crystal bowls to crutches and corn pads.

A man peered over a high counter at the rear of the

store. "Well, hello there, young lady," he called. Before she could reply, he opened a half door and came down the aisle toward her. "Remember me? We met at the airport."

"Oh . . . yes. You're Mr. . . ." The blue fluorescent light from the overhead fixtures gave the skin on his hairless head a greenish tinge.

He smiled. "Pennington. But just call me Will. Everybody does. Can I help you find something?"

"I need a three percent solution of hydrogen peroxide." She pulled off her stocking hat and bent her head. "I have a slight scalp wound."

"Hm-m-m so you do. And not so slight either." He led the way to the back of the room and took a bottle from a shelf. "Want me to give it a bit of a cleaning?"

"Would you? I intended to ask Dr. Chambers, but he's not feeling so well."

Will nodded. "Don't judge him too harshly, he's had a rough time." He drew some peroxide into a dropper and sponged with a piece of gauze as he dripped the antiseptic solution onto her sutured wound. "His wife Mora ran off about ten years ago. Paul hasn't been the same since."

He finished his task and handed her the bottle. "Better keep it handy. You seem to be a bit accident prone."

She nodded and offered a wry smile. "You might say that." She stuffed the bottle in her pocket. "Thanks for the personal service. How much do I owe you?" He quoted her a price and she dug out her wallet.

He rang up the sale. "You're healing nicely. Neat closure. Haven't seen one like that in years. Who did it?"

"A friend."

"Ah, yes. From what I hear, your friend's quite . . ."

he pursed his lips, then his mouth curved into a smile, "versatile."

She kept her face impassive. "Your informant is mistaken."

"Could be." He grimaced and blotted perspiration from his forehead. "But I'd suggest you keep your friend handy, just in case."

She met his steady gaze. "I appreciate your concern, Mr. Pennington, but usually I manage to take care of myself." She left the store before he could say more.

At a combined fabric–yarn–florist shop, she ordered Sarah's flowers and went on her way. A block farther up the street, the whine of a power saw came from a two-story clapboard house. As she neared, Jared Dworski bustled through the open doorway and tossed a board onto a scrap pile on the wide verandah.

She waved. "Hello again, Mr. Dworski. Still building boutiques?"

He grinned. "Nah, not this time." He crooked his finger. "Come on in and take a gander." Inside, a lanky man dressed in patched pants and plaid flannel shirt limped around a large contrivance that filled most of the room.

"Miss Prescott," Jared said, towing her forward. "This dried up old geezer is Frank Reece." Jared's vivid blue eyes creased with a smile. "And this is the Molly Magee," he said with a sweeping gesture.

Reece, who was only slightly more wrinkled than Dworski, shook her proffered hand. "Golly sakes, girl, you're just a slip of a thing. From the stories going round, I reckoned you'd be built like one of them female Rusky sailors."

She laughed. "This is the weirdest town I was ever in. Everybody knows what's happened five minutes after it's happened." She regarded the two men. "Surely there must be more interesting topics than me."

Frank shrugged. "If there is, my wife hasn't gotten wind of it." He wagged his head. "Wanda's a fine woman, but I swear she'll go to her grave with that gol-durned phone stuck to her ear."

The townspeople didn't know about the dead man! How had Chief Pike managed that? She studied the odd-looking structure surrounding her. "What're you building?"

"Ah, Wanda's got the hair-brained notion tourists will pay to see how a mine works." He jerked his thumb at Jared. "And this son-of-a-jackass who calls himself my friend agreed with her. She hasn't given me a minute's rest since."

Jared jostled Frank aside. "This metal tower is the headframe. It's built above the main shaft to raise and lower the cage."

"That's the elevator that takes the men down into the mine," Frank put in.

Jared scowled and went on. "Muck from the stopes comes up the same shaft in a skip."

Frank raised his gaze to the ceiling and gave a long sigh. "Damnit, Jared, if you want people to understand, you have to use their lingo not ours. *Muck* is ore rock and the place where the ore is mined is a *stope*. And a *skip* looks like this." He attached a miniature bucket to a slender hoist cable.

"Only lots bigger." Jared jabbed him in the ribs with his elbow. "Well, show her how it works, so she can tell you how smart you are."

Frank flushed. "Back off you silly old coot, or I'll lay one along side your head." He flipped a switch and tiny lights came on all over the structure.

Amy peered into a hoist shack where a tiny figure

stood in front of levers and buttons. "You've done a marvelous job, Mr. Reece."

"That's nothing," Jared said. "Wait'll he gets it going."

"You mean it works?"

"Sure as hell does." Jared bumped Frank with his shoulder and hooked his thumbs in the band of his pants. "Cut her loose, Frank."

"I will, I will, if you'll throw a twitch around that lip a yours." He grinned at Amy. "He gets a little tetched when he gets around the Molly Magee." He patted the side of the model. "I made this to look like the mountain cut from summit to base."

Amy nodded and touched the clear plastic shield that covered the exposed interior of the mine. "Does the ore come from these tunnels?"

"Nope. And that's not a tunnel it's a cross-cut. A tunnel goes clear through the mountain and comes out the other side. These," he indicated passageways leading off the cross-cut, "are drifts. They're about nineteen feet wide and fifteen feet high."

"Really? I pictured them as small and cramped."

"They used to be. Now many mines have a standard gauge railway system to transport ore, men, and supplies."

"And you have to have room for the mucking machine," Jared added. "Up at the China Lady, we had a big, rubber-tired, front-end-loader with hydrostatic drive and a catalytic scrubber for the diesel exhaust."

Frank removed the ore bucket from the hoist and attached a cage filled with lead replicas of miners. "Cover your ears." He pushed a button and the whole model sprang into action.

The cage descended, men walked along a drift. A siren sounded and a strobe-lit trolley pulling a string of loaded ore cars swayed and clattered by the workers.

In another part of the mine, two men operated a mobile pneumatic drill that hissed and hammered at a rock face. All the while, a fine mist of muddy water and pulverized rock nearly hid the two men from sight.

Vent fans roared, exchanging stale, moist air for cooler drafts from the surface. A chugging motor powered a sump pump sucking water from a shaft. Every few minutes a simulated dynamite detonation shook the structure and added to the deafening clamor.

"How deep are the mines," she shouted.

"Some are two to three miles," Frank said.

"And the deeper you go, the more you roast," Jared yelled.

Amy stared at him. "I never thought of that. How hot does it get?"

"I've seen it a hundred and ten degrees. And the air so heavy you think old Lucifer's got his pitchfork planted in your chest every time you suck in your breath."

"How on earth do the miners stand it?"

Jared shrugged. "That's what they get paid for."

Frank turned off the current and for a few seconds the quiet seemed unreal. "Bad air caused Frank to get his," Jared said. "His pard didn't have his wits about him. They were workin' ratty rock. He brought down a slab with a eight-foot scaling bar. The bar jerked out of his hands and caught Frank's leg. Snapped it like a match stick in three places."

"Are there many accidents?"

"Too many," Frank said. "Most of them because McAllister's too cheap to buy proper equipment. Jared's boys would still be alive, if it weren't for Holt's greediness."

"Yes, Jared told me." She shifted her position so she could see each man's face. "Anyone you know ever get his foot mashed, or lose some toes."

Frank lifted his head, his eyes alert and watchful as a buck deer in hunting season. "Who wants to know?"

Amy contemplated the two men, trying to assess their character. "Can I trust you to keep what I tell you to yourselves?"

Jared leaned forward, his eyes glinting with excitement. "Old Frank and me can be close-mouthed as a priest when the need arises." He swiveled his head. "Ain't that right, Pard?"

"Sure thing. You in some sort of trouble Miss Prescott?"

"Call me, Amy." She smiled. "If we're going to be co-conspirators, we may as well be on a first-name basis."

Jared chuckled. "I already know you're looking for that redheaded fella who was here asking all those questions."

Amy frowned. "Who told you?"

"Edna, the waitress at The Golden Goose." His florid complexion grew a deeper shade of red. "Her and I kinda got a thing goin'."

Amy blew out her breath. At this rate, everyone, including Simon's abductors, would know why she'd come to town. "His name's Simon Kittredge. Some men conned his father into buying phony stock in a silver mine. Simon traced one of them to Rock Springs. Four days ago, he called and left a message that sounded as if he were in trouble. Now he's disappeared."

Frank scratched his furrowed cheek. "Did you talk to Chief Pike?"

"No. I already know Simon stopped in to see him. I doubt Pike offered him any assistance. Your police chief seems more concerned about his job than he is about people."

Jared laughed. "Told you she was sharp, Frank."

Frank picked up a wrench and made a pretense of tightening a nut. "Where does the guy with missing toes come in?"

"So you do know him?"

He lay down the wrench and folded his arms across his chest. "You haven't answered my question."

"Someone dumped Simon's rental car in Silver Lake. We . . . I found a misshapen footprint where the car went over the cliff."

"Is that all?"

She hesitated, then decided she'd have to trust them all the way. "I know Simon went fishing on Colby Creek and that he was taken prisoner by two men. One of the men was tall and lean, the other one weighed about two-eighty and had a deformed foot."

Jared lit a cigarette, took a long drag, and let the smoke trail from his nostrils. His sharp eyes probed her through the veil of smoke. "How do you know all that?"

"Interpreting signs is my job. I'm an investigator."

Jared led out a low whistle. "Holy Joe, a female private eye." He exchanged glances with his friend. "What do you think, Frank? Should we give her some help?"

"We'd better keep our noses clean until she comes up with more proof."

Jared leaned back against the wall. "Yeah, you're probably right. No sense putting ourselves in the hot seat just yet." His steady gaze met Amy's. "Walk easy. Life gets real chancy back in these hills."

Chapter 14

Paul called out to her as she passed his house and asked her to come into the kitchen. "Troy and Dean are out of the hospital," he said. "I'll keep a close watch." A wild light flickered in his eyes. "Take this." He held out a .45 automatic. "If they get by me, use it." His face had a gray cast and the hand holding the gun trembled.

She backed away. "I already have a gun." She paused in the open doorway. "I'm grateful for the help you've given me, but I'd rather you didn't appoint yourself my guardian."

His eyes narrowed to slits. "I might've known it. You're looking for some young stud just like Mora always was."

Amy clenched her fists at her sides. "I've had it, Paul. I'm moving back to the motel."

His shoulders slumped, the pistol slipped from his hand and thumped to the floor. "I'm sorry, Amy. I'm sorry." Tears coursed down his face. "Please don't go. I need you here." He clutched her hand and fell to his knees. "I have to have someone nearby in case . . . in case . . ." He pressed his forehead against her hand. "I'm so scared, Amy. I don't want to die alone."

Pity overcame her revulsion and kept her from shoving him away. "Stop that kind of talk." She helped him to his feet. "What you need is some coffee and a good hot meal." She set about fixing the coffee first. "I'll bet you haven't eaten in days."

Paul put his .45 in a drawer and sank down on a chair. "I've been so depressed."

She plugged in the coffee pot, put bacon in a frying pan, and began to scramble eggs. "That's no excuse, Paul. And you should know that better than anybody." She poured the eggs into a pan and began to set the table.

Paul looked up at her. "I'm sorry I made a pass at you the other night." His head drooped. "Couldn't have done anything anyway. I'm useless. Can't work, can't sleep, can't even have a woman when I want one." He let out a long sigh. "What's the good of it all?"

Amy's temper began to simmer. She poured a cup of coffee and set it in front of him. "Knock it off, Paul." She turned the bacon and gave the eggs a savage stir. "You claim Sarah Wahsise was your friend. And you know damned well George Pike won't try to find out if she died a wrongful death. So quit moaning about your problems and do some investigating on your own." She dished up his food, poured herself a cup of coffee, and took a chair across from him.

"What can *I* do. I'm not an expert like you."

"Have you ever sat in on an autopsy?"

"Sure, lots of them."

"Okay, make certain they do a thorough one and don't let them slack off on the toxicology."

Paul's fork stopped in mid-air. "You think she might have been poisoned?"

Amy spread her hands. "She was taking digitalis. She

handles herbs. Foxglove could induce ventricular tachycardia or fibrillation. Perhaps she made a mistake."

"Not a chance. Sarah labeled her herbs as carefully as a pharmacist and she knew the effect each one had on the body." He chewed thoughtfully. "It doesn't make sense that anyone would want to do her harm. God, her house was the only thing she owned."

Amy peered over the edge of her cup. "I heard her grandson had some property up in the hills."

Paul frowned. "Now you mention it, I remember her saying her husband left some land to Yancy."

Amy took a sip of coffee. "Wouldn't she be executor of his estate?"

Paul nibbled a piece of bacon. "Makes sense."

Amy studied him. She stared into the dark brew, hoping she could talk to Nathan before she made her decision. She took off her glasses and rubbed her eyes. Discussing it with Nathan wouldn't help, neither of them could dig around without causing a stir that'd wreck their search for Simon.

"Suppose someone wanted that land real bad."

Paul laughed. "Ah, come on, Amy, this isn't the Wild West. They'd keep offering more money until she sold."

"What if she wouldn't sell at any price?"

Paul finished his food and set his plate aside. "They'd just have to forget it."

Amy leaned forward. "Maybe it's not that simple. Suppose the people that need the land own the new ski lodge."

Paul turned stark white and let out a strangled cry. "Oh, my God. Oh, my God." He stood up nearly upsetting the table. Dishes crashed to the floor. "It can't be. It simply can't be." He stumbled down the hall to his study and closed the door.

Amy stood gaping at the mess. Why should her suggestion have caused such a violent reaction? She picked up the broken dishes and cleaned the kitchen, thinking he'd return. After half an hour, she gave up and sloshed down the dark, winding path to the cabin.

Once inside, she turned on the lights and put a match to the wood in the fireplace. When heat began to take off the chill, she slid her gun beneath a couch cushion and removed her damp clothing. Naked, she dashed into the icy bedroom, snatched a wool dress and a pair of Paul's wool socks from the closet and raced back to the fire. She donned her clothes and sat down on the couch with her notebook.

She stared into the crackling flames for several minutes. The odds of a town the size of Rock Springs having three mysteries at the same time were one in a thousand. Yet she couldn't find any connection between them.

Her mind wandered back to her talk with Frank and Jared that afternoon. Obviously, they knew the man she sought and considered him dangerous. Before she left, they had cautioned her about questioning anyone else about him.

A sharp tapping on the window made her jump. She turned off the lamp, grabbed her gun, and peeked through the gap in the drapes. Her pulse pounded as she waited for her eyes to adjust to the darkness. Was it the McAllister brothers? She shivered and gripped the gun butt so hard, her fingers ached.

A minute passed, then two. Finally, she recognized Nathan's tall form. Shoulders hunched, he stood in the pelting rain. She unlocked the window and raised the sash. "You're drenched. Get in here where it's dry."

After he'd climbed through, she closed the window,

locked it, and pulled the drapes tightly closed, before switching on the lamp. Water streamed from Nathan's hair and clothing. "What are you doing out on a night like this?"

"Walking and trying to think. Sorry if I frightened you. Last night, I saw Dr. Chambers prowling around outside, so I didn't want to risk coming to the door."

She glanced down at the .38 in her hand. "The McAllisters got out of the hospital this afternoon." She put the pistol back under the cushion.

"Yes, I know." He swiped his hand down his wet face and tried to wipe it on his sodden denim jacket.

"Wait. I'll get some towels." She ran into the bedroom and in a few minutes returned with towels.

"Thanks." He dried his face and wrapped the towel around his neck.

"Let me take your jacket," she said. He peeled it off and she hung it on a line strung near the fireplace. "Now your shirt."

"No, I can only stay a few minutes."

"Don't be ridiculous." As she held out her hand and wiggled her fingers, she remembered him doing the same thing that first night at the bus depot. "Hand it over."

He gave her an amused look. "Stubborn woman."

She smiled. "No more than you, my friend."

He unfastened his top button, took out a brown envelope that lay next to his skin and put it on the end table. Then he parted with his shirt and she put it beside his jacket.

When she turned and saw him standing beside the fire with light from the flames playing over his bronze skin, her bodily reaction took her unawares. "Now," she said quickly, without giving herself time to think. "Let's have your pants."

He folded his arms across his chest. "Is that any way to treat a man who has climbed in your window?"

She laughed at his wry humor. "It seems to fit the occasion. You'll find a sweatshirt and sweatpants on my bed."

"Amy, I'm all right. I don't need—"

"Go, for goodness sake. You're dripping on my rug."

His athletic shoes squishing with every step, he left the room. She quickly dumped a quart of milk into a pan, set it on the stove and began to spoon cocoa and sugar into a cup.

Nathan came back carrying his pants, socks, and shoes. "These sweats must not belong to Doc. They fit." He draped his pants and socks over the line.

"One of Paul's fishing or hunting buddies probably left them." She poured some of the milk into the cocoa mixture and stirred. A cool movement of air across her neck caused her to drop the spoon. Nathan had crossed the room in his bare feet and she hadn't heard a sound. "Don't sneak up on me like that. I'm jittery enough already."

He toweled his hair and flashed an impudent smile. "That'll teach you not to be so bossy." He peered over her shoulder. "What are you making?"

"Cocoa."

"Real cocoa? Not that saccharin sweet stuff you get in a package?"

"Uh huh, the real McCoy. Would you like some cinnamon toast?"

"Yes. I haven't had cinnamon toast since I was a kid." He tossed the towel over the back of a chair. "Let me help."

When everything was ready, they carried the food to the table and sat down. "I'm glad you came," she said. "I wanted to talk to you."

"Me, too." He sipped his cocoa. "Mmm this is good." He bit into a piece of toast and gave her a melting look. "This, too." He wiped sugar from his lips. "I brought the pictures you took. The dead man is a Mexican. None of my people have seen him before."

"I sent his prints and the rest of my specimens to Dad. Good thing I did, too. The police chief barged in here and tore the place apart." She laughed. "Paul chased him off with his rifle. Funny thing is, he asked me what I was doing at the river, but he didn't say a word about the Mexican."

"He and Dr. Leibow hauled the body off to Winterhaven Hospital."

She chewed a bite of toast. "Is Leibow the county coroner?"

"No, he lives in Wallace." He cupped his hands around the blue china mug to warm them. "But I'm bringing in my own man to monitor Sarah's autopsy. I want it done right."

"Paul questions her sudden death, too." She took in a deep breath. A fine trembling had begun inside her the moment she'd taken the chair across from him. Tonight, he wore no disguise and the force of the electricity he created muddled her mind. "I did something you may not like."

He regarded her with one lifted brow. "Like what?"

"I probably shouldn't have said anything, Paul's not very stable these days. He nearly flipped out when I hinted the ski lodge owners may have killed Sarah to get her land."

Nathan sat forward. "What did he do?"

"At first he acted stunned. Then he went into a panic."

"Strange."

"And I also did something else . . ." She corralled some stray grains of sugar and worked them into a neat pile, thinking that as soon as Nathan heard he'd probably explode. Her chest began to ache. She glanced up at him, then back down at the table.

He touched the back of her hand. "This is your investigation, not mine."

"Yes, I know, but . . ."

"You don't need my approval."

She ventured a wan smile. "Sometimes I make a gut decision and it backfires."

He chuckled. "You, too?"

She inhaled and found the catch she'd gotten in her chest had disappeared. "I met a couple of men in town. Frank Reece and Jared Dworski. Frank built the display you saw at The Golden Goose. Jared used to be shift boss at the China Lady mine until an explosion killed his two boys and the mine shut down."

Nathan drank the last of his cocoa and set down his cup. "I've heard their names."

"I told them who I was and why I'm looking for a man with a deformed foot. I'm positive they know him, but they refuse to commit themselves until I come up with more evidence." She let her shoulders sag. "Doesn't look like there's much hope of that."

She mustered her spirits. "I shouldn't be loading you down with my problems. You have enough already. How's Yancy holding up?"

"All right. He hasn't had an easy life. After Sarah's funeral, I'll put him on the bus to Orofino. He can stay with my father." He stared down at the table.

Finally, he shook himself and said, "One of the elders told me of a trail near the place where Simon parked his car. Could I take a look at your forest map."

She brought the map and spread it out on the table. He stood, leaned his weight on his elbows, and ran his fingertip along a road. "We'll start at the base of Star Mountain and hike over the summit. The weather report says this storm'll be over by tomorrow. We can pack in and stay until we find him."

He glanced at her. "Okay by you?"

"Absolutely. Sitting around doing nothing is driving me crazy."

"Me, too." They bent over the map, their shoulders nearly touching, their faces inches apart. "It'll feel good to get back into the woods. I can think better and . . ." his eyes met hers, "things seem much simpler."

"Yes," she said.

"I'll get the food and the stuff to prepare it. You bring whatever you need."

"Paul said I could borrow his gear." Their shoulders touched and she felt the warmth of his body flow into hers. The longing to rest her head against him became so overpowering she could think of nothing else.

"Good." He ran his tongue over his lips. "Amy?"

"Yes?"

"You . . . uh"—he cleared his throat, but when he spoke his voice still sounded husky. "The . . . the terrain gets pretty barren up on the high ridges. You better buy some camo."

She met his gaze and found herself unable to break the contact. "Camo? What's that?"

"Camouflage gear." He straightened and put some space between them. "Try to find universal or tiger. They're best for all terrain." He took a long time folding the map, finally laying it on the table. "I suppose I should be going."

"Why don't you have another cup of cocoa? We'll sit by the fire so you'll be warm when you leave."

He beamed at her. "Good idea."

While she filled the mugs, he put another log on the fire and they settled themselves on the couch.

"Nathan, it's been five days since I heard from Simon. Do you think there's any chance of finding him?"

"We'll do our best." He fell silent for several minutes, then said, "Have you been in love for a long time?"

She hesitated only instant. "When Simon and I met last fall, I'd been through a bad marriage. He was still recovering from the death of his wife and unborn child. We tried to convince ourselves we were in love, but we weren't."

"Then you know about Erika."

She opened her mouth to ask how he knew but closed it again. He wouldn't tell her. "Simon's letters have been full of her the last few months."

"And you don't mind?"

"Actually I'm relieved."

"Oh . . ." His dark eyes swept over her. "That gold color looks nice on you."

For a moment she felt as she had when she'd launched herself off a mountain in a hang glider— giddy, joyous, lighter than air. Excitement heated her cheeks. "Thank you." Laughter bubbled from deep in her chest. She stretched out her legs. "I think Paul's socks make the outfit."

A line formed between his brows as if he'd made a discovery that disturbed him. "Sometimes, you glow as if you've switched on a light inside." His expression softened. "My mother used to do that whenever my father came into the room."

A piercing sweetness filled her, and her lips parted with the wonder of it. "She loved him. Haven't you ever felt that way about a woman?"

He lifted his cocoa mug from the end table and took a long swallow. "Just teen-age kid stuff. I guess some people never find the real thing."

"Your father did, didn't he?"

"My mother was his whole life." He drew in a breath and let it out in a long sigh. "When she died, he blamed her death on Anglo weakness. From then on, he laid into me every time I dated a white girl."

"But that's silly, you're part Caucasian."

"All the more reason. He said our strong bloodline should not be weakened by any more out marriages."

Her stomach contracted with apprehension. "Surely you don't believe such nonsense."

Silence stretched between them, marked by the heavy thump of her heart.

At last, he stirred. "Indians should marry Indians. Anglos should marry Anglos."

"I see." She wrapped her arms across her chest and gripped her elbows. "And . . . which . . . are you?"

He stared into the flames until her nerves grew taut waiting for his reply.

When he twisted his head to look at her, tense lines stretched from his nose to his mouth. "Indian." He pushed himself off the couch, took his clothing from the line, and retreated to the bedroom.

Amy chafed her arms. Although the fire still burned brightly, the room seemed to have grown cold.

Nathan came back and paused in front of her. "Thanks for everything."

She forced herself to raise her head. "Forget it."

"See you Wednesday?"

Did he think she'd abandon Simon just because of him? "I'll be there."

He leaned down and switched off the lamp. "Four-thirty. Same place you let me off."

She heard the window slide up and the soft thud as he closed it from the outside. She sat huddled in the darkness until the fire died and the chill in the room drove her to bed.

The next day she scoured the length of Silver Valley for camouflage gear that would fit her. She settled for a boy's size eighteen and bought suspenders to hold up the pants.

Before starting back to Rock Springs, she phoned her father.

"It's about time," he said. "I've been pacing the floor."

"Come on now, Dad, it's only been two days."

"Well, I've been worried."

"I'm mailing you some photos I took and you should be receiving some physical evidence I've gathered. Will you check out the fingerprints first?"

"Got any new leads on Simon's whereabouts?"

If she told him about Simon's abduction, he'd be on the next plane. "A few. They haven't led anywhere." She shifted to a more emphatic tone. "I've hired a tracker. We're going into the mountains tomorrow. We'll be away several days."

"You think that's a good idea?"

She blew out her breath. "It's the only hope we have."

"Damnit, Amy, I don't like the feel of this case one bit."

"I can handle it, Dad. Trust me."

When she arrived at Paul's house, his car wasn't in the garage. Sarah's funeral had been at two, he should be returning soon. She borrowed his nylon tent and backpack. At the cabin, she crammed the things she would need into the pack, attached the tent and sleeping bag, and carried them back to the jeep.

Just as she finished stowing them away, Paul drove into the yard. He got out of the car and came toward her. He wore a black suit and a white shirt and his eyes were reddened. "Her people really did Sarah proud." He leaned against the jeep. "Every one of them got up and said something about her. Touching, real touching, especially the eulogy given by a man named Blackthorn."

She scowled at the puddle at her feet. So that was what had driven Nathan out into the rain. He could have told her. She'd have listened.

"Amy . . ." Paul moved closer. "Are you mad at me?"

"No, of course not." She straightened and tried to give him her full attention. "It's Simon. Tomorrow, I'm going into the mountains to hunt for him." She jerked her head toward the jeep. "I borrowed some of your camping gear."

"Take anything, dear. Anything at all." He peered at her. "You aren't going alone, are you?"

"A tracker is going along."

The corners of his mouth drooped. "Who?"

"A man I met."

"A man you met!" His nostrils flared. "You're a young attractive woman. It isn't safe for you to be traipsing around the woods with a man you don't even know."

"Now, Paul . . ."

"It isn't safe I tell you. Things are happening around here. Strange, crazy things."

He'd learned about the dead man! She propped her back against the jeep and crossed her legs. "What do they think happened to him?"

"Worthless," he mumbled as if talking to himself. "Plumb worthless. But he didn't deserve to die like that."

She leaned forward and said in a quiet voice, "How did he die?"

"A drug overdose."

"Are you sure?"

Paul's eyes flashed. "Good God, he was stretched out in a shed behind the pharmacy. Still had the needle in his arm."

Amy let out a gasp. "Who overdosed?"

When he didn't answer immediately, she caught hold of his arm and shook it. "Who was it?"

"Dean McAllister."

Chapter 15

"You came." Nathan tossed his gear into the back.

Amy's flesh felt like marble and her ears ached from having had her jaw clamped from the moment she got out of bed. "Did you think I wouldn't?"

"Yes." He climbed into the jeep, folded his arms across his chest, and slumped down in the seat. Dark circles under his eyes indicated he hadn't slept well either.

She noted the set, unyielding cast of his face and body. His mood, like hers, matched that of the gray predawn. "I'm not a quitter."

"I know. I thought you wouldn't want—"

"What *I* want isn't important. *Simon is.*" She filled her lungs with the crisp, fresh scent of pine to dislodge the sense of loss that lay like a lead weight inside her. Soon she would return to her home in Ursa Bay. Once there, she'd forget this man and his stiff-necked opinions. The thought failed to raise her spirits.

The taut silence continued mile after mile, until finally she couldn't stand it any longer. "Dean McAllister died yesterday morning."

"Yes. Will Pennington came and got me. He wanted me to see the body before he called Dr. Chambers or the chief of police."

She peered at him from under the floppy brim of her camouflage hat. "Are you and Pennington friends?"

"Not exactly."

Her fingers tightened on the wheel. *Damn him and his secrets.* "What's that supposed to mean?" When Nathan didn't answer immediately, she ground her teeth with frustration.

Finally, he straightened and faced her. "Will is my contact."

Why? For what reason? Knowing it would be useless to ask, she pushed the questions aside. "What did you find?"

"Slivers of glass littered the area where Will kept the narcotics."

"So Dean broke in to get drugs."

Nathan hitched one leg over the other and scowled. "Maybe, maybe not. I collected fibers from his shoe soles but found no soil fragments or glass splinters."

"What about his hands and clothing?"

He shook his head. "Only a bit of thread that had gotten caught on a torn fingernail."

"Ah, that might be helpful. Which arm was the needle in?"

"Left."

"Did you notice the angle of the needle?"

"Normal—for a right-handed shooter. But Will says Dean was left-handed and totally inept with his right."

"Any other needle tracks?"

"None."

She nodded. "Paul says Dean drank a lot but he'd never heard of him using drugs."

Nathan rubbed his forehead. "Two missing men, two dead men, and one dead woman. They must fit together. But how?" He turned to her. "Any ideas?"

"Not a one." She mulled over what little she knew. "But there has to be a connection."

Ahead, a white mantle of fog blanketed Star Mountain. When she reached the spot on Colby Creek where she and Nathan had discovered car tracks, she parked the jeep. Ankle deep in slippery maple and cottonwood leaves, Nathan shouldered his backpack and started to help fit her arm straps over her ill-fitting camouflage jacket.

She stiffened and moved away from him. "I can manage." A red squirrel, evidently disturbed by her sharp tone of voice, ran out on a maple tree limb and commenced to chatter. Amy ignored his racket, worked her backpack into place, and set off after Nathan. Each step raised an acrid odor of decaying vegetation.

Nathan, despite the swirling mist, took only a few minutes to find the brush-screened head of the trail. He pushed aside dew-drenched cottonwood saplings, bent, fastened his gaze on the rain-gutted incline, and started up.

She followed, her mind teeming with questions. If Simon had come this way, had it been by design or mere happenstance? A sodden branch of leathery mountain laurel smacked her cheek and she abandoned her musing. If she intended to keep up with Nathan, she couldn't afford any clumsy blunders.

They hiked in silence, the white-barked quaking aspen and lodge pole pine gradually giving way to subalpine fir and mountain hemlock. On a craggy escarpment, she broke a twig from a scrubby, twisted evergreen and stopped to examine it with the folding magnifier she'd brought with her. "Rocky Mountain juniper," she said excitedly.

Nathan raised his head and nodded. As they went higher, the trail wound along precipitous cliffs and between jutting stone spires. From time to time shrill bleats and barks pierced the icy air.

She didn't recognize the sounds and kept searching for the animal who made them until Nathan halted beside a shale ledge and pointed to small piles of drying grass. She knelt for a closer look. Black, BB-sized droppings dotted the area. "Pika," she mouthed and smiled up at him.

She started to rise, but he gripped her shoulder and his tensed arm held her immobile. She followed his upward gaze and her heart jammed against her ribs.

On an overhanging crag stood a mountain lion. Deep set green-gold eyes on either side of a long narrow nose stared down at them—keen, thoughtful, speculative. Pale beige fur with a silvery overlay covered the animal's lithe frame. On her belly, where her coat shaded to platinum, a gentle swelling indicated she had recently weaned a litter of kittens.

Seconds inched by and Amy remained frozen, too frightened to even think of moving. Finally, the cat flicked her long, black-tipped tail, bounded to a rock on the other side of the trail, and disappeared.

Nathan let out his breath as if he'd been holding it the whole time and sank down beside her. His face was ashen. *Fear?* she thought. *Surely, not. He'd spent his childhood in the woods. It had to be something else.*

She touched his arm. "Are you ill?"

Nathan ran his hand over his eyes. "The same," he said dazedly. "All the same."

She shook his arm. "What is?"

"My Wey-e-kin."

"Your what?"

"Wey-e-kin, my guardian spirit." He released a long sigh and settled himself in the cross-legged position he seemed to find so comfortable. "When I was ten, my grandfather decided I was ready to go on my vision quest. I went alone into the mountains. I fasted for four days and waited for a vision to come to me."

Amy shivered. "You were only a small boy. Weren't you scared?"

He nodded. "And lonely and very, very hungry. I cried sometimes but not for long. Grandfather had told me the quest wouldn't be easy." He leaned closer, his face intent. "The fourth night a full moon lighted the clearing among the pines where I sat waiting. I felt light-headed, a singing sound filled my ears. I had to have a vision in the next few hours or my quest would be a failure."

Amy pictured him sitting alone in the vastness, his thin legs and arms crossed, his young being straining for some unfamiliar out-of-body experience. "You were too young to be in the forest by yourself. How could your grandfather have done such a thing?"

"All Indian boys must go on a vision quest." A dreamy look softened his features. "That night in the meadow, I dozed off or fainted, I'm not sure which.

"Then, all of a sudden, I came wide awake, every nerve tingling. A silvery-white cougar stood not more than ten feet from me, its pupils glowing with luminous fire in the moonlight. The cat stared into my eyes and I got all quivery inside. It felt as if the big cat crept into my mind and padded through long, dark, twisting halls searching for sins and impure thoughts.

"I prayed my time in the sweat lodge before setting out had purged my body and soul of evil. All the while, I trembled with terror, certain the beast could smell my fear and that any minute it would pounce and tear me to pieces. When I thought I would pass out if I had to sit still an instant longer, the cat rumbled deep in its chest and disappeared in the forest."

Nathan leaned back against the rocks. "A great joy filled me and I knew the moon cat was my guardian spirit." He frowned. "I wonder why she reappeared today."

Amy wriggled. Talk of spiritual things made her uncomfortable. "How long ago was that?"

"I was ten at the time and I am now thirty-two."

"That's twenty-two years. It couldn't be the same cat." She stood up and brushed mud from her knees. When he didn't answer, she glanced at him. He sat motionless, his face as hard and cold as the stone beside him. "Could it?" she asked sharply.

"My people belive a Wey-e-kin lives forever."

She tensed. He'd already made it quite clear they came from different worlds, he needn't keep reinforcing the message. She took off up the trail, trying to set a pace that would keep her far ahead of him.

An hour passed and the terrain grew more rugged with every switchback. A short way from the summit, Nathan caught up with her and gave her a small stone.

"Put it with the others you'll find at the crest."

She stared down at the rock. "What for?"

He scowled at her. "It is the home of Amo'tqEn, the mountain deity. We show respect by placing a rock at the summit. In return, he gives us luck and good health."

Once again, she felt on the outside. She shoved the rock back at him. "You observe your customs, I'll take care of mine." To her dismay, she'd gone not more than twenty feet, when she stumbled. She lurched forward, sprawled and found herself hanging over a sheer hundred-foot drop.

Nathan dragged her to safety and regarded her with an impassive expression. "Taunting gods can be dangerous." He stepped around her and didn't look back as she limped along behind.

She arrived at the top with her dignity in tatters and sat down on a rock. Across the canyon, deep purple shadows still shrouded Mount Grayson's angular slopes. She rubbed her bruised shin and watched the rising sun penetrate the morning mist.

Slowly, glowing fingerlings moved down Mount Grayson's high-domed peak, crept over the face of a cliff, and accentuated an odd-shaped protrusion. Dancing rays picked up a flash of red, then some distance away another. Seams of white quartz swept out through black basalt on either side.

"Oh, I think . . . I think . . ." Afraid to move for fear she'd lose sight of the landmarks, she reached out blindly and caught hold of Nathan's jacket. "We've found it," she whispered, and pointed across the canyon.

He squatted beside her. "What?"

"See the red rocks on either side of that jutting piece of stone?"

"Yes."

"Now, follow the outline of the quartz and use your imagination."

He focused on the mountainside. "I'm not sure . . . Wait a minute. Yes, you're right." He turned, his eyes gleaming with excitement. "Simon's ruby-eyed raven."

Chapter 16

"I brought these for you." Nathan handed her a pair of binoculars. He flattened himself among tufts of bear grass and trained his glasses on Mount Grayson's timbered slopes.

Amy took a position nearby, propped her elbows on a lichen-encrusted rock, and started her own scrutiny. "Odd," she said. "I hear engines. I can see a headframe and tailings, but there isn't a hoist shack. Don't all mines have one?"

"They would have to with a hard rock mine of any depth. And judging from the height of that headframe, I'd say this is not a two-man operation." He moved to a different location, and neither of them spoke for ten or fifteen minutes. "Ah-h-h," he said at last.

"See something?"

"Camouflage netting."

"Are you sure? Why would they use camouflage?"

"Good question. We must get closer." He pointed out the downhill route. "From now on we talk only in whispers. Sounds carry in this thin air. Think, before you make a move. If we're out in the open, follow my lead."

He went a couple of steps and swung around. "Wait."

He took a flat container from his pocket. "Let me put some of this on your face." He tipped her chin and smeared brown streaks along her cheeks. "I keep forgetting about your white skin."

She jerked out of his grasp. "That'll be the day!"

They stood toe to toe and glared at each other. "I'm not bigoted."

"Oh, no?" she countered coldly. "What would you call it?"

He ran his hand over his face. "You wouldn't understand."

She met his hostile scrutiny with her own. "You're right. I wouldn't."

He shoved the camouflage kit in his pocket, sank into a half crouch, and started the downhill trek. Led by the deep-throated throb of massive unseen engines, they darted from tree to tree, rock to rock. In barren stretches, they crawled on their bellies. Pieces of broken rock bruised her knees. A sharp root tore open an unhealed blister in her palm.

Finally, they reached the base of Star Mountain and found themselves in a canyon choked with aspen, box elder, and willow. They cached their backpacks in a thicket and rested.

Nathan cut a leafy willow branch to whisk away stinging flies and leaned against a fallen tree. "We need a signal. Can you do any bird calls?"

"A passable owl or chickadee."

"Good. The chickadee will do for now. You listen for the cry of a hawk." He unzipped a pouch of his pack, withdrew a camera, and got to his feet. "We better get going."

With a groan, Amy rose, stretched knotted leg muscles, and followed him uphill to a rocky ledge. He pointed to where he wanted her to take her position and slipped away. She hid herself in a tangle of wind-twisted juniper and adjusted the binoculars.

From this angle, she could see beneath the interweaving of the multicolored netting. A six-foot chain-link fence with rolls of razor ribbon wire along the top surrounded a rectangular area. Near the base of the headframe lay a number of structures covered with dull, corrugated metal. Three long buildings constructed of rough unpainted shiplap ranged along the fence.

A man with a long canvas case slung across his back came out of a lean-to hut. He climbed a rope ladder hanging from a crudely built platform in the center of the compound. When he reached the top, he pulled up the ladder, leaned on the railing and blew a whistle. Men emerged from an elongated passageway, stretching between two oversized sheds, and straggled into the barren dirt enclosure.

Amy focused the glasses on the men and caught her breath. Mexicans! All of them clad in white caps and coveralls like those worn by the dead man in the river. One of the men turned and shook his fist at the tower. A sharp, explosive report split the air. The sound reverberated off the canyon's rock walls, and a puff of dust spurted at the man's feet.

Amy swung the glasses and a gasp escaped her. The man in the tower held a rifle. Her mind wrestled to interpret what she could clearly see. Miners garbed in white—the idea was ludicrous. Miners, who also seemed to be prisoners—equally preposterous.

She pressed her fingers against her forehead in an effort to concentrate. Perhaps Idaho's Department of Corrections had some sort of agreement with the mine owners to provide workers. That explained the guard, but it didn't explain Simon's connection. Had he seen something happen that triggered his investigative reporter's instinct?

She discarded the notion as too coincidental. A correctional facility couldn't have been responsible for Simon's disappearance.

Unless . . . yes, that has to be it. The operators must be high-grading ore.

Even that theory stretched credibility; however, she could think of no other explanation that made sense.

She moved farther out on the ledge and scanned the mountainside. Below her, the rays of the afternoon sun glinted on something bright. She tried to make it out and failed. Just as she refocused on the fenced yard, a man opened the door of a shed. Five dogs rushed out. The Mexican workers scattered and dashed for the wooden buildings.

Anger churning inside her, she hunkered down and watched the dogs roam the compound. Bony ribs stood out on the animals' gaunt bodies. After patrolling the fence several times, one large Doberman pinscher hastened to the back of the dog hut. When well out of sight of the guard, he started to dig by a fencepost. The flying dirt made a pile behind him.

Aside from the dogs, an occasional ground squirrel, and the infernal black flies, nothing stirred.

Nathan's shrill hawk's cry brought her alert. While she waited for him, she made a last reconnaissance. Again she caught the flash of light. She traced it to a patch of willows where two magpies flitted about. The scavengers' snowy white bellies and shoulders made a spectacular display against their iridescent black feathers.

Nathan appeared, pointed toward the canyon floor,

and indicated she should lead the way. Halfway down, she again sought out the shiny object and located it in a nest built of thorny twigs. Evidently the storm had torn off the nest's bulky dome, exposing the magpie's glossy treasures.

She gestured to Nathan, he nodded, and she began to creep toward the grove of willows. She drew a breath before each step, the slightest noise could send the birds into a raucous flurry that might attract the guard's attention.

As she and Nathan drew closer, he began to mimic the magpies, answering their nasal *mag? mag? mag?* with his own. When the two of them finally stood beneath the willow, Nathan boosted her high enough so she could reach her hand into the nest.

She found a white pebble and a rock encrusted with mica. Unsatisfied, her searching fingers continued, closing over a round, flat object. She brought it to eye level and a tiny cry escaped her.

Nathan eased her to the ground and gave her a questioning glance. She unclasped her hand. In her palm lay the stainless steel identification tag she'd attached to the camera she'd given Simon for Christmas. Nathan's triumphant smile matched hers.

They retrieved their backpacks and hiked along the floor of the canyon. At its entrance, they came to a swamp. She recognized the marshland as the same one they'd crossed three days before while searching for the footprints of Simon's abductors.

Nathan skirted the swamp and continued for another five or six miles. Finally, he halted in a grove of ponderosa pine, near a sheer rock wall that enclosed the site on two sides. "We'll make camp here," he said.

Amy sighed. "Am I ever glad to hear that. I'm pooped."

He shrugged off his backpack and stretched. "It doesn't take long for a person to get out of shape."

She set her backpack alongside of his. "I'll say."

He kneaded a shoulder muscle. "Can you manage your tent alone?"

"Probably. It didn't look too complicated."

He took a polyethylene bag from his pack. "I'll see if I can find water."

She chose a flat spot in a grove of aspen and cleared away the rocks. To her delight, Paul's domed tent went together with no difficulty at all. She had it up and her sleeping bag spread inside by the time Nathan returned.

"Found a nice stream about a hundred yards up the valley." He took a tiny stove nested with cooking pots from his pack. "There's a pool deep enough to bathe in."

"Sounds inviting. If you don't need my help, I'll give it a try."

"Go to it. Dinner will be ready in about twenty minutes."

When she rejoined him, she felt refreshed, and the achiness in her muscles had subsided a little. Nathan dished up a plate of freeze-dried stew that tasted surprisingly good. After a few bites, she said, "Do you think those men are convicts?"

Nathan sipped his coffee. "Never heard of prisoners wearing white, especially in a mine." He ate in silence for several minutes. "Seems likely the dead man in the river came from there."

"Right." She shuddered. "And I'll bet those guard dogs are responsible for the horrible bites."

Nathan set down his aluminum plate. "I'll go back after dark. I want to do some more investigating."

"I'm going with you."

His face grew dark and quiet. "Too dangerous. I can't be worrying about you."

She held herself ramrod straight. "Then don't." She met his angry glance without flinching. "I manage most of my cases without a man's help." She firmed her lips. "And there's always an element of danger."

"Suit yourself." Nathan rolled out his sleeping bag next to her tent, lay down, and turned his back to her.

After washing their utensils at the stream, she changed into dark clothing and crawled inside her own sleeping bag. In her tense state, she hadn't thought she'd sleep but she did.

When Nathan shook her awake, a pale moon had risen. Dark clouds scudded across a vast black-velvet sky, drawing purple veils over rhinestone stars.

"Put these on." Nathan handed her a pair of night vision glasses. The elongated lenses reminded her of a movie director's conception of men from outer space.

"So you expected me to go with you," she said accusingly.

"I hoped you wouldn't insist." He held out his tin of camouflage makeup. "Some women like to be protected."

"They wouldn't last long in my profession." She smeared black goo on her face, wiped her fingers, and took her pistol from her shoulder holster to check it.

Nathan scowled at her weapon. "Too noisy. If something comes up, let me handle it."

The muscles in her shoulders knotted. "Yes, *sir.*" She shoved the pistol back in its holster and buttoned her shirt. "Can we go now?"

He gave her a narrow, glinting glance and strode off in the direction they'd come, his shoes crunching in grass crisp with frost. He set a fast pace, stopping only once to cut and trim a long willow staff. When they reached the slopes below the mine, he assumed his cat-like stance, placing each foot before he raised the other. She tried to imitate him, but impatience kept fouling her up.

The slower pace gave her time to think, and fear rippled through her. Two men may have disappeared inside that place. If that were true, getting rid of two more wouldn't faze the people who ran it.

As they drew closer, her heart throbbed at the base of her throat and her insides quivered. She tried to swallow, but her saliva had dried. She darted a quick glance at Nathan, hoping he didn't suspect.

She squeezed her arms to her sides in an attempt to gain control. *I'm not a weakling.* Even the bravest of men admitted that they, too, had sometimes been afraid. She cleared her mind. She had gotten through this before, she would get through it again. Strength began to flow through her again.

When they reached the compound, it didn't have masses of floodlights as she had feared it would. However, the guard paced round and round in the tower, his gun at the ready. The dogs were nowhere to be seen, but even so Nathan paused frequently to check the direction of the wind.

Satisfied, he wormed forward until the deep shadow of the first barrack closed around him. She caught up in time to see him work his staff through the chain links of the fence.

He tapped lightly on the barrack wall and asked a question in Spanish. Amy recognized only five words:

"gringo," "Henry Cummings," and "Simon Kittredge."
A burst of excited voices responded to Nathan's query.
Nathan snapped a command and the commotion
ceased. After a moment, a single voice answered his
questions.

Nathan touched Amy's arm, shook his head and
pointed to the next building. She raised up enough to
check the guard and immediately flattened herself again.
He'd stopped pacing and seemed to be staring in their
direction. She motioned for Nathan to hurry and drew
her finger across her throat.

At the next barrack, Nathan went through the same
routine and again received a negative reply. At the last
one, a man spoke to Nathan in rapid Spanish.

Nathan put his mouth close to her ear and whispered.
"Henry is dead. Simon is being held captive in the
mine. He has a broken arm."

For an instant, she felt euphoric. *Simon was still alive!*
Then a dozen questions flooded her mind. "Ask him—"
Nathan's finger on her lips shut off the rest. An instant
later, the big lead Doberman galloped past, his feet slap-
ping the dirt-hardened track the dogs had worn next to
the fence. Two more Dobermans followed a few minutes later, with two half-grown German shepherds
bringing up the rear.

Nathan gestured for her to start downhill. Their retreat was quiet and orderly until Nathan hissed, "The
big Doberman has gotten out." He pressed his walking
stick into her hand. "Go. Run as fast as you can." She
didn't move. "Hurry before the rest find the hole he
dug."

"No! I'm not going to leave you to face the pack
alone."

Nathan stood irresolute for a fraction of a second.

Then, he grasped her wrist in a vise-like grip. "Silly, Anglo woman!" His dark eyes flashed. "Do as I say before your foolishness gets us killed."

Rage erupted inside her head. To contain it, she ran—ran as she had never run before, anger energizing her, giving her strength. *Damn him!* She slithered down a bank, bashed into a boulder and careened on. Damn him for making her feel small and insignificant, degrading her intelligence as Mitch had done time and again during their marriage. Thorns tore at her face, her arms, tangled her feet. From now on, she'd go it alone. She didn't need Nathan's help.

She clambered over rocks, squeezed through brush and stumbled over roots. Finally, she made it to the floor of the canyon and stopped to catch her breath.

From a short way up the mountain came the sound of wild barking. She shuddered. The dogs had found her trail.

Chapter 17

She recalled Nathan's remark about the viciousness of wild dogs, and a surge of adrenaline shot through her. She dashed down the canyon, thankful the ghostly white of the aspen trunks made them easy to see.

The tone of the dogs' cry changed to a chilling and triumphant chorus. Instinct told them she'd be easy prey. She ran faster, her gaze darting frantically right and left. A tall tree, a big boulder, someplace where she'd be out of the animals' reach. She found none.

Behind her the shadowy figures of two dogs traveled at an easy, unhurried trot. They would wait for her to tire, then attack.

Terror-stricken, she ran blindly and blundered into the marsh. Ankle-deep water and gooey mud slowed her down. The dogs' barking changed, became higher pitched, more excited. They splashed into the water after her. She tried to move faster, to lift her knees higher.

She glanced over her shoulder and saw their bodies arc into the air like aquatic animals, each giant leap bringing them a yard closer. They'd be on her any minute.

She shinnied up an aspen sapling. The big lead Doberman charged and vaulted upward in one fluid motion. His teeth scraped her ankle and caught in the cloth of her running shoe. He ripped it off as he fell to the ground and backed off for another lunge.

While her attention focused on the Doberman, the German shepherd came at her from the other side. He sank his teeth into her toes. She kicked him in the nose and he let go just as the Doberman launched another attack. She scrambled to a higher branch, heard the aspen crack with the strain and shivered with panic.

Moonlight gleaming on his wet, ebony coat, the Doberman paced, growling and biting the air. He ran off a few yards, turned, and flung himself upward, a snarling mass of fury. His nails scrabbling on slippery tree bark, he climbed higher. His jaws snapped shut only inches from her leg.

The lighter dog followed suit. His fangs tore through her pant leg and sliced into her flesh. The taste of blood drove him into a frenzy. He and the Doberman sprang at her again and again, hitting the sapling with the full force of their bodies.

The top of the tree whipped wildly, then snapped, flinging her into thick, foul-smelling ooze. Instantly, the dogs hurtled after her, tearing at her from both sides, ripping her clothing. Lips curled back from bared teeth, they snatched at her hands, her face.

"Get back," she shrieked. She yanked off the mud-smeared night-vision glasses and flung them at her attackers. The dogs separated and struck again. Screaming, kicking, hitting, she beat them off and plunged into deeper water.

They followed, leaping from one tussock to another, forcing her to retreat until the water reached her chest. The shepherd grabbed her wrist in his teeth and hung on. She wrapped her legs around him and sank into the warm sulfurous soup pulling him down with her. She held him under until her lungs felt as if they might burst. When she came up for air, the shepherd swam away, crawled onto a hummock of bulrushes and lay down.

She'd vanquished one, but the Doberman sensed her fatigue. He attacked from first one side then the other, leaping, snarling, his terrible, slashing, tooth-filled mouth coming so close to her face she could smell his sour breath.

She wrenched a dead branch from a half-submerged log and thrust it at him. He caught the stick in his teeth. She submerged and dragged him under with her. When he let go, she shot out of the water and swung the club. The blow caught him above one eye, splitting the skin. He yelped and slunk into the marsh grass.

She swam to a tiny floating island of tangled willow roots and dragged herself onto it. When she'd rested, she sat up. The toes the shepherd had bitten felt better in the warm water so she let her foot dangle, her lacerated fingers she tucked in her armpit while she gazed around.

On three sides, a clear section of water lay between her and the dogs. They'd have to swim to get at her and they'd learned that could be dangerous. On the remaining side, trees created thick, purple shadows the moonlight couldn't penetrate.

A frog croaked somewhere in the darkness. Up on the hill, a coyote yipped. From far off, another answered, a desolate, lonely sound. She shivered convulsively. *Anglo woman.* The closest thing to a curse she'd ever heard Nathan say. Would he even bother to worry about her?

A horde of stinging insects descended on her. She

slapped with one hand and scooped stinking mush from the water with the other. She spread the stuff on her face, but it ran off and didn't hamper the insects in the least.

She plunged her hand into the mass of roots and grass on which she sat, searching for thicker mud. A snake wrapped itself around her wrist. She shook it off. Another slithered through her fingers and plopped into the water.

She shuddered but continued to dig in the undulating island until she had layered her face, neck, hands and feet with muck. When she finished, she hunkered down and waited. Across the stretch of water the dogs' eyes shone, hard, cold, unwinking. They waited, too.

She wondered about the rest of the pack. *Nathan must have found a way to escape them,* she thought. *A capable person like him would never get himself into a situation like this.* Another thought surfaced, *when they lose his trail, will they retrace their tracks and come after me?* She shivered and gazed into space, trying to decide what to do.

If she fired her gun at the dogs, she might scare them away, or Nathan might hear and come to help her. But shots would also attract the attention of the men at the mine. If they captured her and Nathan, that'd be the end for them and Simon, too. She rested her forehead on her knees and closed her eyes.

Dawn brought fog and a mist-like drizzle. Careful not to move too fast and cause the island to tip, Amy stretched cramped muscles. She whimpered as she unclenched her slashed fingers. Instantly, the German shepherd and the Doberman came to their feet, ears pricked, eyes alert.

Warm air rising off the marsh to meet the crisp air above created a suitable setting for a horror movie. Amy peered through the haze. Sixty feet away lay a tree-lined bank. An easy escape, if the dogs couldn't get to it. She wiped mist from her lashes and scanned the marsh. In every direction, clumps of willows and tall cattails cut off her view.

Once again she surveyed the ancient cottonwoods growing on the tempting bank. She gauged the distance—five minutes to swim to shore, three to climb the tree, ten minutes at most and she'd be safe until the dogs got hungry and went home.

She eased her body into the pond. In the morning light, the water looked and smelled like liquid manure. Clutching her club in one hand, she plunged in and began to swim. With every stroke, the consistency of the water grew more jelly-like. The jelly progressively coagulated to thick, glutinous slime.

She stopped swimming and plowed forward pushing her legs ahead of her. Soon, she discovered the waist-deep muck would support her weight if she didn't linger. Each time she took an exploratory step, she brought her other foot up to join the first.

Gradually, her apprehension faded and she eyed the clean grass ahead with eager anticipation. In a few hours, if the dogs stayed put, she could be at camp bathing in the clean cold pool. She started forward again and found both her feet were stuck.

No problem, she'd worm one loose at a time. She tried to bend her knees. No luck. She tried to move her foot. The mud encased her legs from feet to thigh in a grip as unyielding as concrete. She turned, twisted, and pulled. Then she looked down and gasped. She'd sunk an inch.

A frantic barking made her glance up. The German shepherd stood on a pile of dried litter below the grassy bank. He made wild rushes at her, leaping into the mud, then scrambling back.

She gripped the club she still held and twisted from right to left, searching for the Doberman, but she couldn't spot him. Her movements caused her to sink to her chest.

All of her independent bravado vanished. "Help, help," she screamed over and over. Fog shrouds muffled her voice. "Nathan," she sobbed. "Find me. Please find me."

A yelp from the German shepherd caused her to glance toward shore. Nathan bent over the dog's inert form.

"Don't move," he shouted. "I'll get you out." He dashed among the trees and came back lugging a chunk of log. He heaved it into the pond. The log fell short. "I'll push it out to you." He rushed back to the trees.

After a few precious minutes, he returned with a long pole. "This will do it, Amy. You'll be on solid ground in no time." He lay down on the bank, maneuvered the pole into position against the log, and inched forward until the upper half of his body extended well beyond the lip of the embankment.

She glimpsed a black shadow. "Nathan, behind you, the Doberman! Look out!"

The Doberman sprang, sunk his teeth into Nathan's back, and hung on. Nathan let go of the pole. Without it, he had nothing to support him. The dog weighed him down. He couldn't turn, couldn't even get his knees under him. He reached for the sinking pole and missed. The dog growled, sank his fangs deeper, and braced his front legs.

Nathan tried to hit the beast but failed. His arms sank to the elbows in mud. He jerked his head back to keep his face from going in.

"Save him," Amy prayed. "Please save him."

At the edge of the trees, a sleek silvery form materialized out of the mist. Amy stared. It couldn't be. "The cougar," she yelled. Nathan ceased to struggle, his head sank forward into the muck.

"No! No! No!" she screamed.

The cougar ignored her. Her impotent flailing arms presented no threat and the animal knew it. The Doberman, intent on ravaging Nathan, didn't even sense the predator's presence.

Silent as death, the moon cat advanced, her belly slunk low to the grass. She crouched, muscles tense.

"Oh, God, oh, God . . ."

Letting out a savage snarling cry, the cat sprang.

Amy's blood froze, she couldn't breathe.

The cat's huge paw caught the Doberman in the ribs, knocking him clear of Nathan. The dog clambered backward, but she cuffed him again. A sound of stark terror burbled from the Doberman's throat. The cat's jaws clamped on his neck. Then silence, pitiless and final.

The cat rose to her feet and turned to gaze at Amy. The animal's keen, riveting stare seemed to penetrate her brain, and she trembled with fear just as young Nathan had long ago. If the cougar found her unworthy, Nathan would die. And if he died . . . so would she.

Chapter 18

The cougar padded over to Nathan, pushed her head against him, and sniffed his neck. Then she moved back to the dog, lifted his body, and melted into the fog.

Seconds dragged by and Nathan didn't move. Amy's pulse thundered in her ears. Had the dog's bite paralyzed him? Panic engulfed her. Her time was running out. The mud was up to her chin.

Afraid to hope, she called, "She's gone, Nathan."

He snatched up the pole, jammed it into the mud, and righted himself. Wading in, he pushed the log within her reach. "Catch hold." He worked the pole into the muck.

She clung to the log, but shifting position made her sink lower. She gulped in a mouthful of scummy water and began to cough.

Nathan flung her an anxious glance. "Don't let go." He worked furiously. "I can get you out, Amy. All I have to do is make a hole."

She felt the point of the pole strike her feet, water rushed in, released the suction and she spurted upward like a popped champagne cork.

"Grab on." Nathan shoved the pole toward her. She

caught hold, but her feeble grip kept sliding off as he dragged her shoreward. Finally, he seized her arms and tugged her up the embankment. She tried to stand, but her legs gave way. She sank down on the grass and rolled onto her back.

Nathan knelt beside her. "I had to wait until dawn to track you." He gathered handfuls of wet grass and gently wiped mud from her face.

"Where are the other dogs?"

"Dead. I threw them in the swamp. The shepherd goes in, too, before we leave. The people at the mine may come looking for them."

She caught his hand and pressed his palm against her cheek. "You were right. I *am* silly and foolish." Hot tears overflowed onto his fingers.

His brows drew together in a ferocious scowl. "You are not! You're the smartest, most level-headed woman I've ever met." He drew a labored breath. "You're so softhearted you put everyone else first and yourself last. I had to make you mad so you'd only think about getting away from me."

"I nearly got both of us killed."

He put his finger on her lips. "What is meant to be, will be. Neither you nor I can change it." He helped her sit up. "Can you make it to camp?"

She glanced down at her bare feet. "I'll crawl if I have to. Anything to get away from here."

On the trail, she trudged doggedly forward. Closing her mind to her injuries, she concentrated on avoiding briers and sharp rocks.

After an hour of slogging along behind, Nathan stopped her. "You've punished yourself long enough." Before she could stop him, he picked her up and strode down the path. "Do you ever eat anything?"

She frowned at him. "Of course, I eat."

"Not enough."

For once, she didn't have the strength to argue. She fastened her arms around his neck, lay her head on his chest, and felt consciousness slip away.

She awoke when he laid her down beside the stream near their camp. "I'll get your soap and towel," he said.

"Please bring the small blue bag from my pack, too."

He came back and set her things beside her. "Since I didn't know what clothes you wanted, I brought you my flannel shirt." He sauntered away. A few minutes later, he stuck his head through the shrubbery. "Leave your clothes on the bank. I'll wash them out and hang them to dry."

The water numbed her, but she loved its brisk cleanness. She sudsed her body and hair three times before she felt free of the sulfurous stench.

Downstream, Nathan splashed and made washing noises. The thought of him being nearby filled her with elation. She hummed as she washed her clothes.

After putting them in a neat pile on a rock for Nathan, she dried off and donned his shirt. The sleeves came down over her hands and the tail reached halfway to her knees. The red plaid fabric smelled of soap, sunshine, and fresh air. She loved the feel of the soft flannel against her skin.

She stretched out her arms and turned her face up to catch the sun. Its rays had burned off the mist, heated the pines, and a warm, rich, resinous fragrance filled the air.

"Are you decent?"

She giggled. "As an 1890s bathing beauty."

"I won't fit in," he said, a lilt in his voice. "I'm dressed for bikini beach." He came through the trees wearing olive-drab Jockey shorts. "I'm out of clean pants." He stopped and stared. "I didn't realize you were so short."

She squared her shoulders. "I'm five foot seven."

He chuckled. "That explains it. I'm over six feet."

Being careful not to bump her sore toes, she knelt on the grass and opened the bag he'd brought. "We're both going to need an antibiotic and tetanus shot. Are you allergic to anything?"

"Nope." He sat down beside her.

After the injections had been given, she let him bandage her fingers and toes. "They sure feel a lot better than they did last night. I guess hot mineral baths aren't just hype after all."

He grinned and brushed his fingers across her cheek. "I wondered why you were standing in the swamp wearing a mud pack." He laughed out loud. "I should have realized you were trying to get rid of the freckles on your nose."

She smiled at the delightful sound of his laughter. He so seldom let himself go. She raised one eyebrow. "You're turning into a regular comedian, Blackthorn." She grinned at him.

A smile crinkled around his eyes. "I like your freckles. They give you panache."

She snickered. "Sure they do." She gave him a little push. "Turn around you clown, I want to look at your bites."

While she knelt behind him, cleaning and bandaging the ugly gashes on his back, images of the Doberman tearing his flesh built in her mind. Without any warning, she broke out in a sweat. Small, red dots spun in front of her eyes, and she clutched Nathan to keep from fainting.

He turned in alarm. "What's—" He caught her, lowered her to the grass and leaned over her. "You're pale."

"I'm okay." She touched his face. "And so are you. If your Wey-e-kin hadn't come along, we'd both be dead."

"My Wey-e-kin?" The corners of his mouth twitched. "Oh, come on, Amy. That's only an Indian myth. Surely you don't believe such foolishness."

"You're darned right I do. Wey-e-kins and any other guardian spirit you may have. I may even hike up Star Mountain and put a rock on that pile to appease Amo'tqEn."

He smiled. "How do you know that particular cougar is my guardian spirit. Maybe she thought her kittens preferred a Doberman to a half-breed."

"Don't joke about it."

"Who has a better right? Lady, you haven't lived until you've felt a cougar's nose against your jugular vein."

She gripped his arm. "You should've seen the way she looked at me."

He nodded and his gaze sharpened. "What went through your mind?"

"That nothing comes without a price tag." She shivered and chafed her arms to rid them of goose bumps. "One way or another we're going to have to pay for having our lives spared."

"Hey, enough of this kind of talk." He swept her up and carried her into camp. "Get some sleep, then we'll discuss how to rescue Simon."

"I'm sorry about Henry Cummings."

"Our work is like that. Henry knew the risk." He unzipped her tent. "Rest easy. I'll be right outside."

She flopped onto her sleeping bag and fell into restless slumber. In her dreams, she raced through an endless forest with a pack of howling dogs behind her. On and on she ran until she could scarcely lift her feet. One by one they hurled themselves on her, snarling, biting, tearing. She stumbled and went to her knees. The big Doberman leaped at her face, his long mouth agape, his fangs bared. She screamed and screamed and screamed.

She awakened to find herself cradled in Nathan's arms. He stroked her hair. "Shh shh, I'm here. Nothing can hurt you now."

He cupped her face and, with a gentle expression, placed his mouth on hers in what she knew he intended to be a benign, big-brother kiss. The moment his lips touched hers, however, the kiss ceased to be either brotherly or benign.

His lips grew heated, and she went all hollow and shivery inside. *She loved him.* It was the last clear thought she had. Nathan lifted his eyes to hers, desire smoldering in their depths.

He kissed her eyes, her face, the length of her throat. "I shouldn't be in here," he murmured with each kiss. "I should go back where I belong."

She buried her fingers in his thick hair and held him close to her. "Please stay." She kissed him hungrily, wantonly, as she'd kissed no other man before.

He crushed her in his embrace and caressed her, caressed her entire body, filling her with a glorious, mind-staggering desire.

He pressed his lips against the pulse in her throat. "I want you, Amy. I have wanted you from the first minute I saw you."

"Yes," she breathed. "Yes."

He left her for a moment and rummaged in his clothes outside the tent. When he returned, he poised above her, leaned to kiss her, lifted his lips from hers and regarded her with an expression of such tenderness it made her giddy.

He tilted her chin and kissed her until thoughts of him possessing her completely became a driving urgency. Then he made love to her, wild, riveting, passionate love that obliterated everything except her body and his.

Before either of them could reach a climactic ending, a loud crash in the woods behind the tent yanked them back to reality.

Like a cat Nathan sprang away from her and plunged outside. Her heart pounding, she yanked on Nathan's flannel shirt and her camouflage pants, shoved her feet into hiking boots, and hurried into the woods. Her search proved fruitless. Her nerves taut, she returned to camp and began to pace.

After several minutes, Nathan appeared. Water dripped from his hair and sunshine glistened on drops clinging to his tawny body. During her years in medical service, she'd seen many naked men. She'd seen none she considered spectacular, until this moment. Nathan's broad muscular shoulders and chest tapered to a narrow waist, flat abdomen, slim hips and long slender legs. Such a fine, wonderful man. Happiness filled her chest to bursting.

She moved toward him. "What was it?"

"A bear."

His distant manner triggered an alarm. She reached out to touch him. "Are you all right?"

He backed away from her out-stretched hand. "I shouldn't have made love to you." He avoided her gaze. "I'm sorry, Amy. It was all my fault."

An icy band clamped around her heart. "Don't be ridiculous. I wanted you, too."

"I won't ever touch you again," he said, as if he hadn't heard her.

"Oh . . ." She took a breath, tried to fold the hurting inside. "I see." She pressed her lips together and caught them between her teeth to keep them from trembling.

He swung away from her and stared into the distance, his face taut. "No, you don't. You're not capable of doing the terrible thing that I've done."

A breeze rustled in dry, brittle grass, bringing a scent of dropped pine needles, and she forced down a scream of protest.

She hid a thick swallow in her throat. "What . . . did you do?"

He turned and spit out the words. "I deceived you."

A tiny shred of hope welled up. He demanded such perfection from himself. "Nathan, I'm not faultless either. You're allowed to make a mistake."

"Not this kind," he said in a harsh voice. "Not when I'm to be married in three weeks."

Chapter 19

MARRIED! A gasp rose up from her stomach, clogged her throat, and she shuddered for breath. "Why didn't you tell me?" Her words came out in a whisper.

"In the beginning, I didn't think it was important."

"Good God, if getting married isn't important. What is?"

He made a vague gesture. "Usually I've managed to conquer any temptations I've had."

She clenched her fists. "You knew I wouldn't have let you come near me, wouldn't have . . ." She turned her back on him, yanked off his flannel shirt, threw it from her as if it were something repulsive, and dove into her tent.

Fierce anger driving her, she shoved her arms into her camouflage jacket. Muttering to herself, she stuffed everything else into her backpack, rolled her sleeping bag, threw it outside, crawled through the zippered opening, and began to jerk up the tent supports.

Nathan, clothed in the SWAT-style jumpsuit he'd worn the night before, sat with his back propped against a tree. "Where are you going?"

"Away from here. Away from you."

He stood up. "You can't do that, Amy. Simon needs us. Not just me. Not just you. The two of us working as a team."

She wheeled and flew at him, hitting him wherever she could. "You dirty . . . rotten . . . despicable bastard. I wish I'd never met you."

He gripped her wrist. "We can't change any of this."

"Oh, no? Just watch me." She struggled to free herself.

His grip tightened. "Think, Amy. Think. Together, we have a chance to get Simon out of that mine. Alone, neither of us will succeed."

Her shoulders sagged. He was right.

He let go of her. "I am sorry, Amy. I swear I never meant for any of this to happen."

She bent her head and stared at her feet. "Don't think I let every man I meet make love to me."

"Look at me, Amy."

She kept her head down. "I can't. I'm too embarrassed." She couldn't risk him knowing how deeply he'd hurt her.

He lifted her chin. "That first day, when you got on the plane in Coeur d'Alene, your stockings were torn, your knees were bloody, and you had a smudge of dirt on your face, but you walked up that aisle with your head held high, stood in front of those men, and you smiled that wonderful smile of yours. Right then, I said to myself, 'This is a lady with class.' "

He gazed down at her with earnest intensity. "To me, that's what you'll always be."

She straightened her shoulders and managed to smile. "Cops and soldiers say this sort of thing happens all the time to people who go through danger together."

He beamed. "I've heard that, too. Some sort of survival of the race reaction."

Her lip started to tremble, and she sucked it against her teeth. "Exactly. So, that craziness in the tent meant nothing, nothing at all." She inhaled and let the air out slowly. "Now that that nonsense is out of the way, we ..." she searched for words that floated just out of reach, "we ... can ... get on with what we came here to do."

He stared at her with admiration. "You're really something special. Don't ever let any man make you think otherwise."

Hah! She pulled in the corners of her mouth. "Let's get down to business."

Nathan sobered. "Rico Diaz, the man I talked to in the last barrack, seems to be the workers' leader. I wish I'd had time to ask why they were brought to the mine."

She closed her eyes and attempted to concentrate on his words instead of the ache in her chest. "Are the Mexicans convicts?"

Nathan shook his head and grimaced as if in pain. "They're prisoners."

"That's crazy," she snapped, glad he'd given her a reason to vent her anger. "This is the United States, not some lawless, uncivilized country. Good grief, that mine can't be more than thirty miles from Rock Springs."

"Right. Makes me wonder how many of those people know about this. And why they haven't told the authorities."

"Authorities! That's a laugh." She pressed her fingers against her throbbing temples. The effort of making conversation raveled her nerves. "Probably, Pike has done little except tread water since he took the job."

"They could tell the state police or the FBI."

She shoved her hands into her pockets and clenched them into fists. "Then, why don't we?"

He ran his fingers through his hair. "Because something about Rock Springs's miraculous rebirth stinks." He lowered himself to a thick cushion of pine needles, drew his legs up to his chest, and gripped them so tight his knuckles turned white.

"Mysteries. Too many of them. No rhyme or reason." She sank down on her rolled sleeping bag. "We need to . . ." The rest of the thought drifted away. She frowned and grasped it again. "We need to find out who owns that mine." She picked up a stick and dug the tip into layers of black leaf mold. "I wonder if Jared and Frank would know."

Nathan looked up with a skeptical expression. "Think we can trust them?"

She turned her palms up. "Who knows? Frank's wife is the town grapevine's major broadcaster. And Jared's having an affair with the waitress at The Golden Goose. If we're not arrested the minute we hit town, the two men have kept their mouths shut." She steered a centipede away from her foot. "Frank and Jared may not know where the dung heap lies. Still, I think they've been downwind of it and don't like the smell."

Nathan got to his feet. "With luck, we can make it to town before nightfall."

After a brief side trip to Amy's cabin, Nathan stopped the jeep at a gas station. Amy borrowed the station attendant's phone book and wrote down Jared's address.

"He lives on Spruce," she said when she returned.

Nathan put the jeep in gear. "Most of the miners live in that section of town."

Rock Springs's paint-up, fix-up campaign had not reached the rows of tan cookie-cutter houses on Spruce. When they located Jared's, Nathan pulled to the curb.

Amy tucked the manila envelope from the cabin inside her coat and trudged up the walk ahead of Nathan. She stepped with care to avoid gaping cracks in the concrete. When they reached the front door, Nathan stood in the shadows while she knocked. Dust-dry paint came off on her knuckles Jared opened the door.

"Well, ain't that a corker," He swung the door wide. "Me and Frank were just wondering what you'd been up to."

"Could I talk to you and Frank for a few minutes?"

"Can't think of anything I'd like better. Come on in. We're just sittin' around shootin' the breeze while we make some ore cars for the Molly Magee."

Amy hesitated on the porch. "I have someone with me I'd like you to meet."

"Fine. Fine. Bring 'em on in." He turned and led the way to an all-purpose room at the back of the house. "Hey, Frank," he shouted. "Look who's here."

Frank rose from beside an oblong table cluttered with miniature wheels, a charcoal block, bits of metal, and a propane torch. A smile wreathed his face. "Nice to see you again, Amy." His gaze went beyond her to Nathan and his smile faded.

"You too, Frank." She brought Nathan forward and introduced him.

"Call me, Nate," Nathan said and shook hands with each of the men. Both Jared and Frank greeted his invitation with a cool, appraising stare.

Frank seated himself, fitted two small squares of metal together in a jig, ignited his torch, and began to heat snippets of solder with a thin, blue frame. Across the

combination kitchen-work room, Jared leaned against a
scarred counter strewn with unwashed coffee mugs,
dirty paper plates, and empty beef stew cans.

The silence grew and Amy's nerves began to twinge.
She cleared her throat. "Nathan's a private investigator.
He's searching for a man who disappeared in this area."
She glanced from Jared to Frank. Not a quiver of inter-
est. "His name's Luis Herrera. Have either of you heard
of him?"

Jared tapped a cigarette from a pack of Camels and
lit it. "People hereabouts don't take to Mexicans." He
took a draw on his cigarette and let smoke filter from his
nose. "Or Indians."

Amy took a quick breath and her face grew hot. "Oh,
really!"

"Easy," Nathan said in a soft voice. "It doesn't matter."

"It does to me." She strode across the scuffed green li-
noleum and planted herself in front of Jared. "Is that
why none of you rednecks have mentioned the dead
Mexican Chief Pike pulled out of the river four days
ago."

Jared pooched out his lips and shrugged. "It's news to
me." He ambled over to the table, straddled a wooden
chair, and rested his arms on the back. "How about
you, Frank?"

"Somebody's been feeding you a bunch of bull."
Frank fitted another piece of metal into his jig. "If anything like that had happened my wife would've known
it." He glanced up from his work. "You can bank on
that."

Amy jerked the brown envelope from inside her
jacket, took out several of the enlarged photos Nathan

had brought her Monday night, and fanned them out on the table in front of Jared.

His eyes bulged. "Jee—sus! That's right by the park." He shoved them toward Frank. "He's sure enough dead all right."

Frank studied the photos with an impassive expression. Finally, he raised his head. "Where did you get these?"

"I took them."

"How did you know the guy was there?"

"Some kids told me."

He squinted. "That's a crock. The news would've been all over town in twenty minutes."

"Not if they were Indian kids," Nathan said. "They found him the day the mayor blew the dam."

"So why are you telling us?" Frank asked.

Amy tapped one of the photos. "Notice the white coveralls?" She leafed through the glossies in the envelope and laid one in front of Frank. "The man may have died as a result of these animal bites."

Frank's Adam's apple bobbed and he turned a pale shade of green, but he recovered quickly. "So?"

Nathan rested his hands on the table and leaned toward the two men. "Today, while we were in the mountains looking for Simon Kittredge, we saw a bunch of Mexican workers wearing that same garb. Guard dogs patrolled the fenced-in sector where they were being kept."

Jared took a last drag from his cigarette, snuffed it out in a sardine tin, and lit another. "If you're expectin' me to cry over a bunch of wetbacks, you can forget it."

Nathan's gaze met Jared's and bored in until Jared looked away. "Know where we saw them?"

Jared stood up. "Look, Mister," he kicked his chair

aside and braced his legs, "I don't give a damn. You got that?" He thrust out his chin. "And you've wasted enough of our time."

"Answer one question and we'll leave," Amy said.

"Depends on what you're wantin' to know."

"Who owns the mine on Mount Grayson?"

Jared's mouth dropped open.

Chapter 20

Jared balled his fists. "You're lyin'. Holt wouldn't bring in a bunch of Mexicans to work the China Lady." He swept Amy and Nathan with a challenging look. "Not when half the men in town are out of work." A muscle knotted along his jaw. "The sonuvabitch wouldn't dare."

"I have proof," Nathan said.

Jared's blue eyes flashed fire. "Yeah, like what?"

"I took pictures."

"Oh, hell." Jared slumped onto a chair. "Holt's a shit heel, but I never thought he'd sink to this."

Amy took a chair near him. "A lot of money is being spread around Rock Springs. Where's it coming from?"

"The mayor got a grant," Frank said.

Nathan shook his head. "When I was in college, I combed the grant programs looking for a means to help my people. No way would this place get a grant. The mines are dying and so is the town."

Frank bristled. "Like hell it is. What about the ski resort?"

Nathan seated himself alongside of Amy. "We'll get to that later. First I want to talk about the China Lady. If something was going on there, wouldn't McAllister know about it?"

Frank dug gnarled fingers into his cropped gray hair. "He could have leased it."

"How long has it been closed?"

Frank darted a glance at Jared. "Two years."

"Ever since . . ." Jared scraped back his chair, got a bottle of beer from the refrigerator, uncapped it, and took a long pull. "Ever since an explosion and cave-in on the 2,000-foot level. It buried my two boys right there."

An expression of sorrow came over Nathan's face, and, although Jared stood ten feet away, he put out his hand as if to touch him. "They didn't dig them out?"

Jared took another swallow of beer and wiped his mouth. "His honor the judge said he couldn't risk the men's lives." He hurled the bottle against the wall. The glass broke, spewing beer in all directions. Jared gulped in a ragged breath. "My men would've worked that drift till hell froze over. Holt wouldn't let 'em."

Nathan grew very still. Finally, he said in a gentle tone, "We'll find a way to put your sons' spirits to rest."

Jared's florid complexion deepened to purple. "What the hell do you care?"

"No one should have to wander between worlds."

Jared's mouth wobbled, and he pushed his clenched fist against it until he got control. "I'll get even with that tight-fisted bastard if it's the last thing I ever do."

He settled onto his chair and stared down at the table for several minutes. Finally, he let out a sigh and said, "A stretch limo with tinted windows has been slinkin' through Rock Springs at night for the last year and a half."

"Did you see the limo stop anywhere?" Amy asked.

"Never thought about following it." Jared made a sound of disgust. "Hell, people come through here all the time, all kinds of people. Lots of things go on in these hills no one knows about. Always has, always will."

Amy put her hand on his arm. "Is there any way to get into the China Lady without going in the front entrance?"

Jared smiled for the first time since they'd entered the room. "I know ever inch of that mine." His grin broadened. "Don't even need maps, but I've got 'em. Stole 'em out of the office after they closed the Lady down." He gouged dirt from a scratch in the wooden table with his thumb nail. "Thought I might . . ." He shook his head. "Doesn't matter now. Want to take a look at 'em?"

"Later on," Nathan said. "Tell me about the ski resort. Who owns it?"

Jared shrugged and glanced at his friend. "You know, Frank?"

"My wife Wanda says it's a conglomerate called Stoneridge Corporation."

Nathan regarded Frank for a long moment. "Did you know that Sarah Wahsise owns land up there?"

Frank reared back in surprise. "You mean that old sq . . . woman had property?"

"Yes. Twenty acres. Right in the middle of the main ski runs. Someone claimed she hadn't paid her taxes and confiscated it."

"What else is new?" Jared said with a shrug. "Doesn't matter if you're red or white. If you don't pay your taxes, they take your land. Anybody knows that."

"She didn't owe any taxes." Nathan's flinty glance traveled from Jared to Frank. "She wouldn't sell. Now she's dead." He turned his hand palm up. "Very convenient, right?"

Jared scowled. "Ah-h, nobody would—"

"Don't be so sure," Amy broke in. "Two men have disappeared in the vicinity of Rock Springs—a government man and my friend Simon, who is an investigative reporter."

Nathan nudged her with his foot and added, "And the man I'm trying to find."

Amy sent him a silent message of thanks. "Last night, at the mine, one of the Mexicans told us the government man is dead, and Simon is being held prisoner inside the mine."

"Prisoner!" Frank leaned toward her, his face intense. "Why would—"

Jared bounded out of his chair. "You talked to the Mexicans?"

Amy explained about their aborted visit to the China Lady. "I'm sure the man Chief Pike found in the river came from there. He probably escaped, and the guard dogs ran him down and attacked him." She shuddered. "They're half starved and vicious. They tried to tear me to pieces."

Frank sat back with a scowl. "You don't really expect us to believe this wild story of yours, do you?"

"Yeah," Jared chimed in. "All we got is your say-so. And we don't know either one of you."

"My father and Dr. Chambers are old friends," Amy said.

Jared flung her a doubting look and moved toward the living room. "I'll just give him a call."

"No, wait," Amy said. "When I told him about Sarah, he reacted very strangely. He could be involved."

Jared swung around. "That ties it, girl. Doc's as hon-

est as the day is long. Ain't nobody gonna tell me different."

"Call Will Pennington," Nathan said. "He'll vouch
for both of us."

Frank's scowl grew more fierce. "For a stranger, you
know a lot of people in Rock Springs."

"Sarah was a cousin," Nathan said. "I've visited Rock
Springs a number of times."

Amy envied his cool, self-controlled manner. She'd
have to learn not to get so emotionally involved.

Frank's glance met Jared's and he jerked his head.
"Phone Will. Find out if these two are lying through
their teeth."

Jared's questions to Will carried through the thin
walls. After a few minutes, he came to the doorway. "He
wants to talk to Nate."

Casting a sheepish glance at Amy, Jared resumed his
seat at the table. "Will, says you're both true blue. Sure
am glad to hear that."

Nathan came back. "He thinks all of us should get together. The sooner the better." He frowned and began
to pace. "He suggested Frank contact Officer Hollenbeck." He stopped in front of Frank. "That make sense
to you?"

"Sure does. Norm's a good law man. Used to be on
the Coeur d'Alene police force. And he's fed up with
Pike."

Jared dug a bent cigarette from his crumpled pack.
"Hell." He struck a kitchen match on the leg of his jeans
and held the flame to the tip of his Camel. "I'd a got a
bellyful long before this. Half the time Old Suck-ass has
him baby sittin' those goddamned McAllister boys."

"Careful Jared," Amy said. "Dean didn't give himself

that drug overdose. When Holt finds that out, he's going to lean on Pike to dig up the person who did."

"See?" Frank glared at Jared. "Crazy old fool. What'd I tell you? You know damned well Holt's just itching to get something on you."

Jared gestured impatiently. "I'd like to see him try it."

"Hah! When you going to learn you're either going to have to best him or knuckle under like the rest of us?"

"I'll die first."

Nathan sat down between the two men. "Does that mean you're willing to help us?"

"Damn right." Jared glanced at his friend. "You in or out, Frank?"

"Ain't good for much anymore." He regarded Nathan with a pleading attitude. "Don't suppose you got a job a gimp could do?"

"You ever been in the hoist shack."

"I've done a little bit of everything up there."

"Damned straight. Holt had him workin' everybody's job just 'cause he's handy. Even had him wire in the phones."

Nathan beamed. "What could be better? One man who knows the inside and one who knows the outside. We need you both."

Frank squared his shoulders. "Jared and I figured something was haywire around here. We just didn't know what."

Amy opened her mouth to again question him about the man with the deformed foot, then changed her mind. Later on would do just as well. It never payed to push your luck.

Nathan got to his feet. "It's now six-thirty. Shall we meet at the Indian church on Crystal Creek Road at nine?"

"Sure thing," Jared said, speaking for both of them.

Amy followed Nathan out to the street. A lamp pole made a bleary streak of light around the jeep. "I'll walk to Sarah's house from here," Nathan said and retrieved his backpack. "You'll find the Indian church about a mile up Crystal Creek. Sits on a ridge. Watch for the sign."

"Won't you need a ride?"

"I'll get there on my own. Better that way."

She nodded. "Have Will redress your wounds." She laced her fingers and squeezed her palms together. "And . . . and you should have another antibiotic injection tomorrow."

"Will can give it." He studied her with an air of concern. "You look beat. Try to rest for a couple of hours."

"I intend to." She tried to perk up, failed, and knew she'd pushed herself to what her father called her "refugee child stage"—pinch-faced and big-eyed.

Nathan moved a few steps closer. "Amy . . ."

Her heart quivered at his soft tone. *Don't be kind and gentle. Don't give me hope where there isn't any.* She got into the jeep to put some space between them. "Yes?"

He grasped the door ledge and bent to look at her. Deep within his eyes something stirred. He let out his breath and took another. "Dean's death may have tipped Troy over the edge. So keep your pistol handy."

She swallowed and croaked, "I'll be on guard."

Neither of them made a move to go. The hopelessness of her longing for him wrung a small whimper from her.

He reached for her, stopped, and his face contorted. "I don't dare touch you, Amy."

He stumbled backward and shoved his hands into his pockets. "Please . . . go."

Their eyes met, and the desire she saw eased her feeling of rejection, but only for an instant.

"Go," he said harshly. "Now!"

Chapter 21

On the ridge, ancient cedars rose against a black backdrop of wooded hills. In a moonlit semicircle formed of evergreens stood a salt-white structure resembling an old-time schoolhouse.

Amy followed a graveled roadway into a meadow of dried wild hay and parked alongside three other cars. She vaulted out of the jeep and ran up a winding dirt path.

Damn! She'd wanted to be the first to arrive. The men would have their plans all set and more than likely they wouldn't include her.

She eased open the heavy door and a faint odor of juniper met her nostrils. She slipped inside. In the foyer, a single cord fitted with a low-watt bulb dangled from a ten-foot ceiling.

Through a broad archway lay the main body of the church. Pine walls and floor, no pulpit, statues, or crosses. A branch of autumn leaves and a sheaf of wild oats in a woven rush basket provided the only color. Small overhead fixtures supplied watery light and shadows webbed the far corners. Along three walls, tin candle sconces hung between multipaned windows.

Backless wooden benches flanked opposite sides of the room.

In a cleared area, Frank and Norm Hollenbeck lowered a sheet of plywood onto two sawhorses. As soon as it was in place, Jared tossed a fat roll of maps on top. "That's the works," he said. "The Lady's layout from first draft to last."

"That's great, Jared." Will Pennington clapped him on the shoulder. "Without them, this project wouldn't have a prayer."

"Don't go jumping the gun, Will." Norm lifted his low-crowned Stetson, raked his fingers through his sandy-colored mop, and tilted his hat to the back of his head. "The story Frank told me is the craziest I've ever heard. No way am I getting involved unless I get some answers—the right answers."

Will smiled. "Fair enough. Fire away."

"Who the hell is Blackthorn, how did he and this Prescott woman get teamed up, and how come you know so much?"

Will smoothed his hand over his hairless skull. "Sometime back I worked for the government."

"Doing what?"

"That's classified."

Norm's expression became hard and resentful and Will made a calming gesture. "This much I can tell you—once they've got you on record, they have no qualms about calling on you again." He let out a long sigh. "Regardless of what may be going on in your own life."

"Damnit, Will, you're a sick man. You should've told them to go to hell."

Will's mouth twisted into a cynical smirk. "This was supposed to be just a small favor. Simon Kittredge and a woman companion were poking around some sensitive areas in Central America. Our government put a tail on them. When they suddenly returned to the U.S., an agent named Henry Cummings followed."

"Is he the guy Amy said disappeared?" Jared asked.

"That's right. He called me from Coeur d'Alene to tell me two men had bilked Kittredge's father out of some money. Kittredge had picked up their trail and was headed for Rock Springs. Henry phoned a few days later, said he was in town and would keep me posted. I never heard from him again."

Norm pulled up a bench and sat down. "So where's Blackthorn come into this? Frank says he's some sort of investigator. Is he?"

Will lowered himself onto the bench beside Norm. "One of the best. After six years of government service, Nate had had enough. He was on his way home to Orofino when the agency intercepted him. They asked him to locate Kittredge and find out if he had anything to do with Henry's disappearance."

Norm tugged on one end of his droopy mustache. "Okay, I got that part straight, but that doesn't qualify this Blackthorn to come in here and . . ."

"For God's sake Norm who could be better? The man's a trained jungle fighter. He can put a man out of commission with his bare hands."

"Who the hell cares?" Jared took a pack of Camels from his pocket, started to put a cigarette in his mouth, glanced around, frowned, and stuffed it back in the pack. "This here ain't no damned jungle."

"That's what you think," Will said. "From what Nate says, the people out at the China Lady aren't likely to welcome visitors."

"So what?" Norm said. "I'm a good shot and I've been on raids."

"Whoa there, Norm," Frank said, shaking his head. "Guns and mines don't mix. If the rock's rotten, you could trigger a cave-in."

Amy grimaced. When she'd been with the mobile unit of the Washington State Crime Lab, she'd often listened to the law officers go through the same purposeless wrangling. These men would never work together if they didn't have a strong leader.

Where was Nathan anyway? It wasn't like him to be late. Imitating Nathan's cat-like walk, she moved farther into the church, tuned out the men's voices, and forced herself to center down.

After several minutes, faint tendrils of warmth brushed her right cheek. She turned slowly, testing each air current. Then she saw him. Still as a stalking panther, he and the dark shadows blended into one. She smiled. Her senses were sharpening. A week ago, she wouldn't have been able to see him or feel his presence.

She eased back to the door, gave it a slam, and strode toward the men. Four pairs of male eyes swung in her direction.

Norm jumped to his feet. "Don't tell me she's going to be in on this, too."

"Miss Prescott is . . ." Will began.

Amy held up her hand. "Let me, Will." She smiled at Norm to defuse some of his hostility. "As Frank probably told you, I'm a private investigator. I came here to find Simon Kittredge."

"Yeah, yeah, the guy came into the station to ask for help."

Amy regarded him with a steady, even gaze. "And?"

Norm folded his arms on his chest. "He wears silly

hats. Talks like a blooming professor. The chief didn't take him serious."

Amy's face flushed. "What kind of a cockamamie police department is he running anyway?"

Norm squirmed. "I tried to tell George we should put out a bulletin. He wouldn't hear of it. Said the guys on the force over in Wallace would laugh us out of the county if we listened to every kook who came in."

Amy expelled an explosive breath. "Simon's a top-notch investigative reporter for *Global News* for God's sake. How could Pike doubt his word?"

Norm spread his hands. "You should know George doesn't always make a lot of sense. You've been buttin' heads with him ever since you got to town."

"The man's a jackass." Amy made an impatient gesture. "If it hadn't been for my evidence, we'd never have known where to look for Simon."

"What evidence is that?"

Amy narrowed her eyes. "I found mud from Star Mountain and Colby Creek in his room at the Riverview Motel."

"Ah-hah!" Norm braced his fists on his hips. "So it was *you* who broke into one of Zeigler's rooms. That's against the—"

"Norm!" Will snapped. "Be quiet and listen, or we'll be here all night. Miss Prescott isn't one of your run-of-the-mill investigators. She's a forensic scientist. With her skills and Nate's combined, they could probably tell you every place you've been for the last week."

Norm threw up his hands. "Indians, Mexicans, and women. What's next?" He hunched his shoulders and leaned forward. "Where's the pictures Frank says you took?"

She removed the envelope from inside her jacket and

fanned out the glossies on the table. "Someone dumped Simon's car in Silver Lake . . ."

Norm slapped his forehead. "Jesus H. Christ, don't you people ever tell anybody anything?"

She stopped him with a hard stare. "Nathan didn't find Simon in the lake. So when he told me about the boys finding a body, I feared it might be Simon."

Norm studied the photos silently. Finally, he lifted his gaze to hers. "What day did you take these?"

"Early Monday morning. When I finished examining the corpse, Nathan called your office."

Norm nodded and his face set in deep, strained lines. "The phone rang as I came on shift. George answered it. Afterwards he went into his office and made some calls."

Norm flipped through the photos again. "Chicken-livered bastard took the van. Stayed away a couple of hours. Never said a goddamned word about a corpse when he came back." His hazel eyes flashed angrily. "Being a piss-poor cop is one thing. Covering up a possible homicide is a whole different ball game."

She was about to comment when she heard a faint sound. An instant later, Nathan appeared at Norm's side.

Norm jumped. "What the hell . . ." He reached for his gun.

Nathan caught his wrist before he could complete the draw. "I didn't mean to startle you. I'm Nate Blackthorn." He smiled and put out his hand.

Norm glanced up at him, then over at Will.

"Go on, Norm. You've been telling me what you could do around here if you got the chance. This may be the only one you'll get."

Norm studied Nathan narrowly before he stuck out

his hand and gave Nathan's a brief shake. "What've you got in mind?"

Nathan unbuttoned his shirt, brought out an envelope and dumped the contents on the table. "These'll give you an idea of what we're up against."

The four men bent over the enlarged photos.

"What a set-up," Will said. "Camouflage netting hiding the whole operation."

"Jesus." Norm flattened his hands on the table and leaned down for a closer look. "No wonder nobody knew anything about what was going on up there."

Jared's breath wheezed in and out. "Holy balls! It doesn't even look like the China Lady." He punched a close-up showing oblong buildings in the foreground. "What the hell are these?"

"Barracks." Nathan spread out the pictures so everyone would have a better view. "The Mexicans sleep and eat there. Any of you men got any ideas what kind of work they would be doing in white coveralls?"

Frank shifted his weight off his bad leg. "What they're wearing isn't important, Nate. All of us miners changed out of our mucking gear in the dry."

"The dry?" Amy said. "What's that?"

"This." Frank indicated a building opposite the hoist shack. "The men undress, shower, and put on their going-home clothes."

"Hm-m-m, perhaps that could be the answer." Nathan glanced at her. "What do you think?"

"Sounds reasonable. The white coveralls make the workers easy to keep track of when they're off shift."

Nathan frowned. "Could be." He turned to Frank. "Is there a way to cut off the phone service without going into any of the main buildings?"

Frank smiled. "Sure is. When I wired the place, I installed all the switchboxes in a utility shed."

"Good, bring the tools you'll need and a flashlight. Anybody have a heavy-duty wire cutter?"

Frank glanced at Norm. Norm ignored him until everyone's attention focused on him. "Yeah, I got one at the ranch."

"Fine. That'll save us time and money." Nathan pushed one of the pictures toward him. "Cut the wire here so I can get in." Nathan indicated a spot behind one of the barracks. "Then go back to the front gate and wait there with Frank. When you hear my signal, cut the chain at the front gate."

Nathan regarded Frank. "You take care of the phones." He swung back to Norm. "You speak any Spanish?"

Norm glowered. "Enough to get by."

"That's all you'll need." Nathan smiled warmly at the scowling Norm. "Cut the locks on the barracks' doors. Let the Mexicans out and load them in the trucks." He caught Will's eye. "We're going to need two large trucks and a good-sized van. I figure there may be thirty or more Mexicans and six to eight guards."

Norm thrust out his chin. "And what're you going to be doing while I'm herding a bunch of beaners around?"

"I'll take care of the dogs and the guards." Nathan's flinty gaze honed in on each one of the in turn. "There will be no killing unless it is absolutely unavoidable."

Nathan straightened to his full height. He towered over all of them. "People's lives being at stake does not make a wildcat mission like this legal. We'll be treading on the FBI's toes. They'll make it mighty hot on all of us if we screw up. Everyone agree?"

For the first time since he began to speak, Nathan got a unanimous "yes" vote. He nodded and smiled in appreciation. "Norm, when you and Frank finish, meet me at the hoist shack. Okay?"

Frank's face lit up and his eyes snapped with suppressed excitement. "Sure thing, Nate." He jabbed his elbow into Norm's ribs. "You got any problem with that?"

The muscles bulged in Norm's neck. "I can manage a hell of a lot more than that any damn day of the week."

"Glad to hear it," Nathan said. "We might run into a regular hornet's nest down in the mine."

Nathan peered at Jared and reached for the roll of maps. "I hope there's something in these that'll give us an edge. We're going to need it."

Chapter 22

Everyone crouched over the schematic drawing, while Jared explained the layout of the mine. "The China Lady's main shaft goes straight down." He glanced at the others. "Not all of them do."

"A vertical shaft makes the whole operation easier," Frank added and gestured to his friend to continue.

Jared eyed Frank with a sour expression and hitched his jeans over bony hips. "Nine-foot square cross-cuts are driven every two hundred feet. Drifts branch off the cross-cuts. After we remove the ore from the stope—"

Frank cleared his throat. "That's the working face."

Jared's face turned vermilion. "Butt out Frank. This is my show." He expelled a noisy breath. "Then the stope's backfilled with deslimed mine tailings to make a floor for the next level."

"Where do you think the men are most apt to be?" Nathan asked.

"Hard to tell. They could be working a new heading." Jared turned to Frank. "Let 'em down slow so they can signal when they spot something."

"Sounds good," Nathan said. "Earlier you indicated you knew of another way to get into the mine."

"Right." Jared spread out another map. "When they started the mine, they drove a tunnel clear through the mountain. Been boarded up for years."

"Could you find your way to where the men are working?"

"Easy."

Frank grabbed Jared's shoulder. "When the hell you going to learn to stop grandstanding? You know damned well that tunnel's got to be chock-full of fire-damp."

Amy moved closer. "What's that?"

"Gas, that's what," Frank said.

"Methane," Nathan put in. "Dangerous to breath and very unstable."

"Decaying timbers make it," Jared said. "You strike a match in there and most likely you'll come out blind and hairless—*if* you come out at all."

Nathan ran his hand over his face. "We can't use it."

"Who says," Jared said, squaring his shoulders. "I've got an OBA."

"A what?" Norm asked.

"A self-contained oxygen breathing apparatus." Jared spoke slowly as though he were explaining to a child.

Nathan shook his head. "Too dangerous."

"Humph," Jared said. "You and Norm could be walkin' into worse."

"I'm going in with Jared," Amy said. Dead silence followed her announcement.

Jared's glance darted from Amy to Nathan. When he didn't react, Jared glowered and jammed his hands in his pockets. "No way. I'm not baby-sittin' no woman."

Amy set her jaw. "The matter isn't up for discussion. I'm going and that's that." She scanned the group of un-smiling men. "If Simon's alive, he'll need a doctor."

No response.

She avoided Nathan's gaze. He wouldn't be pleased. She'd challenged his command in front of the other men. And both of them knew he could give emergency care, if he had the time. An idea struck her. "I can be getting Simon prepared for travel, while the rest of you are mopping up."

The roll of maps crackled beneath Nathan's clenched fingers. "Do you have another respirator, Jared?" His quiet voice held a steely note.

"Holy jumped-up Christ, Nate. This ain't a damned tea party."

"I have one she can use," Frank said.

Nathan jerked his head toward Amy. "Get together with Frank. Make certain you know how to use an OBA." He began to pace. "There must be people in town who know what's going on at the China Lady."

"Have to." Jared smacked the plywood with his palm. "And if any of us gets a loose lip, we'll get our asses shot off."

"And likely get Simon and the Mexican workers killed as well," Amy said.

Nathan stopped in front of them. "I'm going to call your names. If any of you are not behind me one hundred percent, please say so now. Jared?"

"My boys are up there. They wouldn't rest easy knowin' their dad was a coward."

"Will?"

"I'd rather go out on my feet then spend my last few months in a hospital."

Nathan's gaze brushed Amy's, moved on, then returned. "Amy?"

"Until the very end."

"Frank?"

"You bet! Even a crip needs to feel useful." He squinted his eyes at Norm. "What do you say lawman? You going to climb out of the manure pile or wade in it?"

Norm went rigid. "Don't push me old man." He took hold of the curled brim of his hat and set it more firmly on his head. "Pike's going to be at a convention in Boise for the next three days." He peered at Nathan. "When do we go?"

Nathan smiled. "Good man! We'll meet here at seven tomorrow night. Anyone have a problem with that?" No one spoke.

Will rose from the bench. "Norm will be on duty during the day, so I'll need you and either Frank or Jared to help get the transportation."

"I'll do it," Jared said. "We don't want Frank's wife wondering what's keeping him away from home so much."

The men agreed to meet at Will's house at 8 A.M.

The next morning, every muscle and bone in Amy's body protested each time she moved. She shuffled around the room, gathering supplies she would need for Simon or others who might get injured.

After breakfast, she decided to have Paul give her a penicillin injection. She opened the cabin door and found a plastic bag thumbtacked to the wooden panel. The bag contained two labeled envelopes, two large bird feathers, and a note from Nathan.

Knowing he had come and gone without bothering to knock triggered her temper. Probably, he was nursing a grudge because she'd insisted on accompanying Jared. She stomped back inside. What right had he to assume she'd sit back and let him and the other men take over her case?

She reread his instructions and put the feathers in her knapsack along with her emergency kit. Eager to examine the physical evidence he'd sent, she got out her field microscope.

The fibers Nathan had taken from Dean McAllister's shoes proved to be sheered burgundy wool. The thread from Dean's torn fingernail was a strand of shimmering peacock-blue silk. She recorded her findings, hid her forensic satchel in the root cellar, and went to Paul's back door.

When he answered her knock, she was pleased to note he wore a fresh shirt and a pressed suit. His face had a pasty cast, but his eyes were clear and his pupils normal.

"You need something?"

"Yes, a penicillin shot." She showed him where the dog's fangs had gashed her fingers.

He took a breath and exhaled noisily. "Come in." He hobbled over to the kitchen table and sank down on a chair. He gestured toward the hall. "Get what you need in the exam room and I'll give it."

"Thanks, Paul."

She had to go through several cabinets before she located everything she needed. In the process, she came upon a vacuum splint and some pain medication—just what she'd need for Simon. The problem would be finding a way to ask Paul without telling him the truth. She decided to do some probing before she broached the subject.

She fitted a 22-gauge needle onto a syringe, dunked a cotton ball in alcohol, and carried the vial of penicillin into the kitchen. "Did you learn anything from Sarah's autopsy?" she asked as she drew up the medication.

"The results aren't in yet." He glanced at the clock.

She swallowed and began again. "You said you knew the person Simon was looking for."

He avoided her gaze. "I lied."

She lay the filled syringe in front of him, rolled her short sleeve a little higher and sat down on the chair next to him. As he pulled the needle from her skin, she turned and met his eyes. "Do you know a man with a deformed foot?"

He turned white, dropped the syringe and stumbled to his feet. "Leave it alone before you get hurt." He glanced at the clock again. "My attorney's waiting. Lock up when you're through." He rushed out the back door and a few minutes later his car roared out of the driveway.

She returned to the exam room, removed emergency care supplies from the shelves and left a note on the cabinet telling Paul she would explain when she could. If her luck held, he wouldn't see the note until after Simon's rescue.

In the kitchen, she did the dishes, dusted, and mopped the grungy floor. Her guilt partially relieved, she sat down at the phone and called her father collect.

"Good to hear from you," B.J. said. "How are thing's going?"

She crossed her fingers. "Fine, Dad. We've found Simon."

"Is he all right?"

She scrunched her eyes closed. Her father always caught her half-truths. "He's . . . still up in the mountains. We . . . uh . . . they are going to try and bring him out today or tomorrow." She thought fast. "It depends on when the weather clears."

"Is someone with him?"

"Yes," she said, making it sound as positive as she could. "He's suffering from shock and a broken arm. Otherwise he's . . ." she ushered up a silent prayer, "okay."

"That's a relief. Say, I got all the stuff you sent, ran most of the tests, and documented them. Those fingerprints belong to a Jorge Alvarez. He's from Toppenish, Washington. Arrested two years ago on a vagrancy charge. Hasn't been seen since his release. What's he got to do with Simon?"

She gulped. "Probably nothing."

"You sure? I talked to a lieutenant over there. He says the farmers are having trouble getting migrant workers to come to the valley. The Mexicans maintain that last year someone offered their young men jobs with big money. They claim the men haven't been heard from since."

Her pulse thrummed in her head and her fingers shook. "Sounds like a job for Prescott and Prescott." She forced a laugh. "We'll have to check into it when I get back."

"No way. I've got all I can handle on this side of the mountains."

"Take care, Dad," she said quickly. "I'll call when I know more."

After stowing the medical supplies in her pack, she braved the raw, gusty wind and trudged into town to see Frank. A newly painted sign above the door read: *The Molly Magee Mine, Frank Reece, Prop. Come see the miniature mine. An astounding spectacle with all the lights, sounds, and action of the real thing. The experience of a lifetime.*

As she entered, several people filed out, each exclaiming about the exhibit. She found Frank checking a section of track inside an improvised drift made of Portland cement.

"Hey there," he said with a broad smile. "Didn't expect you so early." He locked the front door, put up a "Closed" sign, and ushered her into a back room. "Wanda's gone to visit her sister for a few days." He grinned and his eyes sparkled like a kid's at Christmas. "So I'm free to do as I please."

She stared at him. "You're looking forward to this, aren't you?"

He laughed out loud. "Damned right." His expression grew serious. "It's not something a woman would understand."

"Try me."

"A man needs to feel like a man. If he doesn't he might as well be in the scrap heap."

"But you're smart and creative. Why do you need danger?"

"A miner plays dice with the devil every day." He shrugged. "You miss it." He squinted at her. "You shouldn't'a done what you did to Nate."

She slumped down on a chair. "He'd have left me out if I hadn't made a stand." She raised her head. "A woman has things she has to do, too, you know."

"I suppose." He removed a gas mask from a cupboard and fitted it on her.

A black snout extended out from her face, making her resemble something out of a horror movie. She slipped it off. "It isn't too flattering," she said.

"Wasn't made for pretty." He explained the controls of the small tank that she'd sling on her back. "They hold thirty minutes of air." He put mask and tank in a large shopping bag and covered them with a newspaper. "Good luck."

She took the bag from him. "Same to you. Make sure you wrap your tools before you put them in your knapsack. You don't want anyone to hear you coming."

"Right." He took a handful of screws from his pocket and poured them from one hand to the other, scattering a good many on the floor in the process. With a sheepish expression, he stooped to pick them up. "Guess I'm a little jittery."

"Aren't we all?" She opened the door and stepped out.

"See you in church," he called from the doorway and grinned mischievously.

Wind-driven rain struck her in the face and flattened her clothing against her body. Ahead of her, a man hurried from a sportswear store carrying a large paper sack. He wore a red hunting shirt with matching cap and blue denims, all with the shelf creases still showing. He seemed vaguely familiar, but she couldn't figure out why.

He came down the sidewalk toward her and she noticed his long face, his sharp features. Where had she seen him before? As he drew abreast, he glanced at her from beneath half-hooded lids. The instant his chilling gaze swept over her, she remembered. He'd been on the plane from Coeur d'Alene.

She turned to look into a shop window so she could watch him. He got into a blue pickup with gray trim. When he cruised by, she noticed the cab's gun rack held two rifles.

She jogged to keep his car in view. On the plane, he had worn an expensive suit. Now he was dressed as a hunter. No grounds for suspicion there. Businessmen often became hunters in the fall. She felt foolish with the cumbersome shopping bag banging against her leg with each step, but she didn't slow down.

Several blocks outside of town, the pickup turned off on a side road. Amy rushed to the sign post and read: *China Lady Mine 30 miles.*

Chapter 23

Wind lashed the cedar trees, showering the pathway to the church with broken branches. She dodged them and clambered up the wooden steps. She tugged the door open a crack, thrust her leg between jam and door, then shoved the heavy panel open wide enough to squeeze through. After she switched on the light, the men began to straggle in.

Jared gave her a yellow hard hat with a battery light attached. "You can get yours out of the dry at the mine," he told the men. "There are lots of 'em."

Norm and Nathan wore dark blue jumpsuits with half a dozen cargo pockets. Norm's badge gleamed on his chest.

"Better ditch the badge," Nathan said. "The Mexicans might panic."

Amy sidled closer. "The dead man in the river came from Toppenish, Washington."

Norm frowned at her. "Who says?"

"I sent his fingerprints to my associate. The victim's name is Jorge Alvarez. He and the other men at the mine may have been abducted in Yakima Valley a year ago."

"Bull crap." Norm spit a stream of tobacco juice into a coffee can he carried. "Nobody would be that stupid."

"It's happened to illegals before," Nathan said. "They're scared to go to the police. If any of them do get the nerve, nobody listens."

"Humph," Norm said and retreated into himself.

Nathan unzipped a pocket, brought out several of the black, slit-eyed hoods he'd worn the night Amy had met him in Simon's room, and pulled one over his head.

The effect brought instant silence. "These have two advantages," Nathan said. "They make a small force appear larger," he pulled off the hood, "and they scare your enemy."

"That's for sure," Frank said.

Nathan handed them out, admonishing Norm not to put it on until after the Mexicans were in the trucks. "You speak Spanish, Will. Why don't you help Norm? Between the two of you, the operation should go smoothly."

He took a handful of flexible plastic handcuffs from another of his pockets and demonstrated how they worked. "Everyone take some," he said. "They're faster and more reliable than rope."

After they'd discussed who would ride with whom and Amy had stated she'd follow them in the jeep, Nathan strode off to a shadowy corner.

A few minutes later, he called her over. "I want you to wear my body armor."

"No," she said in a loud voice. All the men gawked at them and immediately she cursed her short fuse.

Nathan angled his body to obstruct the men's view. "To do what I do, I have to block out everything else. I can't do that and worry about you, too."

"Then put me out of your mind."

He stared into space and a muscle bunched along his throat. "I tried." He swallowed noisily. "And still I came to your cabin last night."

Her breath trembled out of her. "Why didn't you come in?"

"I couldn't have left."

Her heart gave an enormous thump. Did that mean his marriage wasn't as definite as he'd implied? She dropped Paul's jacket on the floor. "Give me the blasted thing." She stretched out her hand.

Nathan ignored it and held the Kevlar vest while she slipped her arms through. The garment hung over one shoulder. His attempts to make it fit better didn't succeed. "Stop fussing," she said, as his frustration mounted. "Chances are I won't need it anyway."

His fingertips brushed her neck. "Promise me you won't take foolish risks."

His worried expression kept her from arguing. "I won't. I'll get Simon out and leave the rest to you men." She studied his face. "What about you, Nathan? What's going to keep you from harm?"

"I've always come through before."

A lump filled her throat. She tilted her face and looked into his eyes. In a thin, constricted voice, she whispered, "I didn't know you then."

"Amy . . ." He made a helpless gesture. "We'd better join the others." He wheeled around.

Amy snatched her coat from the floor and caught up with him in time to hear him as he drew alongside Jared.

"Remember what I told you," Nathan said softly.

Jared's head bobbed. "Yep, just call me Superman."

Amy let out an exasperated breath. Nathan had probably instructed Jared to keep her out of any action that happened to come their way.

Nathan's gaze swept over the group. "Okay, team, let's head for Will's woodlot."

The drive to a clearing in the midst of towering pines took twenty minutes. When they arrived, Norm got behind the wheel of the parked van. Frank and Will each chose one of the sixteen-foot rental trucks.

Amy pulled the jeep under thick pine boughs and took out her gear. A gust vibrated the pine and rain hissed through a screen of needles, showering her bare head.

While she waited, her mind skittered like a mouse in a maze. Nathan could get killed. She might never see him again. An icy band clamped around her chest.

Nathan dashed from one vehicle to the other giving last-minute instructions. After he finished talking with each of the men, he came to her. Ducking under the pine's protecting boughs, he removed his glove, interlaced his fingers with hers and pressed his warm palm to her cold one. *"Toksa ake WaN ciNyaNkiN kte."* He twisted his mouth into a half smile. "That's Shahapti for until we meet again."

His words worsened her fears. "Hold me." His fingers tightened on hers, but he made no other response. "Please . . . it's all I'll ever ask of you."

He gathered her to him, fitted her body to his until she could feel his warmth, his strength, his need for her. His heart pressed to her cheek beat so heavily it seemed to echo her own. Suddenly, he uttered a groan and brought his mouth down on hers in a feverish kiss. Then he let loose of her so abruptly she almost fell. "I must go."

She caught hold of his arm. "Be careful."

He put his hand over hers. "You, too." He hurried away and a heavy sadness settled inside her.

She slogged through wet grass to Jared's ancient station wagon, tossed her supplies into the backseat, and slumped down beside him.

Norm and Nathan headed the procession in the van. Will and Frank followed in the trucks at ten-minute intervals. Jared and Amy's destination lay two miles this side of the mine's main entrance, so they brought up the rear.

Wind, rain, and potholes slowed the station wagon's progress on the one-lane track. They traversed steep canyons, edged sheer cliffs, and slithered sideways on snake-like switchbacks ascending Mount Grayson.

More than an hour passed before Jared backed the car into a patch of brush. "The tunnel's not far." He gathered his paraphernalia, settled his hard hat on his head, and started up a narrow gulch.

Guided by the bobbing flashlight he carried, Amy stayed right on his heels. He'd not be able to tell Nathan she'd been a hindrance. *Damn!* She grabbed her precariously balanced hard hat as an updraft tipped it over her eyes. She repositioned the aggravating contraption and tried to hold her head at an angle that would adjust the weight of the head lamp.

After struggling through rain-drenched juniper and thick chokecherry, Jared clambered up an incline of tailings and entered a tunnel.

Twenty feet inside the portal, he handed her the flashlight and took a prybar to the barricade. Rusty nails shrieked and the wood fell to the ground. As the opening widened, a horrible stench filled her nostrils.

"Phew," Jared said. "That's one smell you'll never

forget." He turned on his light and reached for the flashlight. "Better get your OBA on."

He waited until she'd finished and turned on her light before he put on his own gear. "Ready?" he asked, his voice muffled by the respirator. He fitted the flashlight and prybar in among the other tools hanging from a wide belt he wore low on his hips.

"Lead the way." She shuffled a few feet and let out a gasp. Their light beams illuminated a scene so grotesque she felt as if she'd entered a tomb. Monstrous, white, worm-like strands of fungus dangled from the ceiling, writhing slowly in the air current. On the walls, thick lengths of the growth clung like mummy sheets. The mucous seeping from them reminded her of body fluids oozing from a putrefying corpse.

"Creepy damned stuff." Jared ripped aside the obstruction and motioned her forward. "We may not run into firedamp," he said. "We mined a lot of the China Lady bald-headed."

"Without a hard hat?"

He chuckled. "That means untimbered. You can do that with solid rock. Now, 'ratty' rock, you gotta use timber or you won't live long."

"Oh . . ." She caught her foot, fell to her knees, and swore under her breath. Jared could have warned her about the ore-car track.

Righting herself, she started in pursuit of Jared and ran smack into a post. In the intense darkness, peripheral vision and sense of space didn't exist.

"How you doing back there?" Jared called.

"Fine. Just fine," she said between clenched teeth.

"Don't wander off. At the ends of some of these drifts, there are deep shafts."

"How deep?"

"Eight or nine hundred feet."

A chill climbed her spine. "Wait for me." One hand in front of her, the other stretched out to the side, she hurried to catch up with him. Everywhere she stepped, she encountered water. An ankle-deep stream cascaded between the rails.

For a time, orienting herself kept her too busy to think of anything else, but as they progressed, she began to hear a snapping, creaking sound. All at once, she became conscious of the tons of rock above her head. The feeling pressed on her chest, smothered her. She took in great gulps of oxygen and began to feel light-headed.

Jared grabbed her shoulders and gave her a shake. "Take it easy. Most everybody panics the first time down." He made her breathe easy and concentrate on the way ahead.

After what seemed like a long time, Jared allowed her to remove her respirator. "My signal will go off if we run into any gas pockets."

A short while later, he guided her into a crosscut. "My boys are in here." He lowered his backpack to the floor. "Nate asked me to bring something each of them loved." He draped a red satin shirt over a protruding rock. "That's Steve's. He bought it with his first pay-check." He set a pair of western boots nearby. "Those are Judd's. He always wanted a pair of snakeskin boots with silver-toe caps. Worked for six months to get 'em."

Amy took the two feathers from her bag. "Nathan says eagle feathers have great power." She attached the feathers to the boys' belongings and stepped back. "Now, we're supposed to clear our minds and silently ask the eagle spirit to guide Steve and Judd home." Jared looked embarrassed, but he bowed his head. Silence settled around them, broken only by the drip-drip-drip of water from ceiling and walls.

In the glow of their lights, first one feather fluttered, then the other. "What made 'em do that?" Jared asked in a hushed voice. "There's no draft in here." The feathers came loose and floated slowly to the floor.

Following the instructions Nathan had given in his note, Amy picked up a rock from beside each feather's resting place. "Nathan says, you are to take these home and put them some place where your boys were happy."

Jared stared down at the gray stones. "You sure this isn't a bunch of Indian hocus pocus?"

She put her hand on his shoulder. "Trust Nathan. Your boys are at peace now."

Jared scrubbed his sleeve across his eyes and cleared his throat. "I sure as hell ain't gonna tell nobody about this. They'll think I've gone off my nut."

"What others think isn't important, Jared. You're the one who must believe in your heart that Steve and Judd are somewhere out there in the sunlight." She placed the two feathers in his hand. "Keep these, they'll help you build your faith."

He carefully stowed away the things she'd given him and shouldered his bag. "We'd better git to gitten." He set off at a fast pace.

After half an hour of stumbling through rubble, he came to a sudden stop. "Something's damned strange. The Lady's never had good air, but it never stunk like this before."

"I wondered about that. It smells like . . ." she drew in a hefty breath, "like my dad's compost pile." She giggled. "How's that for weird?" She adjusted her hat for the fiftieth time and asked, "What's the noise I've been hearing for the last half hour?"

"Motors. A mine has all kinds. Drills, muckers, pumps, vent fans, you name it." He frowned. "Only thing is, these engines don't sound right to me."

Ten minutes later, she noticed the darkness had receded and she no longer needed her cap light.

Jared put his mouth close to her ear. "Walk soft. Must be something going on ahead." As they eased around a corner, Jared grabbed her arm and yanked her behind him. "Jesus! What the goddamned hell is that?"

Chapter 24

Light so incredibly bright it hurt her eyes shimmered through a plastic sheet attached to timbers at the top, bottom, and sides of a glistening barrier that bulged and undulated in front of them like a giant, translucent jellyfish. A murmur of soft Spanish seeped from within.

She slowed her breathing and tugged on Jared's sleeve. "Got a knife?" He nodded. She dug hers out of her pocket. "Let's go."

They crept to one side and each cut a small hole. "Holy balls," Jared breathed.

Amy stared in disbelief. Milk-white plastic lined the ceiling and walls, completely enclosing a sixty- to seventy-foot section of tunnel. All the whiteness combined with megawatt, high-pressure halide lamps hanging from the ceiling reminded her of an operating room. Three men dressed in white caps, coveralls, and face masks completed what seemed like an illusion.

But these men were not attending a patient. Rows of tall plants filled long wooden planter boxes that rested on the concrete floor. The three Mexicans moved along a narrow walkway between the boxes, spraying, weeding, and watering.

She clutched Jared's sleeve. "They're raising marijuana."

"Nah, they couldn't be. Are you sure?"

"I know pot when I see it."

"I'll be damned." He beckoned her off a safe distance. "Why in thunder would Holt let 'em come in here and do that?"

" 'Cause marijuana brings in big money, and this mine provides a perfect cover. They're probably hiding the bales under loads of ore and transporting it to the nearest airfield."

Jared made a guttural sound. "That two-faced sonuvabitch has his own airstrip out at his ranch." He clenched his fists. "I'm gonna nail him, Amy. He's gotten away with too much for too long."

She held up her hand. "First, we find Simon. Deal?"

Some of the feistiness went out of him. "Yeah, that's my orders."

"Did you see any guards?"

"Nope, just the Mexicans."

She chewed her lip as she thought through a plan. "The guards could be in the next growing room, so we have to keep this as quiet as possible. If both of us barge in at the same time, the workers may raise a rumpus."

"That's for sure."

"You speak any Spanish?"

He wagged his head. "Nothing useful."

"Then I'd better go first. I had to learn a few basic words when I was an intern."

He stroked his chin and gazed into space. "We-e-ll, I don't know. Nate——"

"Forget what he told you, Jared. He means well, but I've got a gun, I'm a good shot and I'm quite capable of looking after myself."

"You heard what Frank told Norm about gunfire."

She unglued her tongue from the roof of her dry mouth. "Yes. I'll only use mine as a last resort." She moved back to the peephole she'd made. After assessing the situation, she slit the plastic and stepped into the warm, humid room. An earthy skunk-like odor permeated the air.

The throb of the ventilation system and a sucking sump pump covered her entry. She tapped the nearest worker on the shoulder. *"Buenas noches, señor."*

He pivoted and let out an oath. She put her finger to her lips and whispered that she was a doctor. The workers, goggle-eyed at seeing a woman, flung rapid-fire questions at her.

She motioned for silence and asked if any of them spoke English. All three men shook their heads.

She thumped her chest. *"Mi companeros* want . . ." she searched her memory, *"la ayda* you." She pointed to each of them. *"Mi companeros captura malo hombres."* She made a circular motion, pointed overhead, and asked them if they understood.

The men's heads bobbed in unison. *"Sí. Sí."*

She smiled broadly, went to the opening she'd made, and beckoned to Jared.

He eased through the slit and the workers beamed but kept glancing toward the entry as if waiting for others to follow. When no one else appeared, the men shuffled back to their work.

Jared's gaze darted to the wide double doors at the end of the enclosure. "Find out where your friend is?"

"Not yet." She turned back to the workers and asked the whereabouts of the guards and the dogs. The men shrugged their shoulders and indicated they were everywhere. She let out an exasperated breath and inquired if they'd seen a white man with a broken arm. They shrugged again. One pointed at the double doors and said Rico Diaz's name.

She urged them to help her find him. The men ignored her. She swore under her breath and turned to Jared. "Guess we're on our own."

He scowled. "Don't these jokers want to get out of here?"

"They know what'll happen to them if we fail." She screwed up her courage and opened one of the double doors a crack. Jared leaned in beside her. The next section was a repeat of the first, except that a single white-clad worker rotated potted plants that sat on wooden pallets. She took out her gun. Jared pulled the prybar from a loop on his belt.

The man looked up as they barged in. She quickly gave her friendship speech and asked for Rico Diaz. He rattled off a stream of words she didn't understand and motioned them on.

"I don't like this set-up," Jared muttered. "We stick out like turkeys in a henhouse."

The adjoining enclosure was longer and held three-foot-tall plants in five-gallon buckets. Two workers moved along the rows, pruning branch tips. Two more followed, dunked the pruned tips into rooting powder, put them in small pots, and covered them with plastic bags.

The steady, high-pitched hum of the high-pressure light ballasts wound her taut nerves a notch tighter. She and Jared sidled up to a man engrossed in checking a barrage of instruments on the wall.

"Por favor, señor," she said. The short, sturdy Mexican wheeled around and his black-eyed stare flashed from

her to Jared. Amy asked where she could find Rico
Diaz.

"I am Rico. Who are you?" Apprehension pulled his
skin tight over young, attractive features.

Relieved that he spoke English, she explained in as
few words as possible and said, "The injured white man
is my friend. Can you take us to him?"

He folded his arms across his chest. "How many people you got?"

"Six," she said, and outlined their plan.

As she talked, an expression of disbelief came over his
face. "Four up there," he jabbed his forefinger upward,
"and only a woman and an old man down here." His
lip curled. "You crazy?"

Jared thrust out his chin. "Who the hell you callin'
old?"

Amy's gaze skittered to the next set of double doors,
and she put a calming hand on his shoulder. "Not now,
Jared." She turned back to Rico. "How many guards
are on duty?"

"Four, six, eight." He lifted his shoulders. "Who
knows?"

"Did they get more dogs?" The man spread his
hands, palms out.

Hurry. Hurry. Her nails bit into her palm, as she tried
a different tack. "Nathan Blackthorn, the man who
talked to you, is our leader. He took care of the other
dogs."

"He is Mexican, no?"

She shook her head. "Indian."

He pursed his lips and tilted his hand back and forth.
"The Indian killed all of them?"

Amy clenched her jaws and fought down a surge of
impatience. Without Rico's help, they stood little chance

of finding Simon. "A mountain lion killed the big Doberman when he attacked Nathan."

Rico's mouth dropped open. "A white puma?" When she nodded, his eyes widened. "The spirit cat!" He scratched his head. "Why did she not kill the man?"

Amy's steady gaze met his. "She's the Indian's guardian spirit."

"Ah," Rico said with a nod. "This I know." He smiled, led them to a small enclosure, gave each of them a white uniform, and went back to his panel of instruments.

Amy holstered her pistol, tossed her jacket in a corner, and hurriedly fitted the coveralls over her clothing. A workman had left a weeding fork in the back pocket. She kept it.

Since Jared had to remove his boots, he took longer to get dressed. He was zipping up his coveralls and about to put on his boots when she heard a door slam.

"What's goin' on over there?" yelled a tall, skinny guy wearing a felt hat and bib overalls.

She ducked behind a row of plants.

Rifle in hand, the man loped toward Jared who stood in stocking feet, his crowbar clutched in his hand. "Willard," Jared roared. "What the goddamned hell you doing here?"

Willard skidded to a stop. "Shut your yap, old man. I'll ask the questions."

Jared's face turned purple. "I don't have to answer to you. I'm the shifter . . ."

"Not anymore you ain't." Willard's lips parted in a sneering, gap-toothed smile. "I'm the head honcho now." He gripped the rifle. "And I'm going to make you sorry for every lousy thing you ever said to me."

"Yeah?" Jared bowed his sinewy arms. "Ain't my

fault you're a lazy, blockheaded screwup." He charged. "Gimme that gun." He swung at Willard with the pry bar and grabbed for the rifle.

Willard swerved and swatted Jared alongside the head with the rifle barrel. Jared staggered, caught his balance, and lunged at his opponent.

Amy didn't wait to see more. She crawled along in the shelter of the plants. When she got beyond the guard, she peeked out in time to see Jared go down.

Willard kicked him. "How do you like that, big man?" He kicked him again. "I'll teach you to come nosing around where you don't belong." He aimed another kick.

Amy pulled the weeding tool from her pocket, crept up behind him and jabbed the butt end of the tubular handle against his back. She lowered her voice and barked, "Drop the rifle."

His weapon clattered to the floor, but in the same instant he swiveled and his fist grazed her chin. She swung the tool, embedding the curved steel tines in his cheek and raking them downward. Willard let out a screeching howl.

Before he could recover, she shoved the wooden handle against his throat, stepped in close and rammed her knee into his groin with every ounce of strength she had. He collapsed into a groaning heap. She cuffed his wrists and ankles with the plastic restraints Nathan had given them, got out her emergency bag, and slapped a strip of tape over his mouth. "That'll hold you."

She steadied her shaking legs and flung an apprehensive glance at the door. Another guard could show up at any minute. She dragged Willard into the enclosure and rushed back to Jared who was trying to sit up. "Are you hurt?"

"I'm fine." He took a breath and wiped the perspiration from his forehead.

"Lie still." She checked the door again, unzipped his coveralls, pulled up his shirt, and felt along his rib cage. "You've got a fractured rib." She taped it and tried to get him up, but his left knee gave way under him.

He slumped onto the floor. "Guess I twisted the damned thing during the fight."

Silently cursing the delay, she wrapped his knee with an elastic bandage, put on his boots, and got him to his feet. "Can you walk?"

"Sure. Sure. I've had worse than this lots of times."

Rico trotted over. "This lady," he beamed at Amy, "she's one mighty fine street fighter."

The corners of Jared's mouth tucked in among his wrinkles. "Yeah, she'll do."

"Come," Rico said, beckoning to them. "We go see your friend now."

Amy peered at the dark-haired young man. "You know him?"

"I bring him food. We talk some." He pushed a sheet of plywood aside, exposing an unlined and unused cross-cut lighted with ordinary bulbs. "He let them through and slid the plywood back in place. "This way," he said.

Jared grunted, clamped his lip between his teeth, and limped along beside Amy.

Dampness oozed through the rock walls, dripped on her head, sloshed under her feet, and her heart beat in slow fearful beats. *How long could an injured person survive under these conditions?* she wondered.

"How is Simon?" she asked in a tremulous voice.

"Not so good. When Willard and the big one they call Bear bring him here, he get loose and find a telephone. Then, everybody mad." He grinned. "And scared, I think. Willard and Bear they hit him, try to make him tell who he called. Simon think if they know, they ..." he drew his finger across his throat, "so he don't tell." Rico splashed through a puddle. "Today, a man named Quint hurt him real bad." He wagged his head. "I worry for him."

A cold chunk gathered in her stomach. He couldn't die, not when she was so close. She lengthened her stride. "Who's in charge of all this?"

Rico's shoulders rose and fell. "When the big bosses come, they lock us in our houses. I look through knot-hole and see men's legs."

"What color cars did they have?"

"One white, one gray. Today blue-and-gray pickup come."

Her pulse leaped. The same color the man from the plane had driven. "Did you see the driver?"

"A little. He have a red shirt like that Quint fella."

She added the man to her mental list of things to investigate later. "How about the others? Did you notice what they wore?"

"Black city shoes."

"Anything else?"

"A ring," Rico pointed to the third finger of his right hand. "Here. Flashed in the sun."

"What happened to Henry, the other prisoner?"

"Tomas Garcia say two men take him into tunnel. Henry not come back."

"Were the men guards?"

Rico shook his head violently.

"Would Tomas know them if he saw them again?"

"Oh, yes. Tomas he say he never forget them." He halted beside a padlocked stockade. "They don't let me have key."

Jared hobbled up to them. "I'll take care of that." He unfastened a bolt cutter from the tool belt he'd insisted on wearing, clamped the cutter's jaws, and bore down on the handle. A groan wrenched from his throat and he clutched his ribs. "Can't do it." With a frustrated growl, he passed the tool to Rico. "See what you can do."

Rico made short work of the lock and pulled open the wooden door so she could peer inside. Simon, clad only in a pair of dirty briefs, sprawled on a thick layer of large, empty plastic sacks. She muffled a gasp when she saw his face and body. His captors had pounded him to a pulpy purple mass.

She knelt beside him, her stomach knotted with fear. "Simon, it's Amy." Her voice broke and a sob escaped her. "I'm . . . I'm here."

Chapter 25

Amy touched Simon's shoulder. He let out an anguished cry and flung up his arm. "No! No! No more!"

Jared knotted his fists. "You shoulda rammed Willard's balls so far up his ass he'll hafta use 'em for earmuffs."

"He's mean," Rico said. "Like the rest of the guards."

"They'll pay," Jared said. "We'll see to that."

Amy turned cold with apprehension as she took Simon's thready pulse and felt his clammy skin. She lifted his head and spoke close to his ear. "Simon, it's Amy. Can you hear me?"

"Amy?" He stared at her from between swollen lids. "Amy?" He clutched her hand and brought it to his lips. "Thought ... you'd ... let me ... dow—." He sagged against her.

She straightened. "He'll have to be carried."

"No problem," Jared said. "There's a stretcher just a short ways farther on." He started to leave.

"Wait." She laid out the emergency supplies she'd brought. "Roll up your sleeve. I'm going to give you a shot for pain."

He backed up. "I don't need none of that stuff. Give it to your friend."

"I can't, he's in shock. And if you aren't able to get him out of here, he's going to die." Jared grumbled but submitted to the injection before taking off down the passage.

Amy took Simon's blood pressure and looked up at Rico. "We can't wait for Blackthorn to get here." She fitted the vacuum splint on Simon's fractured arm and adjusted the velcro strips. "Can you get three men to help you carry him? He'll have to go out the way we came in."

"No," Rico said, shaking his head to emphasize his refusal. "Water in shafts. They say we drown if we go into tunnel."

"Bullshit!" Jared stood in the doorway, holding a molded plastic stretcher and some musty smelling blankets. "Me and the doc got here, didn't we?" He set down his burden and emptied the contents of a bunched-up blanket. Several hard hats with attached head lamps fell out. "I worked in this mine for twenty years, I know every inch of it. Ain't nobody gonna die so long as they stick close to me."

Filled with foreboding, Amy watched Rico chew his full lower lip and stare into space. If the men couldn't overcome the fear the guards had drilled into them, they wouldn't help her and Jared. Only Rico could convince them.

Rico glanced down at Simon, then centered his suspicious gaze on Jared. "You speak the truth?"

"You damn betcha. You got my word on it."

Rico's gaze darted to Amy. "What he say is true?"

She nodded. "Follow Jared. He'll get you out."

A slow smile spread over Rico's face. "Then we go."

Jared clapped him on the back. "You're my kinda man, Rico."

Amy positioned the blanket in the stretcher. Simon moaned when the three of them lifted him in, but he didn't come to. She wrapped the blanket around him and glanced up at Rico. "Put your shortest men in front so his head stays lower than his feet."

"We take care of him, doctor."

Jared jerked his head at Rico. "Let's go get some respirators."

While they were gone, Amy ran to the enclosure where she'd left her things. The bound and gagged guard made angry noises at her. She glowered at him. "If Simon dies, I'll see they put you away for life."

After gathering what she needed, she hastened back to Simon, put her oxygen breathing apparatus on him, adjusted the oxygen intake and draped a pair of white coveralls over him. The camouflage might fool a guard long enough for them to overpower him.

Jared and Rico returned and Rico selected his men. They set off and made it to the last room without incident.

After they maneuvered the stretcher through the plastic barrier leading to the tunnel, Amy walked up to Jared. "I'm not going with you."

He glowered and thrust out his jaw. "Now wait just a damned minute. You know Nate doesn't want you down here by yourself."

"What any of us wants or doesn't want isn't important, Jared. We came here to do a job. It's only half finished. Someone has to look after the men who are still here."

Jared expelled a noisy breath. "Nate's right. You've got too damned much spunk for your own good."

She stared back at him. Couldn't he tell her flesh quivered inside her skin, that she had to stiffen her legs to hold them steady? She managed a wan smile. "Worse things have been said about me."

"Well, since I can't talk you out of it." He stuck out his hand. "Good luck."

She gripped his hand. "Take him to Silverton. We don't want anyone in Rock Springs alerted."

"Gotcha."

"How do they call the workers together?" she asked Rico.

"A signal button on the post by the elevator shaft."

She raised her hand. "God be with you."

She sped through the sections she'd been in thus far, slowing at each door before dashing to the next. The men wore no ear protectors and she wondered how long it took to get accustomed to the chugging pumps, the whine of fans, the brain-numbing noise of the ballasts. The pungent odor filled her nose, her lungs, clung to her hair, saturated her clothing.

When she reached unfamiliar territory, she grew more cautious. Fortunately, as she progressed, tall, luxuriant plants reached to her shoulders nearly concealing her.

She entered a long expanse of flowering cannabis bathed in a Halloween glow of sodium lamps. White-garbed men appeared and disappeared among the shrubbery, looking as ethereal as graveyard ghosts. She shivered at the thought and hurried on.

In the adjacent section, men wielded pruning shears, cutting matured plants off at the base and piling the bushy stalks in rubber-tined pushcarts. They'd already harvested more than half the room, leaving few places to hide.

To make matters worse, the camouflage colors of her knapsack decreased her chances of blending in with the workers. Yet she dared not leave it, others might need medical care.

She took a deep breath and ventured in. Midway through the room, she passed a supply bunker. She darted a glance at the dark interior and hurried on.

"Hold it right there, Mex," someone barked.

She broke into a run and heard him thudding after her. She made it to the unharvested rows and zigzagged through the potted plants, tipping them over as she went.

"I'll get you, you weasely bastard and when I do—" The man leaped over the scrambled pile of vegetation, caught his foot, and fell.

Amy yanked her pistol from its holster and brought it crashing down on his head. One more down. She put the restraints on, fastening his wrists behind his back and attaching ankles to wrists as she had with Willard. A few more times and she'd be good at it. She taped his mouth and got him into the bunker.

When she came out, six Mexicans gaped at her. All of them started speaking at once and she couldn't understand a word. She got them quieted down and launched into her help and friendship speech. Suddenly, the double doors burst open and a big man filled the doorway. Protuberant eyes peered through a bushy thatch of curly brown hair. More hair bristled from his open shirt.

"Bear." The word whispered like a long-drawn sigh from the lips of the terrified workers.

Oh, my God. Ted Zeigler, the motel owner. A trickle of cold sweat coursed down her back. She had to get away before he recognized her. Her feet refused to obey.

Zeigler held a .45 in his ham-like hand. "What the

hell's going on in here?" Swinging his head from side to side, he shambled into the room.

She took a cautious step backward, then another. Her foot struck a plastic pot and it clattered across the concrete.

Zeigler's big head swiveled and his eyes narrowed. "You're not . . . how'd you get in here?" His gaze shifted and skittered around the room.

She dodged around him and scuttled through the door he'd left open. A group of harvesters scattered as she plowed into the bushes, leaving mashed and broken stalks in her wake.

Zeigler thundered after her. "Stop or I'll blow your damned head off."

He fired. The blast hurt her ears, reverberating from rock walls and ceiling. The bullet struck a metal cart, ricocheted and hit a lamp. The lamp burst, spewing fine splinters of glass. A rivulet of blood dribbled down her cheek. She bolted for the door to the next room, couldn't get it open, swerved, and tried to go around him. He backed her into a corner.

She yanked her pistol from its holster. "That's far enough, Zeigler."

His eyes widened. "Christ almighty! A goddamned friggin' woman." He pointed a sausage-sized finger. "You're the slut who moved in with Doc. Been stirrin' up trouble ever since." He swung his pistol at her head.

She jumped sideways. Before she could recover, he knocked the gun from her hand, grabbed her, and slammed her head against the wall. Her ears rang and red dots spun in front of her eyes. "City-bred bitch!" Saliva spattered her face. "Think you're pretty smart don'tcha? Getting in here and causing a ruckus."

Behind Zeigler, the door opened. A hooded, black-clad figure slipped through and crept toward them. In the eerie light, Nathan appeared to be seven feet tall. Although he carried only a sturdy five-foot staff, he looked deadly. The Mexicans shrank into a far corner. One man let go of his pruning shears. They clanked on the floor.

Zeigler wheeled, dragging her with him, and sucked in a wheezing breath. "You!" He raised his .45. "You ain't gettin' the best of me this time." He fired.

Nathan dropped to the floor, rolled into a crouch, and swung the staff.

Zeigler let out a howl and his gun flew from his fingers. "Dirty bastard." Zeigler snatched her in front of him, looped his arm under her chin and hoisted her off her feet. "I'll break her neck."

She kicked him, hit him, jabbed her elbows against his chest, but layers of fat cushioned the blows. His arm tightened, shutting off her air supply, her head reeled, the room turned hazy.

"Let her go." Nathan feinted to the right, then to the left.

To keep him in sight, Zeigler kept shifting his ponderous body. Her extra weight threw him off balance and he staggered. Nathan darted in and clouted him in the back of his thigh. Zeigler screamed and toppled over like a felled tree.

Amy gulped in air and crawled over to help Nathan secure Zeigler. "How did you make him go down like that?"

Nathan's eyes glinted in the slitted hood. "Hit his nerve motor point. Hurts like a crotch kick for a few minutes." He trussed Zeigler up like a cowhand would a calf.

"Look Nathan." Amy pointed to Zeigler's twisted shoe. "He's one of the men who kidnapped Simon."

"It figures. How many more guards?"

She held up two fingers. "I took care of them." She saw a flash of white teeth and felt as if he'd given her an award."

"Simon all right?"

She shook her head. "Jared and Rico Diaz took him out the back way."

Another hooded man appeared in the doorway and Nathan motioned him over. "Your man ready for travel?"

Norm nodded. He nudged Zeigler onto his side with the toe of his boot and peered down at him. "Always wondered where this lazy bastard got the money to buy that motel."

A look of recognition came into Zeigler's eyes and his face turned livid. "You sneaky sonuvabitch. When George and the judge gets through with you and your pals, you're all gonna wish you'd never been born."

Chapter 26

The caravan careened down the side of Mount Grayson, two trucks in front and the van bringing up the rear. Nathan drove while Norm read the seven guards their rights.

"Christless bastards," Willard muttered. "If McAllister's mine floods, you'll hear from him."

Norm grinned. "Radical shame ain't it fellas, all that high-grade grass going to waste?" he squirted a stream of tobacco juice into an empty Pepsi can. "Have no fear, Drug Enforcement will be all over the place tomorrow." He met the venomous looks of the tightly secured guards. "The Feds'll go easier on you guys, if you name the one's who masterminded this operation." He took out his notebook. "Who wants to go first?" Dead silence met his question.

He shrugged and put his notebook away. He and Amy moved up behind Nathan. Speaking in a low tone, she recounted Rico's story about Henry Cummings's killers, Simon's arrival at the mine, and the men who tortured him. "I saw the one called Quint on the plane and yesterday in Rock Springs." She described him.

Nathan nodded. "Quint Petrovich. He's a field man

for the rackets. Will and I wondered what business he could have in this part of the country."

"The "rackets!" Norm shoved his fingers through his hair. "Holt's hurting for money. But good God I never thought he'd go that far." He stared into the darkness. "Soon as I get these prisoners settled in, I'll take a run up to his house."

"We'll go with you," Amy said.

"No way. I'm playing this one by the book."

"You'll get killed," Nathan said quietly. "The judge knows if he goes to prison, somebody he's sentenced may try to get even."

"Damn, never thought of that." Norm rubbed his chin, his fingers rasping on a day's growth of sand-colored whiskers. "I'll bet that wily old buzzard started planning his getaway the day he went into the deal. Probably has money and a blonde stashed somewhere in South America." He let out a long sigh. "What do you suggest?"

"You and Amy go to the front door, I'll come in the back."

"Sounds good."

When they reached Will's woodlot, they found Jared, Rico, and Rico's three men waiting. Jared jumped out of his station wagon, pulled his coat up around his ears, and hobbled over to Amy's side of the van.

"Simon'll make it," he said. "They stuck a bunch of needles and tubes in him." He peered in at Nathan. "Where you sending the Mexicans?"

"Sandpoint Naval Air Station. Will asked the FBI to send agents to tape the men's stories. After that they'll be sent home."

"Let me drive instead of Will."

Amy frowned. "That's a long haul for someone with a fractured rib and a sprained knee."

"I'm in a lot better shape than Will. Besides the doc gave me a knee brace, a rib belt, and some pain pills."

Nathan turned the wheel over to Norm and climbed out of the cab. "Fine with me, Jared. I'll go talk to him."

He returned in a few minutes. "It's all fixed. Will's decided to come with me."

"But Nathan, he's . . ." she began.

"He only has a couple of months left, Amy. This last mission means a lot to him."

Half an hour later, Nathan parked the jeep under a weeping willow overhanging an arched gateway. It led to a long driveway edged with tall oak trees. A white rail fence divided the grounds of the two-story house from stables and pasture land.

Nearby, Amy sat in the van with Norm and watched as Nathan and Will got out of the jeep and slipped into the shadows. She took Nathan's Camo-Compac from the pocket of her white coveralls. Earlier, she'd started to remove the coveralls in the van. Nathan and Norm had stopped her, they had a plan.

Now, it was up to her to carry their plan through. She swiped a fingertip over a portion of mud-brown Camo-Creme and began to apply a light coating to her face and hands. While she worked, she questioned Norm.

"Why would a man of McAllister's standing link up with criminals?"

"Oldest reason in the world. Holt inherited money and the mines from his parents. He's never worked a day in his life. He married a woman who loves expensive clothes, jewels, and travel. He's got two boys that cost him a bundle to keep out of trouble. To top it all off, Holt's addicted to fast cars, beautiful women, and Arabian horses."

He turned his palms up in an expressive gesture. "Ore deposits dwindled. The smelter and two of his mines closed. The underworld heard of his predicament and offered him a way out."

He grimaced. "Holt's an expert at covering his ass. My bet is he decided to filter some of his loot into Rock Springs so all of us would look like accomplices in his scheme."

"You think anyone in Rock Springs knows?"

"George does, that's for sure. The mayor and council members must have had their suspicions. The rest of us went along with the flow."

"Didn't you wonder why anyone would give a place like Rock Springs a grant?"

He expelled a long, noisy breath. "Shee-it, what do any of us know about grants? Besides, new business puts money in everybody's pocket." He cocked his head. "Bet you wouldn't have gone around looking under rocks either."

"Maybe, maybe not." She studied her new coffee-colored complexion in the compact's mirror, pressed a bushy mustache Nathan had given her into place, and smiled at Norm. "Okay?"

Norm scowled. "It'll do." He glanced at his watch. "Guess I'd better get on my horse." He checked his .45. "I'll jam the lock. Give me five minutes before you make your move."

Amy left the car and dashed from one gnarled oak to the next. Meanwhile, Norm eased the car down the drive, got out, and banged the brass knocker. She hid behind a camellia bush near enough for her to overhear what was said.

The door opened and McAllister stood in the doorway. He wore a maroon velvet smoking jacket over pinstriped trousers. Light from a crystal chandelier behind him glittered on his silver hair.

"Well, well, Hollenbeck." His lips curled in a mocking smile. "What brings you out on in weather like this? I figured with George out of town you'd be lifting a few at The Green Lantern."

Norm squared his shoulders. "Something has come up, Holt. I need to ask you a few questions."

"Oh?" McAllister scrutinized the officer's stern countenance for a moment, then swung the door open. "Come on in, Norm. I'm always eager to be of help in any way I can." As the lawman went through the doorway, he pressed a piece of putty into the striker plate.

Amy pulled the hood of Paul's roomy coat farther over her forehead and paced a small circle, her boots squishing as she walked. Five minutes passed. Time to go. Quickly, she slipped out of her coat and shoved it under a bush. Donning the white cap that all the Mexicans wore, she hurried across the wide veranda and slipped through the door.

She paused in the foyer. Norm said the hired help left at eight o'clock, but one could never be sure. She glided forward, setting her feet down in the same careful manner Nathan did.

Straight ahead, a circular staircase gave access to the second floor. A living room, decorated in shades of peach and green, lay on her left, to her right a paneled hallway. Voices came from a half-open door. She eased it farther open and glimpsed McAllister leaning against against the marble fireplace. Norm stood beside a massive leather chair, his body angled so he could see the door.

"Sorry about what happened to Dean," Norm said.

"Yes, he was a fine boy. We're going to miss him."

Norm settled his hat straighter on his head. "Hard to believe he did what he did. I trailed around after him and Troy for quite a few years. Never heard of Dean doing drugs."

"No way! I raised my boys right." He narrowed his eyes. "I've made enemies. Lots of them. They're trying to get back at me through my boys." McAllister shook his finger at Norm. "And I want you and George to drop everything and find them. You hear? Nobody's going to kill my boy and get away with it."

"We'll do our best, Holt. But we've got a number of strange cases on our hands right now."

"Like what?"

"Well, there's the body George found in the river the day after you and the mayor blew the dam."

McAllister's attempt to register surprise wasn't convincing. "A body! Man or woman?"

"A man in his late twenties or early thirties. George and Doc Leibow took care of him."

"Hm-m, wonder how come neither George or Miles mentioned it."

Norm glanced toward Amy and quickly away. "The man was Mexican."

"You don't say. We don't see many of them around here."

"That's right, Holt." Norm took a step forward. "So what're you doing with a bunch of them at the China Lady?"

McAllister drew himself up. "Somebody's putting you on. I hire Rock Springs's men." He clapped the officer on the back. "You're a good man, Norm. A damned good man. High time the mayor gave you a raise. Yes, sir, I'll speak to him first thing tomorrow." He turned toward a rosewood liquor cabinet. "How about a shot of my best bourbon for the road?"

McAllister set out two glasses and uncapped a bottle. "Beats me how a wild story like that got started. I'm not even using a full crew at the Lady these days. Only run an ore truck every couple a weeks." He handed Norm a filled glass.

Norm set his drink on an end table. "No ore trucks have gone through Rock Springs in months."

McAllister rested his hand on Norm's arm. "I know that, son," he said in a syrupy voice. "I thought it best to send them out the old road past the ranch." He smiled and ran the tip of his little finger over the edge of his small, neatly trimmed mustache. "Saves wear and tear on our town's newly paved streets."

Norm braced his hands on his hips. "You sure that's the only reason, Holt?"

"Of course, I'm sure. What other reason would I have?"

Amy pushed the door fully open. McAllister's eyes bulged when he saw her. "You've been to the mine," he croaked.

"That's him," she said pointing at McAllister. "I see him take gringo in tunnel. Gringo never come back."

Norm curled his hand over the butt of his holstered gun and moved toward McAllister. "I'm taking you in Holt." He started reading him his rights.

"Like hell you are." McAllister yanked a gun from his jacket pocket. "Drop your weapon."

"Don't be a damned fool."

"Drop it, boy, or I'll kill you. I've got nothing to lose."

Amy inched closer to a floor lamp with a glass shade and bumped it with her hip. The lamp fell to the floor. Glass splintered, bulbs popped. Norm sprang at Holt. The two men wrestled. Holt's gun went off and the bullet smacked into the floor.

Amy drew her pistol. "Freeze," she shouted. They ignored her warning. Her finger tightened on the trigger. "Freeze, McAllister, or I'll shoot."

Gunfire erupted in the hall. She swiveled around. Will lay on the floor, a pool of blood spreading around his head. Quint Petrovich grappled with Nathan. Nathan grabbed his neck with one hand and gave him a karate chop with the other. Quint went down.

Nathan trussed him up and came toward her. Out of the corner of her eye, she caught a movement in a doorway farther down the hall. Troy crouched in the shadows his gun aimed at Nathan.

She leaped in front of Nathan and fired at Troy. Troy's bullet knocked her to the floor. Nathan dived over her, rolled, and bounced to his feet. He kicked Troy in the ribs and Troy's next shot thunked into the wall. Nathan whirled and struck the man's extended arm. The bone snapped. Troy screamed and his gun fell from his hand.

Nathan bound him, rushed back, and knelt beside her. "Did he get you?"

She evaluated the peculiar numb feeling she had. "I think the vest took it. Help Will." She got to her knees and started to stand. Blood streamed down her left hand. She braced her back against the wall, unzipped her coveralls, and got her right arm free ... her left wouldn't respond. She worked the heavy fabric over her left shoulder. The sodden material slid off of its own accord. Blood gushed down her arm. Quickly, she squirmed out of Nathan's ill-fitting body armor. Then, as if she'd flipped a switch, the pain hit her. She cried out and sank to her knees.

Nathan hurried to her side. "What's wrong?"

"Left shoulder. Bullet must have nicked an artery. Losing lots of blood."

Nathan snatched his knife from his boot. He slashed her shirtsleeve at the shoulder seam, ripped off her shirt, crammed it against the wound and tied it in place with the sleeve.

Norm prodded his manacled prisoner through the library doorway. "Everything under control out here?"

"Amy took a bullet in the shoulder." Nathan dashed down the hall, opening doors and peering into rooms on the way.

Amy struggled out of her coveralls and scrubbed her face with them, ridding herself of the brown make-up and silly mustache.

Nathan returned with a blanket and wrapped it around her. "Got to get you to the emergency room."

"What about Will?"

"He's dead."

Chapter 27

At Winterhaven Hospital, Amy lay in a light-headed haze, watching the movements of the emergency room doctor. Each time he turned his attention to the X-ray viewing box, his thick eyebrows shot upward, nearly reaching his chestnut-colored hairline. A moment later, his brows slid down to droop over deep-set green eyes as he probed her wound for the bullet visible on the film. "I'll have to report this," he said.

Nathan stood at the foot of the examination table. Earlier, Miss Babcock, the stout, gray-haired nurse, had told him to leave. Instead, he planted his feet, folded his arms, and flashed his dark eyes. She took one look, backed off, and left him alone.

"Fine with us," Nathan said. "Officer Hollenbeck was there when it happened."

"I see." The doctor glanced at Miss Babcock. "Did you take care of that matter we discussed?"

She flushed and peered behind her. "Oh, absolutely, Doctor. He . . . uh . . . wasn't too happy about . . . um . . . being disturbed this late in the evening."

The doctor pulled his mouth down at the corners. "Tough. I'm fed up with him and his power trips."

The nurse peered over her shoulder. "Shhh Doctor. What if he heard you? You know how angry he gets."

"Hah!"

Amy turned her head. She detested the habit some medical people had of talking over, around, and through patients as if they were inanimate objects.

Across the corridor a light came on, revealing an office decorated in burgundy and gray. *Burgundy carpeting.* The fragmented thought floated around in her fogged brain. *Something important. Something she needed to remember.* She tried to grasp the fleeting impression but didn't succeed.

A man in a gray raincoat came through the office's private entrance. He smoothed wind-blown hair, his mustache, and a scraggly beard that accentuated his thick neck and double chin.

Dr. Leibow! Amy made a wry face. She'd hoped she wouldn't run into him. His racist attitude toward Nathan when they were coming in on the plane from Coeur d'Alene still infuriated her.

He jammed his hands into the pockets of his raincoat, waddled across the office, and slouched in the doorway. Thick rimless glasses magnified his small, close-set eyes. "What's going on, Hatcher?"

Dr. Hatcher didn't raise his head. "This is Dr. Amy Prescott."

"I know who she is. What's she doing here?"

Dr. Hatcher switched the probe to his left hand and reached for a forceps.

Dr. Leibow stalked into the emergency room. "Well?"

"Dr. Prescott has a gunshot wound. I've never treated one before. Thought you ought to supervise." Strands of blood clung to the bullet he withdrew from the wound.

He brought the forceps closer. "Seems to be intact." He started to drop the bullet on the tray.

Nathan stepped forward with a labeled evidence bag. "Initial it and put it in here, Doctor," He sealed the bag with red, tamper guard tape and put it in a zippered pocket.

Dr. Leibow ignored him and glowered at Dr. Hatcher. "What's a goddamned Indian doing in my operating room?"

"He brought in Dr. Prescott."

"Get him the hell out of here . . . now!"

Dr. Hatcher's sharp gaze met Leibow's. "If it hadn't been for Mr. Blackthorn's expertise, I wouldn't have attempted to remove the bullet."

Dr. Leibow pooched his fat lips and studied Dr. Hatcher's work. "Shove in a drain, close it up, and fill her full of antibiotics."

He rounded on Nathan. "What you doing in Rock Springs? You're not one of those shanty-town Indians."

Nathan stared down at the obese little man. His eyes grew blacker, his cheekbones higher, the curve of his nose more pronounced. "Someone killed my cousin," he said quietly.

Leibow's lip curled. "You hot-blooded bucks are always doing in one of your own. Who got it this time?"

Nathan's disdainful look would have caused a less thick-skinned man to cringe. "Sarah Wahsise."

Dr. Leibow blinked owlishly, then a jeering laugh joggled his double chin. "You mean that old squaw who thought she was some sort of healer."

Nathan's eyes narrowed. "Sarah had supernatural powers. She will not rest easy." Each word dropped into the silence like chipped steel. "The ones who killed her for her land will come to regret it."

"Heathen poppycock! This town doesn't cotton to Indians. You'd do well to remember that."

Anger cleared Amy's befuddled mind. She raised her head. "What'd you do with the Mexican, Leibow?"

He wheeled around. "What's that?"

"The corpse you and Chief Pike pulled out of the river."

"Ridiculous! I never heard of anything so preposterous. You're both a couple of crazies." He stomped across the hall and slammed the door of his office.

Amy let her head fall back on the table. That ought to give the old phoof something to think about.

Dr. Hatcher cleared his throat. "An Indian and . . ." his voice rose an octave, "and a Mexican died? When . . . uh . . . did all this take place?"

Nathan's gaze met Amy's. A half smile appeared and he drooped an eyelid. "Don't forget the Anglo."

"Anglo?" Dr. Hatcher's Adam's apple bobbed. "Which Anglo?"

"Dean McAllister."

"He gave himself an overdose."

Nathan raised an eyebrow. "Did he? Or is that what someone wants us to think?"

Amy's memory bank clicked in. The recall struck her with such force she voiced her thought without thinking. "Dean had burgundy rug fibers on his shoes."

Dr. Hatcher bumped his sterile tray, spilling forceps, and hemostats onto the blue tile floor. He recovered his composure. "You mean their deaths are all connected?"

Nathan's quick glance told her they were on the same wavelength. "All the evidence indicates they may be."

Beads of perspiration gleamed on Dr. Hatcher's forehead. "Have you . . . uh . . . gone to the authorities about this?"

"Not yet. We still have some loose ends."

Dr. Hatcher lay down his needle holder and stripped off his gloves. "Miss Babcock will apply a dressing and give you some injections. You'd better spend the rest of the night in the recovery room." He hurried out the door.

When the nurse finished, Nathan lifted Amy onto a gurney and pushed it to the recovery room. He turned his back while Miss Babcock helped her into a hospital gown. Amy submitted to the gown but balked at taking off her jeans.

"It's up to you," Miss Babcock said. She bustled over to the window and raised it a few inches. "Our ventilation system is on the fritz again."

Amy's tongue clung to the roof of her mouth. "Could I have a drink of water."

Miss Babcock set a blue plastic water carafe on the nightstand and poured Amy a glassful. "I'll bet you think a hospital with only ten beds is a joke."

"It's the skill of the doctors and nurses that counts."

Miss Babcock's deep sigh undulated her ample bosom. "Ain't that the truth." She patted Amy's arm. "Your pain medication should take effect soon. I'll check in later."

"How do you feel?" Nathan asked.

Amy grinned. "Like I've got wings."

His eyes twinkled. "That'll never happen. The other angels wouldn't be able to handle the stress."

He wandered over to the window, peered out, came back, and checked inside the closet. "We may have stirred up a mess of trouble for ourselves."

She smirked. "Won't be the first time."

He brushed tendrils of hair off her cheek and tucked

them behind her ear. "I asked the lab to phone Dr. Chambers with the results of Sarah's autopsy."

"Call him. Maybe we can wrap up this case."

"Are you sure you'll be all right?"

"Pos-i-tively." She waved her hand airily. "I'm as fine as frog hair." She giggled at her slurred words. "If I need a white knight, I'll yell." She closed her eyes. "Whoo-e-e, I'm on a roller-coaster ride." He switched off the light, the door thumped closed, and she drifted off.

Someone shook her and said in a husky voice, "It's time for your pills."

She pried open her leaden lids. The person held a flashlight beam directed at her face. She could only see a dark shape. "Open your mouth," he whispered.

Automatically she obeyed. He dropped in several capsules and held the drinking tube for her. She sucked in some water and with the breath came a distinctive odor of rain and cold night air on the person's clothing.

No, that shouldn't be. She fought him.

Letting go of the flashlight, he forced water down her throat, clamped her jaw closed, and held her nose until she swallowed. He shoved in more capsules and made her swallow again. Rays from the flashlight on the bed illuminated his right arm. She saw the ring on his finger, the pulled blue silk threads on the sleeve of his suit jacket. *Dear God.* She fastened her teeth in his hand and bit down until she tasted blood.

"Bitch." He whacked her across the face.

"You killed Dean," she yelled and scrambled away from the fist he drove at her jaw. He grabbed the five-cell torch and swung it at her. She ducked and let out a resounding shriek. The man leaped out the open window. She leaned over the side of the bed and tried to make herself vomit.

Nathan burst in, flipped on the light, and dashed over to the screenless window. "Who was it?"

"His suit jacket," she swallowed some water, "had blue silk threads," she gulped more water, "like the one you found on Dean's torn fingernail." She emptied the glass, poured another, and drank it down. "He has . . . a large diamond . . . on his right hand." She tried to gag herself again. Her stomach tipped, but nothing came up. She grimaced. "He forced me to take a bunch of pills."

He scooped her up, blanket and all. "We're getting out of here." As they neared the front desk, two police cars careened into the parking lot with their sirens screaming. "Someone sicced the state police on us."

"Go, Nathan. We don't have a chance against Leibow."

He whirled, rushed back down the hall and out the rear door. He hid her behind some shrubbery, crept to the jeep, and in a few minutes they were rocketing down a back alley.

She clung to the bucking seat. "Try the main highway. I've got to get to a doctor."

Police cars blocked all the thoroughfares. Nathan swerved and tore through another alley. "Try Paul's house," she said. "He has some bottles of emetic."

"Dr. Chambers won't be much help, Amy. He's roaring drunk. He became lucid long enough to tell me Sarah died from a massive doze of digitalis. Then he started raving about me trying to steal his wife."

He skidded the jeep to a stop beside the garage and helped her to the porch. Lights glowed all over the house, but Paul didn't answer Nathan's thunderous knock.

"Maybe he passed out." She tried the knob. The door opened and she shuffled to Paul's chair.

Nathan stopped beside her. "Where does he keep the emetic?"

"In his exam room." She pointed. "The cupboard over the sink."

He brought back a bottle of ipecac. She swallowed the proper dose, gulped down several glasses of water and waited beside the bathroom door.

"I'll phone Norm and have him call off the cops."

She nodded, clapped her hand over her mouth, and plunged inside. In the midst of her vomiting, she heard a crash somewhere in the house. She was too sick to care.

Gradually, the waves of nausea receded and she ventured out. Nathan wasn't in the kitchen. She heard a scraping sound farther down the hall and traced it to Paul's den. She twisted the knob and slid the door open a few inches.

Across the room, the fireplace stood oddly askew. To one side a tunnel-like opening had been cut in the rock cliff that abutted the house. No wonder she'd felt cold when Paul had shown her the room that first day.

She pushed the door inward and gasped at the sight of Paul dragging Nathan's body toward the tunnel.

"Men, always men," Paul mumbled. "She just won't stay away from them."

Amy seized a stone doorstop and threw it at Paul's back. It struck him between the shoulder blades and he went to his knees.

He turned and looked at her with accusing eyes. "Mora, I only put you in there to punish you for trying to leave me. But you won't learn will you? You keep getting out and doing the same rotten things."

She shuddered at what his words implied. "You're out of your mind." She snatched one of his rifles from the rack, tottered over and rapped him on the head. He sank down in a pitiful heap. She found he had a strong pulse and transferred her attention to Nathan.

When she touched his face, he groaned and levered himself off the floor. "He clubbed me while I was on the phone."

She leaned against the wall. "Did you reach Norm?"

"No. The night man didn't know where he was. Did you get rid of the pills?"

"Some." A cramp knotted her stomach and perspiration bathed her body. She wiped her damp forehead with trembling fingers. "We'd better go. Won't take them long to think of looking here." Her legs gave way and she slid down the wall.

Nathan picked her up. "I'll take care of you, Amy."

"I know . . ." She went limp in his arms.

Chapter 28

She awakened to find herself laying naked on a ledge at the base of a rock wall. Peeled saplings curved from an anchored beam to the floor. Steam billowed up from a bubbling hot spring and condensed on the cedar-bark ceiling.

Nathan, stripped to bikini briefs, stood beside her. He raised her head and held a cup to her lips. "Drink."

She swallowed and made a face. "What is it?"

"Bayberry bark and boneset." He brought the cup to her lips again. "Drink some more."

A few minutes after she finished, she started to retch violently. He got her up, supported her body with his, and flattened his palm against her stomach while spasm after spasm tore through her insides.

When she could get nothing more up. He lifted her onto the ledge and began to knead her muscles. Steam filled her lungs. Sweat poured from her skin. She moaned and cried and pleaded for him to stop. He ignored her and continued like a man possessed.

Finally, he bathed her with icy water, carried her to a log hut nearby, lay her on a thick bed of dry grass, and covered her with a blanket. Every part of her hurt, inside and outside, every tissue, every bone, every muscle fiber. It even hurt to blink.

He lit a fire in the small wood range and put on water to heat. He noticed her watching, and his tense features softened into a gentle smile "We're in Sarah's medicine hut." He searched along shelves lined with jars filled with leaves, berries, and murky liquids. "You won't like this, but there's no other way."

She nodded and turned her hand palm up.

He took down several jars, measured spoonfuls of their contents into a pan, poured in boiling water, and put on a lid. While the concoction steeped, he came to her and slipped a leather thong over her head.

She looked down at the tiny white chamois skin bag dangling between her breasts and then up at him.

"Medicine pouch," Nathan said. "The objects inside protect you as you travel through the spirit world." He went back to the table, strained the mixture and brought her a huge dipperful.

She gulped the bitter stuff, closed her eyes, and fell asleep. Teeth-chattering chills woke her. Nathan wrapped her in the blanket and held her to his warm body until the chills subsided. She'd no sooner dozed off than fever ignited inside her. The blazing heat seared her nerve endings until the lightest touch caused raw, burning pain. Nathan bathed her again and again with liquid that cooled her dry, papery skin and made it tingle. After each episode subsided, he urged her to drink another of the endless cups of odd-tasting teas.

Night became day and each time she awakened she found him sitting cross-legged beside her. The gaze he fixed on her face held such intensity she felt a palpable life force flowing between them.

He sang strange songs in his own tongue to the beat

of a small drum. The cadence pulsed inside her head, a blood throb so compelling it penetrated the fathomless depths of her subconscious and brought her back each time she felt herself slipping away.

Once she awakened and longed to touch him but didn't have the strength. "Love you," she whispered and sank into oblivion again.

Slowly, her head cleared and pain no longer racked her body. She opened her eyes and smiled at him. "I think I'm going to live."

Dark circles smudged his bloodshot eyes. "No fever?" She shook her head. "No chills?"

"None."

His eyes grew large and moist and he blinked to clear them. Reaching out, he caught her hand and pressed her palm against his chest. "Amy, Amy." His face contorted with anguish. "How am I ever going to do what I must do?"

"Shhh. All things in their time." She drew him down beside her, held his head against her breast, massaged his back and shoulders in long, soothing strokes. His tension eased and he fell into a deep sleep.

She tried to memorize the curve of his long lashes on his cheek, the look of his beautiful, sensual mouth, the feel of his body against hers.

She pressed her lips to his forehead. "You gave me back my life. How can I live it without you?" She closed her eyes and drifted off.

Sunlight streaming through the window roused her. She smelled food and sat up. Nathan was bent over the stove stirring something in a pot. "Hey, what's for breakfast? I'm starved."

His face lit up. "The soup's almost ready. Would you like to get dressed?"

Her few pieces of clothing had been washed, dried, and placed by her bed. On the bottom of the small stack lay a pair of deerskin moccasins and his flannel shirt. The same one she'd worn the day they'd made love. Tears filmed her eyes and she could scarcely see to fasten the buttons.

After they'd eaten, Nathan insisted she get some sun while he cleaned the cabin. She stretched out on a bench hacked out of a cedar log. A slight breeze soughed through the pines, and overhead fluffy, white clouds floated across a brilliant blue sky. Knowing each passing second brought Nathan's departure a little closer, dimmed her appreciation.

When he finished inside, he came and squatted beside the bench. "Think you're strong enough to travel?"

She swung her feet to the ground and sat up. "I'll manage."

Nathan opened the back window of Paul's cabin, crawled inside, and hoisted her up. While he peered cautiously out the front door, she studied an unfamiliar notebook. A note stuck to the front said: *Amy, forgive the mistakes of a weak old man.* It was signed with Paul's name.

She opened the cover and scanned the first page. "Oh, my God," she breathed.

Nathan whirled around. "What have you got there?"

"A confession," She said hurriedly. "Quick, we must find Paul." Nathan strode out the cabin door and took off up the path toward Paul's house. She trotted along at his side, her breath coming in little gasps. "This time, he'd going to do away with himself for sure."

They dashed in Paul's back door without knocking

and ran from room to room. Nathan flung open the door to the den and they stood stock still.

"Oh, my God," Amy gasped. Blood spattered walls and floor and Dr. Leibow lay dead near the tunnel entrance, a gun still clutched in his hand.

"Maybe Paul's inside the tunnel." She started forward.

Nathan caught her sleeve. "Let me go first." He padded over, found a switch that triggered a light and stared inside with an expression of disbelief.

"What is it?" Moving with slow, hesitant steps, Amy joined him, peered into the dimly lit stone cavern and gripped his arm. "Oh, Nathan, how awful."

Two skeletons sat with their backs propped on stacked luggage and trunks. One woman's clothing looked to be a hundred years old, the other not more than ten.

Amy knelt to open a pocketbook. The black leather had grayed with age. Pieces of the covering cracked and crumbled away as she twisted the catch. Among other bits of female trivia, she found a yellowed clipping. "She's Martha Humphreys. Fiancée of Michael Chambers." She shivered. "Paul said his granddaddy had some peculiarities."

"You can say that again." Nathan worked open the corroded zipper of the other woman's purse. "This one's name is Mora Chambers." He glanced at Amy. "Dr. Chambers's wife?"

Amy nodded. "The other night he said he'd put her in here to punish her for trying to leave him."

"The guy must be crazy."

"Only when he's saturated with alcohol and drugs." A cry came from somewhere. "Paul." They hurried into the hall. "He must be in his bedroom." She pushed open the door.

Paul lay on the bed holding a blood-soaked bath towel over his stomach. "Glad you made it in time." He drew a shaky breath. "I've been putting the whole thing on tape." He pointed to the recorder on his night table. "Just to make doubly sure."

"Paul, we'd better get you to the hospital."

He wagged his head wearily. "Didn't have the guts to do it myself. Figured if I pushed Sarah's killer far enough he'd do it for me." He coughed and blood flecked his shirt front. "Holt suspected I killed Mora. He's been holding it over me for years."

"You know about the marijuana he's growing in the China Lady?" Amy asked.

"Marijuana! Good Christ! No wonder Holt and Leibow didn't want anyone to know they owned the ski resort."

Amy frowned in confusion. "Holt and Leibow own the resort? I heard it was a corporation."

Paul's mouth twisted. "I'm the corporation, they blackmailed me into letting them put everything in my name."

"It figures," Nathan said. "They needed a means of laundering their dirty money." He moved closer to the bed. "I'm Nathan Blackthorn, Sarah's cousin."

Paul stared at him. "Nice tribute you gave at her funeral. I understand that you're Yancy's guardian."

Nathan nodded. "He's staying with my father."

"That's good." Paul ran a hand over his ashen face. "Sarah and I were friends for thirty years. If I had known those two sonsabitches were going to cheat Sarah out of her land, I'd have killed both of them." He coughed again and the red stain on the bath towel spread.

Amy put her hand on his shoulder. "Please, let us take you to a doctor."

Paul shook her off. "Let me along, girl. I got things I have to say before I die."

Amy sighed. "How do the McAllister boys fit into all this?"

"Holt cut off their allowances. Troy needed money so he helped work that phony mine scam on Simon Kittredge's father. Dean wasn't as quick-witted as Troy. When Leibow offered him money to set a bottle of elderberry wine laced with digitalis on Sarah's back porch, Dean thought it was easy pickings. His big mistake was trying to squeeze more money out of Leibow."

A spasm crossed Paul's face and he motioned to Nathan. "Get the large envelope in the top drawer of my dresser."

Nathan did as he directed and started to hand it to him. Paul waved him away. "It's a copy of my will. My attorney's got all the legal angles sewed up tight. Nobody will be able to contest a single clause."

He gazed at Amy and Nathan. "I've made my peace with Sarah and I fixed the lot of them good."

Amy swallowed the lump in her throat. There was no way he could correct all the harm that had been done, but she humored him anyway. "How'd you do that?"

He pulled his mouth into a painful caricature of a smile. "That tunnel in the den leads to the richest silver deposit ever found in these parts. Granddad put his unfaithful sweetheart in there and built the house in front of the entrance to hide what he'd done." His glance shifted to Amy. "Mora deserved what she got. Will can vouch for that. She jilted him for me."

"Will's dead, Paul."

"Good. Poor bastard suffered long enough." Another spasm of coughing shook him, and when he straightened blood trickled from the corner of his mouth. "Blackthorn, you see that McAllister and this town doesn't cheat Yancy of his heritage."

"What heritage?" Nathan's face darkened and a muscle bunched along his jaw. "Sarah didn't own anything except that piece of land Holt and Leibow stole from——"

Paul silenced him with a quick gesture. "The boy has a heritage now, I'm leaving him my silver mine, my house, my land, and the whole damned resort." A laugh gurgled from his throat. "Let's see how those bigoted bastards like that."

Chapter 29

Norm completed his crime-scene investigation and asked the coroner to remove the bodies of the two doctors. He, Nathan, and Amy gathered in the kitchen.

Amy sank onto a chair, then pushed herself upright again. "I'll make coffee."

Nathan put his hand on her shoulder. "Let me do it."

Norm let out a long sigh. "I haven't been this busy since I came to Rock Springs." He sprawled in Paul's recliner.

Amy idly turned the pages of Paul's detailed confession. Dr. Hatcher's name leaped out at her and she stopped to read. "Nathan," she said, after a few minutes. "Our charade in the emergency room paid off. Dr. Hatcher had seen the Mexican's body in their refrigeration room. He didn't think much of it until we started needling Leibow."

"I had a hunch he might know something. When you mentioned the color of the fibers on Dean's shoes, he got the shakes."

"A good thing, too. The next day he consulted Paul. Told him what he'd seen and that the evening before Dean died he'd passed Leibow's office and overheard

Dean and Leibow arguing. Paul already suspected Leibow of poisoning Sarah. Hatcher's story pushed him into taking action on his own."

"Damned shame he got shot doing it," Norm said.

"No." Amy let the pages slide through her fingers. "There's nothing ennobling about constant pain. Will found relief his way, so did Paul."

Norm cracked his knuckles several times. "Amy . . . and, uh . . . you, too, Nate. I owe you both an apology." He cleared his throat. "There's no way I could've cleared up this mess without the two of you."

"It's part of my job," Amy said.

Nathan finished measuring in the last spoonful of coffee and plugged in the percolator. "Mine, too. Anything new on McAllister?"

"Soon as I jailed Holt and Troy, the guards started singing like a bunch of canaries. Amy was right about them taking the baled marijuana out to Holt's airport. Oh, and by the way, I had the state police pick up Chief Pike. Charged him with criminal negligence for starters."

Nathan set out cups. "How did things go at Sandpoint?"

"Real slick. The men gave their stories, and their families are being notified they're alive and well." He snorted. "The State Department is mighty red-faced over this affair. They're going to have one sweet time explaining to the Mexican government how twenty-five aliens were kidnapped, made to work as slaves in McAllister's marijuana farm for two years, and none of the authorities did much to find them."

Amy leaned her elbows on the table and cupped her chin in her hands. "What're the workers going to get out of this?"

"Well, they're crime victims. Eventually they may get something from the government, but it sure as hell won't compensate for what they went through."

He laced his fingers behind his hand. "Frank and Jared have gotten real chummy with Rico. Seems all of those men are from the same depressed area in Mexico. They need schools, clinics, new wells, better roads, and most of all cottage industries. Frank's real handy—"

"I'll vouch for that," Amy broke in. "He recycles things other people call trash and makes them into something useful."

Nathan laughed. "Like Rock Springs's rocks."

"Right. Anyway, him and Jared are going to take a trip to Mexico and see what kind of equipment they can scrounge up."

"Good thinking," Nathan said. "Who's going to finance the project?"

Norm sat forward and regarded them with an earnest expression. "This is to go no further, okay?" Amy and Nathan nodded. "Folks in Rock Springs like to keep things in the family, so to speak." A grin twitched the corners of his mouth. "I just happened to discover the briefcase full of money Petrovich delivered to McAllister. Seems fitting the Mexicans should get it. Don't you agree?"

Amy smiled. "Poetic justice, I'd say."

"If you run into any snags, let me know," Nathan said. "I know a few government men who are experts at clearing paths in cases like this." He got up and poured the coffee. "Can you get the state police off our necks?"

Norm waved his arm. "I already took care of it. You're both in the clear." He sugared and creamed his coffee, took a swallow, and opened his notebook. "Now, let's go over this crazy case right from the beginning."

After he finished questioning them, he stowed Amy's forensic reports and the box of casts in the patrol car and leaned on the door. "Guess that about wraps it up. You folks going to be around for a while?"

"I'm leaving for Orofino first thing in the morning," Nathan said, avoiding Amy's startled gaze.

She breathed shallowly in an attempt to loosen the knot in her throat. Her chest hurt something awful and she had to force the words out, "As soon as I can get a plane . . . I'll be on my way home."

Chapter 30

Nathan glanced at Amy, then quickly away. "I must go. I have to get my things together."

Amy swallowed to ease the ache in her throat. "The jeep belongs to you and Yancy now. Right?"

"I suppose it does." He raked his fingers through his hair. "That's some mess of worms Doc handed me. I guess I won't have to worry about what I'll be doing for the next year or two."

He'd be married to Angela, that's what he'd be doing. Sleeping with her. Making love to her. Amy kicked a rock, hurt her toe, and swore under her breath. "Do you mind if I use the jeep to visit Simon at the hospital?"

"No, of course not." Nathan shoved his hands into his pockets and stared at his feet. "Can I go with you?"

"Why? You don't even know Simon."

His gaze inched up and met hers for an instant. "He and I have some unfinished business."

"I see." She wrapped her arms around herself, became aware that she still wore his shirt, and clutched a handful of the soft flannel fabric. "I'll return this when you come by."

"Keep it. Wearing it would only remind me of you."

A diversion he obviously didn't intend to indulge in. She ducked her head to hide her bitterness. "Give me enough time to get cleaned up."

"Will an hour do?"

At her nod, he plodded down the driveway, his head bent, his shoulders sagging.

Amy hurried into the cabin. *Keep busy. Don't think.* She took a shower, donned a rose-colored blouse and a burgundy skirt.

Her reflection in the small bathroom mirror gave her little confidence. She sighed, put in her contacts, added eye shadow, a hint of blush to her already glowing cheeks, and a bit of lipstick.

When Nathan's knock sounded, she slipped on her high heels and opened the door. He wore a white, open-throated shirt with blue trousers and sports jacket and looked so marvelous she could scarcely take her eyes off him.

She swung the door wide. "Come in. I'm almost ready." She took her coat from a hook on the wall. When she turned, she found Nathan standing behind her. "Would you help me with this? It's hard to handle with my sore shoulder." She held out her coat. His gaze grew more intense, but he didn't speak or move. She laughed nervously. "Hey, I'm the lady from the swamp, remember?"

He touched her cheek. "You're so pretty."

Suddenly, she felt luminescent, incandescent, light as air. Laughter bubbled out. "Those mud packs did it. Some enterprising entrepreneur could turn that swamp into a mint."

He helped her into her coat and adjusted the collar,

his fingers grazing her nape. "I doubt it. That mud didn't help my appearance."

She glanced up at him. "You're perfect just as you are."

He laughed out loud. "You need to get your eyes checked."

On the way to the hospital, she forced herself to keep up a lively chatter. Oddly enough, the more animated she was, the quieter Nathan became.

At the hospital, he took forever to park the car and lingered in the reception room until she fidgeted with impatience. They started down the corridor toward Simon's room, but the closer they got the more glue-footed Nathan became.

Halfway down the corridor, he stopped and turned to her, his body stiff, his face rigid as stone. "I suppose, since you got all dressed up for Simon, you'll want to see him alone."

His accusation seared her tense nerves. "Sure. Why not? After all we are—"

"Former lovers!"

Her shock gave way to anger. "I was going to say, 'friends.' But you're right, we were lovers."

"Nice of you to correct me." His black eyes snapped. "Stay an hour."

She lifted her chin. "Thanks, I will."

He strode forward and yanked open Simon's door. "Spend the night."

She bit her lip, backed against the corridor wall, and blinked back tears.

"Well?" Standing tall and formidable as a palace guard, Nathan scowled at her. "Your *friend* is waiting."

She glared at him, straightened, and entered the open doorway. With her mouth stretched into the semblance of a smile, she walked toward Simon's bed. "Hi there," she said in as cheery a voice as she could muster. "You're looking a lot better than when I last saw you."

Simon grabbed the metal headboard with one hand and yanked himself to a sitting position. "Where the hell have you been?" He thrust back his auburn hair and his eyes shot green fire. "You get somebody to dump me here, then you disappear. That's a hell of a way to treat a guy."

Before she could recover from his unexpected attack, Nathan rushed in. "Hold it right there, Kittredge." He marched over and put a protective arm around her. "If it wasn't for Amy, you'd be dead."

Nathan's hostile stance and the proprietary way he continued to keep his arm around her only fueled Simon's rage. "Who the hell are you? And what gives you the right to barge in on a private conversation?"

Nathan tensed. "I'm Agent Blackthorn. I followed you and Henry Cummings to Rock Springs. Amy and I met when we both decided to search your motel room."

"So butt out, Blackthorn. I want to talk to Amy. Alone." Nathan took a magazine off the bed stand and retreated to the far end of the room. Simon eyed him narrowly before turning his attention to Amy. "Sorry, I snarled at you, angel. I was worried."

She went to his bedside. "How are you feeling?"

"Okay now except for this," he thumped his short arm cast. "But the first day, I was really out of it." He took Amy's hand. "Would you do an old buddy a favor?"

"Just ask."

"I've been trying to reach Erika Washburn in New York. I believe I may have mentioned her in my letters."

Amy laughed. "Only on every other line."

Simon flushed. "I meant to tell you about her when I stopped off in Seattle." His flush deepened. "I lost my nerve."

Amy put her hand over his. "Don't worry about it. From the tone of your letters, I knew our relationship had changed." She glanced at Nathan who was leafing through a magazine. Simon probably thought he was out of earshot, but she knew better. "To be quite honest, I'm glad you found someone else."

"You mean it?" A glowing smile spread over his face. "Man, that's great. Just great." He drew her down and kissed her cheek. "I wasn't good enough for you anyway."

Amy blushed. "That's nonsense and you know it." She raised her head and caught Nathan's gimlet stare. She pulled over a chair and sat down with a heavy sigh.

Simon peered at her. "You okay?"

"I'm fine."

"That's good. Say, hon, would you see if you can find out why Erika hasn't been answering her phone?"

"Erika's not there, Kittredge." Nathan walked over and tossed his magazine on the bed. "She and the rest of her organization have been arrested."

Simon sat forward. "Arrested? What the hell for? She was working on a story."

"Wrong. She's a courier for a drug cartel. Has been for two years."

"That's a dirty lie. Erika wouldn't—"

"Drug enforcement has had her under surveillance since she left the States."

Simon flopped back on his pillow. "She couldn't be, she . . ." he lifted his hand and let it fall in a helpless gesture, "she said she . . ." He drew his hand over his face. "Oh, hell, I sensed something off-key about her. I just couldn't bring myself to believe she was faking." He put his hand over his eyes.

"She hooked up with you to provide herself with a cover," Nathan said, his tone hard, flat, and cold. "The Feds had to make sure you were clean. So they assigned Henry Cummings to tail you."

"Those goons at the mine took him prisoner," Simon said dispiritedly. "What happened to him?"

"The DEA men found him at the bottom of a mine shaft with two bullet holes in his head. *That's* what happened to him."

"I didn't ask him to follow me, damnit. I went to Rock Springs to find the men who ripped off my father." He groaned and slid down in bed. "I screwed that up, too."

Amy reached out and put her arms around him. "No, you didn't. Troy McAllister is in jail."

A muscle knotted along Nathan's jaw. "If you had used some common sense, Henry might have—"

"Stop it, Nathan." She eyed him over Simon's head. "Simon has been hurt enough."

Nathan's nostrils flared, then he wheeled, strode out, and watched her from the hall with a brooding expression.

Later, in the car going home, Nathan broke the stiff silence. "Will you be seeing a lot of Simon?"

"Possibly. He's a good man, Nathan."

"And an expert lover?"

She frowned. "I couldn't say. I haven't had enough experience to judge." She stared into the tunnel the headlights bored in the darkness. "Will your wedding be in Orofino?" Heat flared in her cheeks. She hadn't meant to bring it up.

"Probably."

She chafed hands, feeling no blood flowing in them. She couldn't leave without knowing. "Are you sure this . . ." her voice gave out and she had to start again, "this marriage is right for you."

For a time the swish of tires on the damp blacktop filled the car. Finally, Nathan let out a long breath. "I'm positive. You and I will survive. I doubt if Angela would."

Amy frowned. Strange. According to his father's theory, Indian women were stronger than white women. She knotted her fingers together. "Do you love her?"

Nathan clamped his lips in a tight, hard line and spoke in a harsh voice. "What *is* love? Do you know?"

She willed steadiness into her voice. "I think I do *now.*"

"Well, *I* don't. I've heard men rave about women they claimed they loved and couldn't do without. A few months later, they're with someone else."

He scrubbed his hand over his face. "Angela and I have known each other since college. We're friends, good friends. We observe the same customs, have the same beliefs." He signaled and passed a slow-moving car. "So she and I have a lot more going for us than most couples." His eyes met Amy's for an instant and slid away. "I want a marriage that'll last."

"I can understand that. My marriage flopped and I've never gotten over the feeling of failure."

Neither of them spoke until Nathan parked the jeep in Dr. Chambers's driveway. Then he came around to her side, opened her door, and took her arm. "Amy, there's nothing noble or romantic about being an Indian."

Amy moved away from him and mounted the steps of

the cabin. "You've certainly done your best to convince me of that."

Nathan joined her on the porch, hunched his shoulders, and shoved his hands deep in his pockets. "I didn't want you to get hurt."

"I know." She glanced at his pinched face. "Would you like a cup of coffee?"

He shivered. "Maybe I should. I feel so . . . cold."

She stared at him with alarm. "Why didn't you tell me?" All the while he'd taken care of her, he'd set in that unheated hut wearing practically nothing. He could have pneumonia.

She flung open the door. "Light the fire. I'll get the coffee started." She stepped out of her high heels, tossed her coat on a chair, and ran water into the percolator. "Little wonder you're chilled. "You've scarcely slept in days."

Nathan hung up his suit jacket. "I think it may be mental, not physical." He folded up his shirt cuffs and touched a match to the kindling.

Amy turned to check on him and lost track of how many spoonfuls of coffee she'd put in. She dumped out the grounds and started over, but the tension inside the room made her fingers clumsy and she spilled grounds into the water. To fill the silence, she switched on the ancient radio. The only clear station played western music. She didn't care. Patsy Cline's ballads of love and loss and heartbreak reflected her mood.

When Nathan settled himself on the couch in front of the fire, she came back with a couple of quilts. "You should take better care of yourself." She leaned down to spread a quilt over him.

Nathan reached out, pulled her into his arms, and kissed her. "I should leave." He lifted his head and made a low moaning sound. "Amy . . ." He cupped her face in his hands and kissed her so hungrily it took her breath away. "Can I spend the night with you?"

She hesitated for an instant, thinking of all the reasons she should say no. Then, she covered his hands with hers. "Yes."

Amy arrived at the beach house on Lomitas Island in the late afternoon and called her father in Ursa Bay.

"How come you're over on the Island?" he asked.

"I need to be alone for a few days."

"Why? What's going on? Are you all right?"

"I'm tired. A little rest and I'll be fine."

"Okay, but don't take too long. I'm involved in a case that's got me stumped."

Amy spent the next two days charging along Otter Inlet's cliffs, cursing Nathan, herself, and fate.

Gulls screamed. Winds howled. Waves boomed against the rocks. Lonely sounds. Sounds that made a fitting accompaniment to her grieving.

When she'd shouted herself hoarse and could cry no more, she took a ferry to the mainland and went back to work.

"MIND-BOGGLING . . . THE SUSPENSE IS UNBEARABLE . . .
DORIS MILES DISNEY WILL KEEP YOU
ON THE EDGE OF YOUR SEAT . . ."

THE MYSTERIES OF DORIS MILES DISNEY

**NOWHERE TO RUN . . . NOWHERE TO HIDE . . .
ZEBRA'S SUSPENSE WILL *GET* YOU —
AND WILL MAKE YOU BEG FOR MORE!**

NOWHERE TO HIDE (4035, $4.50)
by Joan Hall Hovey

After Ellen Morgan's younger sister has been brutally murdered, the highly respected psychologist appears on the evening news and dares the killer to come after her. After a flood of leads that go nowhere, it happens. A note slipped under her windshield states, "YOU'RE IT." Ellen has woken the hunter from its lair . . . and she is his prey!

SHADOW VENGEANCE (4097, $4.50)
by Wendy Haley

Recently widowed Maris learns that she was adopted. Desperate to find her birth parents, she places "personals" in all the Texas newspapers. She receives a horrible response: "You weren't wanted then, and you aren't wanted now." Not to be daunted, her search for her birth mother — and her only chance to save her dangerously ill child — brings her closer and closer to the truth . . . and to death!

RUN FOR YOUR LIFE (4193, $4.50)
by Ann Brahms

Annik Miller is being stalked by Gibson Spencer, a man she once loved. When Annik inherits a wilderness cabin in Maine, she finally feels free from his constant threats. But then, a note under her windshield wiper, and shadowy form, and a horrific nighttime attack tell Annik that she is still the object of this lovesick madman's obsession . . .

EDGE OF TERROR (4224, $4.50)
by Michael Hammonds

Jessie thought that moving to the peaceful Blue Ridge Mountains would help her recover from her bitter divorce. But instead of providing the tranquility she desires, they cast a shadow of terror. There is a madman out there — and he knows where Jessie lives — and what she has seen . . .

NOWHERE TO RUN (4132, $4.50)
by Pat Warren

Socialite Carly Weston leads a charmed life. Then her father, a celebrated prosecutor, is murdered at the hands of a vengeance-seeking killer. Now he is after Carly . . . watching and waiting and planning. And Carly is running for her life from a crazed murderer who's become judge, jury — and executioner!

Available wherever paperbacks are sold, or order direct from the Publisher. Send cover price plus 50¢ per copy for mailing and handling to Penguin USA, P.O. Box 999, c/o Dept. 17109, Bergenfield, NJ 07621. Residents of New York and Tennessee must include sales tax. DO NOT SEND CASH.